I0685791

young & bulletproof

Janet Poisonner

ISBN: 978-1-7379671-5-6
eISBN: 978-1-7379671-7-0

To found families everywhere.

TRIGGER WARNING

This book contains references to:

- Addiction
- Suicide
- Domestic Violence
- Unplanned Pregnancy
- Child Abuse & Abandonment
- Severe Mental Health Issues
- Gore/Blood
- Casual Drug Use

If you or someone you love has been struggling with any of these issues, there are resources available:

The National Domestic Violence Hotline:
1-800-799-SAFE (7233)

National Suicide Prevention Lifeline:
1-800-273-8255

Substance Abuse & Mental Health Services Helpline:
1-800-662-HELP (4357)

prologue

Honey

THE ALARM ON HER MOTHER'S PHONE WENT OFF AND Honey got up, dressing in the clothes her father packed for her. She brushed her teeth, standing on the pink footstool at Nana Kathy's pedestal sink, listening to the staccato of rain pattering on the windowsill, underscoring the wailing alarm. How could her mother not hear it? She'd been right there in bed next to her. Drifting back into the room, Honey touched her mother's shoulder.

"Mama?" Honey shook her, tingles of icy apprehension rushing over her scalp. "Mama, I'm hungry."

She didn't stir. Honey gave her shoulder a good two-handed *shove*, and she flopped onto her back. She was cold. There was a grayish tint to her ordinarily tawny olive skin, and a speckling of white foam at the corner of her lips. Her espresso-brown eyes were wide and glassy, tinged with red, and her chest didn't rise and fall with tiny snores the way it should.

Honey crept closer, hoping her mother was playing a joke on her. Any second now, she would snatch her up and tickle her to make her laugh. They'd make bowls of cereal and spend the day watching cartoons and...

Honey whimpered, knowing her father would be angry.

Mama wasn't supposed to see her without him there, but as soon as he was gone, Nana was stuffing clothes into a case, fretting about changeable desert temperatures. She'd barely recognized her mother when she arrived, but Nana prodded her forward, telling her to give her mama a hug before she hurt her feelings.

Mama held her tight, telling her how much fun they were going to have on their special girl's weekend. Nana rolled her suitcase to the airport van, reminding her of the food money in the drawer and how the bathroom sink would drip if she didn't turn it just right. Mama laughed, insisting she could watch her own kid for a couple nights.

A low rumble of thunder sounded in the distance, the storm moving away, reminding her she couldn't stay here. Baba wasn't coming home for two more days. Squeezing her hands together, she searched her thoughts for safe places close enough to walk to. The community center wouldn't be open yet. There was a little corner store where Nana sometimes bought her ice cream bars, but she didn't have any money. Her mind was blank, save the graphite brick building near the library, the one with the ornamental wrought iron cresting on the roof and triangle-shaped sign. It was a long way off, but she was sure she could find her way there if she walked the same route.

Her coat was hanging on the wall next to the door. She couldn't reach high enough to pull it free, so she went back to the bathroom for the stool and carried it into the kitchen. Her hands were misbehaving. She couldn't get her thumbs to work, so she had to leave the snaps unfastened. Reaching for the dented brass knob on the kitchen door, she looked over her shoulder again, to where she could just see the tip of Mama's big toe hanging off the end of the bed. They'd painted their toenails last night. Mama chose a creamy coral color, like ripe cantaloupe. Unlatching the deadbolt, she let herself out.

one
tura

THE COBBLESTONE SIDEWALKS STILL BORE THE LAST vestiges of the morning's storm as Tura turned the corner on a row of antique storefronts and froze, catching sight of the tiny body huddled under the black awning of Polymatrix Consulting. It was too early for a child her age to be out on her own, especially in the unstructured hours of late summer, but here she was, a diminutive squatter in a red rain slicker with ladybug pockets, sitting balled up with her arms around her legs. The scene was so eerie that if it were any closer to Halloween, she might've assumed this was a prank executed by her demented office assistant Rikki. Tura turned to scan the street, checking the area for concerned-looking adults or hide-and-seekers, then crouched to address the visitor.

"Hello?" Gathering her dark hair over one shoulder, she tilted her head to the side. "Are you lost?"

The creature on the stoop flinched, evidently startled by Tura's presence. A little hand flew to the top of the hood, pushing it back as the child lifted her face to look up at her. Fearful blue eyes locked on hers, and Tura felt her stomach lurch. Those eyes, blue as the Adriatic and fringed with gold-tipped lashes so thick a person could stand under them for shade, set into a sweetly rounded, sun-kissed face. That resolute crinkle in her forehead, as if she were already eons older than she appeared, and the hereditary cleft in her chin.

Something was very, *very* wrong.

Tura stepped back as the child scrambled to her feet, the hood sliding off the top of her head to reveal a corona of corkscrew curled bronze hair. Clutching her hands in front of her chest, she gazed up at her, hesitating for just a moment. The buttons on her jumper dress were misaligned, her socks mismatched. *She must've dressed herself.* Tura cleared her throat, praying she was wrong. "Are you Jack's little girl?"

This was apparently all the confirmation of familiarity the child needed before throwing her arms around Tura's hips in a crushing embrace. Balking at the uninvited contact, Tura reached down, gently removing her hold. Crouching to eye level, she searched her angelic face once again, checking for signs of injury. "What are you doing here, sweetheart? Where are your parents?"

"Mama wouldn't wake up," the girl said softly. Her eyes darted to the scuffed toes of her saddle shoes, and Tura felt all the air punch out of her lungs.

"I'm sorry?" She put her hands on the girl's delicate arms, looking for some hint of emotion. Any other child's eyes would be brimming with tears, but her face was oddly calm. *She's in shock.* "What happened? Did someone hurt her?"

"No." The girl's gaze sailed over Tura's shoulder, fixing on the wall behind her. "I think she took too much medicine, like before."

"Did you call for help?" Tura's voice took on a ragged edge, her fingers gripping the child's upper arms tightly enough to make her wince. Realizing what she was doing, she released her hold. "Where is your *daddy*?"

"Baba went to Jamaica for the wedding." The little girl swallowed hard, shaking her head. "And Nana went to Palm

Springs, and I don't know the unlock code for Mama's phone."

"But you could still dial 911." Tura stopped herself, realizing too late she was dealing with the logic of a frightened child. Taking a deep breath through her nose and blowing it out from between her teeth, she concentrated on keeping her tone even. "Okay. Let's start over. What's your name?"

"Honoré Elisabetta Aldridge," the child answered between sniffles. "But everybody calls me Honey."

"All right. I can work with that." *Elisabetta.* Tura repeated mentally. So, Birdie had a namesake. She straightened, entering the security code into the little black box next to the door and ushering the child inside. "Come on. We're going to find someone to get your mama some help."

"Can you call Baba?" Honoré asked, her chin wobbling as Tura guided her up the stairs.

"Do you know his number?" Tura asked, a tide pool of self-condemnation pitting in her gut. There was no decent reason for her not to have Jack's number, except she'd never deemed it important enough to write down. They weren't *close,* after all. The girl rattled off a series of numbers without hesitation, and Tura nodded gratefully, taking out her phone as she unlocked the door of the office. She directed her to the empty chair behind Rikki's desk and made the call, pacing in the limited well of the front room. Predictably, it rang several times and went to voicemail. Because why would anyone answer a call from an unfamiliar number? Cursing under her breath, Tura took the phone away from her ear, weighing the best course of action. The thought of handing this girl over to the authorities turned her stomach, but what else could she do, if no one answered? Drawing another calming breath, she tapped out a message, glancing at the little girl. "How'd you know to come find me, Honoré?"

"Baba showed me." The little girl pulled free of her coat

sleeves, wiping her nose on the arm of her long-sleeved tee shirt. "We were driving to the library, and he said that's where your Aunt Tura works."

Tura paused, caught off guard. She hadn't realized Jack was keeping such close tabs on her life. Not a pressing concern now, though. "And you said your mom is home?"

The child shook her head, blinking as if she didn't fully understand Tura's confusion. "Mama can't live with us."

"Oh." Tura swallowed the lump threatening to bring her morning tea up with it. Had things really gotten this fucked up over the last six years? Returning her attention to the phone in her hands, she shook her head, clearing her thoughts, and sent the message, praying wherever he was, Jack would see it and be able to respond.

Taking a cautious step toward her assistant's desk, she lowered herself into one of the visitor's chairs facing the little girl. She didn't have a lot of experience with kids, which was partially by design. She didn't know the protocol for dealing with a child in the midst of a serious trauma. Should she be trying to console her?

She suddenly ached with the loss of Aunt Birdie, the long-healed wounds reopened by this unexpected brush with mortality. What would she have done? Tura buffed her palms over the knees of her jeans, casting around the room for something to occupy her hands while they waited. Her eyes landed on the display of teabags and hot chocolate packets Rikki kept arranged next to the coffee maker. Aunt Birdie would be feeding everyone.

"You want some hot chocolate?" Tura got up and crossed to the counter, selected a mug, and ripped the top off a packet of cocoa.

"Do you have marshmallows?" Honoré asked as Tura shook chocolate powder into the cup and bent to fill it from the hot spigot on the water cooler. Tura reached for a stirrer, pasting on a smile as she turned back.

"No, sorry." She looked down into the mug and wondered if it was safe to give a kid her size a cup of hot liquid. Turning to the counter again, she set down the mug to cool and bent to open the cabinet below, rifling through the jumble of office supplies. "Are you hungry? We usually have microwave popcorn or..."

Disco! Her hand closed on the box of frosted strawberry toaster pastries at the same time her phone rang. Tura stood up so fast she whacked the back of her head on the top lip of the cabinet and sucked in a sharp hiss, massaging the tender lump already forming as she dove to answer the phone.

two
tura

November 19th, 2015 - St. Patrick's Cemetery

It was an abominably beautiful day. The cloudless blue sky created a sharp contrast to the vibrant explosion of the autumn treetops as they pulled into a gap at the curb and Rikki killed the engine, speaking in a honeyed Georgia twang. "You okay?"

"No." Tura gazed across the rolling green expanse of the cemetery. A sizable crowd of mourners converged in the crisp sunlight, a set of six pallbearers traversing the strip between the hearse and the open grave, hefting a gleaming white casket between them. She recognized her foster brothers, Noel and Jack, at the front, the sun blanching Jack's sandy blond hair to cornsilk. Folded in amongst the other mourners, she saw Jack's stunning new wife Vanessa, conspicuously pregnant in her stylish black sheath dress and sensible ballet flats. Poor Birdie. She'd been looking forward to meeting Jack's child, always gushing about what a perfect baby he'd make.

The driver's side door of the antique Chevy creaked open. Rikki cut a nimble, androgynous figure in their three-piece pinstripe suit and debonair auburn pompadour, their underlying distress shown only in the ruddy patches coloring their ashen cheeks. They circled the front of the car and opened her door. "Don't worry. I got you, sweet pea."

Trudging through the plush grass of the burial ground, she kept her hands in the pockets of her jacket, ignoring the look of disapproval Noel shot her as they edged into the crowd alongside the grave. He'd had some choice words for her when she showed up at the church service in black tactical pants and combat boots, as if this day wasn't tough enough for all of them. That was Noel though, always taking his pain out on others.

The priest started to speak, using the same dulcet tone he'd employed when he came to the house to give her the news. She looked on numbly, the voices of the speakers blending together into a distant buzz. Someone handed her something, nudging her forward. She looked down and realized it was a rose. Pink, for love and gratitude. She laid it on top of the casket as Jack did the same. Standing opposite her, he pressed his palm to the frigid surface of the coffin, pausing for a long, poignant moment.

Seeing the pain written on his face, she swallowed, retreating into the crowd. Rikki put their hand on her shoulder, patting in a way meant to be comforting, but all it made her want to do was scream at them to *stop touching her*.

The priest invited everyone back to the house for a final remembrance, and a cemetery worker activated the motorized crank lowering the casket into the ground. People started to wander away. Lifting her gaze from the dark hole engulfing her mother, she caught Jack watching her with that cerulean blue gaze, grief tugging the corners of his lips downward. He turned away, taking his wife's arm and walking with her toward the row of waiting cars.

Rikki took her hand as they left, lacing their graceful

fingers through hers. They canted their head. "How you holding up?"

"The service was way too long." She gave her friend a wan smile. "She would have hated it."

"True." They pulled her into the pacific gulf under their arm. "She never was one for jawing on." Leaning in, they murmured into her ear, "But Jack and Noel are *as advertised*."

She pushed away from them with an appalled laugh. "I'll take unhelpful topics for *all* the money, please."

"Sorry to interrupt the levity," a disapproving baritone cut in, and Tura turned to look at Noel, tucking her hands into the pockets of her leather jacket. He wore an especially pinched expression today, his ordinarily ochre-tanned countenance washed out and drawn. His equally sour-faced wife stood off to the side, coifed and top heavy, oozing the entitled detachment that often accompanied generational wealth. He raked a dismissive gaze over Rikki, then looked at her. "You'll be at the house? We still need to discuss the dissolution of the estate."

She nodded curtly, already on edge from their last interaction. "I will."

"Good." He turned to leave without acknowledging Rikki again.

Her friend snickered, opening the door of the car for her. "My goodness, he's got that stick so far up there, if you tickled his throat he'd throw it up."

Tura hesitated before getting in. Rikki didn't want to be at this drab little ceremony anymore than she did, and there was no reason to subject them to a bunch of meaningless small talk with strangers when Noel dragged her away to talk business. "You can head home, if you want. I can catch a ride with the priest."

"If you're sure." Rikki swung the door closed. "But you

warn me if he tries to talk you into taking the veil. I'll need time to set up the intervention."

"Bite your *tongue*." She accepted a final peck on the cheek and watched her friend circle the front of the car.

"Hey." They paused to address her above the roof. "She was a great lady. You keep her in mind when you deal with the boys, all right?"

"I will." Tura felt her face heat, knowing the truth in their words.

"I'll be waiting when you get back." The door creaked open again. "Maybe we can all go out somewhere nice for dinner. Give Birdie a proper send-off."

"I'm not sure I'll be hungry." She shrugged. She'd barely eaten since she got the news.

"No mind, we'll figure something out," they said, leaning into the accent because they knew its power. "What d'ya say I stop off at the Asian market and get some of those thousand layer ube cakes you love?"

"Moon cakes won't get you laid, you know." Her paltry joke was rewarded with a velvety laugh.

"Love you too, turtle dove." Rikki grinned. "Keep ya chin up!"

The door slammed, and the engine turned over, a cannonade of old school seventies punk blaring through the aftermarket speakers as they sped away. Tura wrapped her arms around herself, turning to regard the priest. He was speaking to another set of mourners. There was still time to catch him, and she was pretty sure ferrying sad people to funeral luncheons was a prescribed duty for a priest, but she really didn't want to sit through a rehashing of his canned speech from the services. He'd already tried to tell her Birdie was in a better place when he came to see her the first time and she'd all but thrown him out of the house. It wasn't that she didn't want to believe him, but... Fuck it, she could use the walk, anyway.

At least the weather was good. She walked the three or so miles to the house, savoring the cool air and solitude, then let herself in through the kitchen door, listening to the clamorous tenor of a few dozen Sicilians speaking over one another.

The kitchen was isolated, and she exhaled until she felt her shoulders sag. Nothing changed here. This was the same house where she'd spent her childhood, right down to the owl-shaped sun catcher in the window above the sink. Unthreading the S-hook securing the ornament to the suction cup, she slipped it into her pocket.

three
jack

The Terrible Present

JACK STARED ACROSS THE CAR RENTAL COUNTER AND quashed the urge to reach over and grab the attendant by the front of her polyester uniform vest. "Ma'am, I truly don't care what kind of vehicle it is. I will take a box van if I have to. I just need to get home *tonight.*"

"I understand that, sir," the woman drawled, unconcerned by the wild look in his eyes. It was obvious she was accustomed to being overlooked in life, and now relished the opportunity to wield her gossamer thread of power over any hapless individuals with the misfortune to face her at this desk. "But they're tracking an early hurricane off the coast and we had a rush on rentals when they started canceling flights."

"Listen, I know you're just doing your job, but my wife killed herself last night and my five year old daughter is alone, being cared for by *strangers,*" Jack pleaded, holding his hands open in supplication. "Please. Is there *anything* you can do?"

The woman pursed her lips, pushing the square frames of her glasses up, and typed something into the keyboard. The printer whirred. She laid a slip of paper on the counter. "Sign here, sir. Then I can walk you out to your vehicle."

"I'm sorry?"

"It appears we're experiencing a computer glitch." She looked up, her expression indecipherable. "Hopefully it will be ironed out by morning. As compensation for the inconvenience, I'll be waiving the fee on your booster seat rental."

The goddess in the ugly vest led him out to the rental lot and put him in a silver sedan, bending to give him a tight-lipped smile as he pulled out of the parking space.

"I know, I know," he whispered to the air, checking the clock on the dash against his watch and exhaling a tremulous breath. It would be a six-hour drive back to Providence, if the weather didn't slow him down. "I'll get her."

Before he got the call, Jack was straightening his tie, anticipating finding a willing woman and spending the post-reception hours fucking all the cobwebs out of his system. His phone rang as he prepared to head down to the resort's botanical garden to help set up for the ceremony, a strange number popping up on the ID. He let it go to voicemail, then a few seconds later, it chimed, signaling a new text message. He ignored it at first, reasoning that it was probably his business partner Genie making sure he hadn't forgotten the ring for the eighth time that morning. Fastening the top button of his jacket, he stared at the phone in the mirror, waiting for the display to darken. Seconds ticked by, his intuition howling at him to read the message before he surrendered, skirting the bed and grabbing it off the side table.

This is Tura. I have Honoré. Please answer your phone.

He'd never hit the green return button so fast in his entire life. A split second later, his foster sister answered, sounding uncharacteristically unstrung. "Jack, I'm so sorr—"

"Where's Honey?" he demanded, beginning to pace. "What happened?"

"She's right here, and she's okay. But you need to come home." She released a long, wavering breath, dropping her voice to a whisper. "I think Vanessa may have passed away when your daughter was with her."

"No. This has to be some kind of mistake." Jack's heart felt like it was about to implode. Sitting down on the end of the bed, he pressed his thumb and forefinger to the bridge of his nose as his brain went into a tailspin. "My wife doesn't have contact with Honey. She was supposed to be with her grandmother this weekend."

"I don't know what to tell you."

"I need to speak to my daughter," he bit out, his voice breaking under the strain of holding back a flood of tooth-cracking panic. "Right now."

"Absolutely."

There was a muffled pause, and Honey's weepy voice came on the phone. "Hi Baba."

"Listen very carefully, baby girl." He swallowed against a fist of strangling dread. "Are you safe right now? Are you hurt?"

"I'm okay." Honey sniffled, making soft puffing sounds into the speaker. "I don't want you to be mad."

"I'm not mad at you." He felt his pulse slow exponentially, knowing she wasn't in any immediate danger. "Honey, did you go see your mom?"

"She was taking care of me, because Nana Kathy went to Palm Springs. But she wouldn't wake up."

Kathleen, you thoughtless bitch! Jack's jaw flexed, and he closed his eyes again. "I'm sorry. She wasn't supposed to do that, but I love you and I'm coming to get you, okay?"

The dam broke. She answered between blustering sobs. "Uh-uh-uh-huh."

Jack wrestled a wave of helpless torment back. "Can you put Tura back on the phone?"

Another muffled pause, and Jack heard heavy footsteps echoing down the line. An unfamiliar voice filled the background, reformed deep south, by the sound of it, tinged with amusement. Tura uttered a few clipped syllables he couldn't quite make out, and then she came back. "I can watch her for a little while but I'm supposed to catch a flight—"

"Is there someone else there?" he asked, feeling his pulse mount. It was a small thing, but he couldn't take anymore change right now.

"Just my assistant." She seemed to be adjusting her speech to work as a counterbalance to his, her tone as unvarying and measured as a metronome. "We're contacting the police right now, to see if they can do a wellness check."

"Oh. That's good." Some of the tension slipped from his shoulders. He hadn't even considered what was being done for Nessa.

"Is there anyone I can call? Anyone who can take care of Honoré?" He heard his daughter raise her voice in the background, screeching that she wanted to stay there, with *her*.

"No. Noel and Denise moved to Denver a while back, and —" *Birdie's dead.* He swallowed as a sudden wave of anguish washed over him, blending with the anxiety. Would his daughter have to spend the night in foster care? Wasn't that the *one* thing he promised himself he'd *never* let happen? Resting his bent elbow on his knee, he pushed his shaking fingers through his hair. How could he be so stupid? Kathleen was a lot of things, but she was always good with Honey. He'd been foolish to believe she wouldn't do anything to put her granddaughter at risk. "Kathy was it."

A long pause echoed from the other end.

"Listen, Jack... I realize it is *not* my place and I will follow your instructions, whatever you decide, but Honey felt safe coming here," her sedate tone cut through the fog in his brain, even as shit was spiraling out of control and he was more scared than he'd ever been. "In light of what she's been through today, I think it would be best to avoid compounding the trauma by sending her away."

"Are you sure?" Jack sat up as a balloon of salvation expanded in his chest.

"Under the circumstances, I can reschedule," she said this without a hint of hesitation, but then, Tura knew better than anyone what awaited a child in emergency care.

Back in the present, Jack rubbed his eyes with the palm of his hand and turned on the radio as loud as it would go, telling himself there were no good options in this situation. He could call Family Services. They would rip his daughter out of the place she felt safest on the worst day of her life. Instead, he chose to trust the voice on the other end of the phone. The voice of a woman who'd been all but a stranger to him for eighteen years.

four
jack

November 19th, 2015 - After the Services

IF HE HAD TO, HE COULD HAVE MADE THE TRIP blindfolded. Straight up the hill from the offramp. Right at the gas station. All the way to the very end of the dead-end street. The sun was sinking over the scraggly trees forming the noise barrier between the neighborhood and the highway, tinting everything an ornate Titian yellow and casting bands of light between the tightly packed buildings along the street. His hands itched to turn the car around and point it in a safer direction, but he remembered why he was taking the risk when Birdie's house came into view, with its faded green siding and bathtub Madonna standing watch over the sidewalk.

Somewhere in the distance, a crow perched on a rooftop, its sharp calls echoing on the breeze. He caught a phantom whiff of Shalimar through the open car window, despair grating in his chest. Birdie was the heart of this place. Now she was gone, it looked hollow and lonely.

He was glad he'd dropped Nessa at home first. The trip back to their place in Providence ate up enough time that the guests had already filtered out. He recognized Noel's sensible minivan and pulled up next to it in the unpaved lot next to the house. Killing the engine, he took a deep breath. On some level, he'd hoped to avoid this forever, but life had a way of kicking a guy right in the balls.

A strange electric current worked its way through the halls of the house, with its carpeted floors and faux-paneled walls. Not even the dust would settle. Jack felt as if someone were holding a cattle prod to the back of his neck. Of course, that might have been because he'd just walked in on a very intense conversation between Noel, his best friend since the second grade, and the woman he'd avoided for the last decade.

Noel sat at Birdie's vintage dinette table, chewing air and staring daggers at Tura. Surprised how quickly the sight of her dredged up memories better left in the past, Jack noticed she'd cut her hair. Where it used to lay in a stick-straight sable black curtain down her back, it now fell in textured, uneven waves above her chin, showing off the long, alabaster column of her neck. Noel stood up when Jack came in, never taking his eyes off her. "I can see we're not going to agree about this."

"It would appear so, yes." She leaned against the counter, every bit the immovable object Noel was.

"I'll call tomorrow and set up a time for all of us to meet with the lawyer." Noel turned to leave. "Maybe he can help you make the smart choice."

"I can't decide, Noel," she said coolly, the corners of her wide, finely chiseled lips turning up in a mocking smirk. "If you're giving the lawyer too much credit, or selling me short. Why do you think that is?"

"God damn it, this isn't a game!" Noel exploded. "Birdie had a reverse mortgage! We have to—"

"Do. Not. *Yell*. At me," she cut him off, her voice never wavering from its throaty pitch. Noel's face flushed, and he turned on his heel, his footsteps thundering through the house. The front door slammed. They stood in silence for a moment, listening to the sound of his car turning over, and the crunch of the tires as he drove away. She turned back to the place where she'd been assembling a sandwich from a leftover deli tray, speaking to him over her shoulder. "Sorry. Apparently Noel was hoping I left my spine at home."

"Don't worry about it. This is nobody's best day." Jack pulled open the old round-topped refrigerator to get a bottle of water and caught a whiff of her subtle, almost masculine cologne, citrus zest and rosemary, with a cedar base note.

She tucked a piece of hair behind one slightly oversized ear, the cartilage embellished with stacks of silver hoops. "Where's Vanessa?"

"She got sick of people trying to rub her belly and her feet were starting to hurt." He cleared his throat. "Pregnancy makes it hard to stand for a long time."

"I've heard that," she murmured. "Too bad. I would've loved to meet her."

He swiveled his head, stealing another glance at her profile. She was still fascinating, with the sharp, animal-eyed cunning of a woman forever ten steps ahead. She had a proud, diamond-shaped chin, betraying a strong tendency toward obstinacy, and there was a graceful hump at the bridge of her nose, suggesting a trace of Mediterranean or Middle Eastern blood somewhere in her uncharted lineage. Her cheekbones were high and angular, without a hint of blush. *Still a heart-breaker.* The irony was, for the first ten years of their acquaintance, she was one step up from a piece of furniture. He couldn't determine when that started to change.

An indomitable little shit, even at the tender age of eight, Tura came along when the boys were in their sophomore year of high school. She was far too young to take up much headspace beyond the occasional inconvenience of having to babysit. Still, Birdie never let them forget she was their little sister by proxy, and it was their responsibility to look out for her.

Never an official foster child, Jack was one of Noel's friends, just another neighborhood stray with a fucked-up home life. He turned up at the kitchen door with bruises and split lips on nights when his latest stepdad got violent. Birdie would bring out the first aid kit and clean him up, tutting over the ruination of his beauty. One day, he stopped trying to go home, and no one thought anything of it. He became another one of Birdie's kids, and sometimes when his guard was down and he wasn't thinking too hard, it was easy to forget there was a time before.

Then one fateful Christmas Eve, when they were all home for the holiday during Tura's second year in college, the gawky little urchin was transformed into someone else. A grown woman bearing only a passing resemblance to the child he'd long ago learned to take for granted. Sure, she could be oddly intense at times, and she dressed like she expected to be sucked into a dystopian wasteland at any moment, but she carried herself with confidence and could verbally eviscerate him without breaking a sweat. There was no defending against that.

"He wants to throw it all away." She kept her eyes down, the dark fringe of her lashes fluttering against her skin as she avoided his gaze. "Just wants to throw it all away without even looking at any of it. Can you believe that?"

"I don't like it either, but it's not like there's much to choose from anyway. If you lift up the doilies on the living room side tables, you'll see they're cardboard." Jack took a step closer, leaning one hip against the counter. She seemed to forget her resolve and pinned him with a glare, those mesmerizing obsidian eyes slicing right into him. He'd never forgotten the way the dim kitchen light leeched all the color from their centers, turning them a dusky slate gray. "What? We all have lives. We don't have time to sift through all this."

"And I get that." She looked away again, reaching for the mustard. "But I feel like we owe her a little consideration, rather than throwing away her whole life."

"You're right. We do." He took a long drink, studying the way her hair laid against the nape of her neck. "But we're in a bad position."

"I know." She sighed, seemingly losing her appetite. She turned away from what she was doing, the look of anguish in those big eyes leaving him gutted. Two points of pale pink rouged her cheeks, the way they did when she was little and winding up for a real barnburner of a tantrum. "I don't think I'm ready to let her go yet."

Damn it... He reached out and pulled her in, crushing her against his chest. She buried her face against his clavicle, and he rested his chin on the crown of her head, trying to calculate when Tura got this tall. He'd wager she was taller than average, even without the platform Docs. "Neither am I."

She didn't cry. She relaxed into him, wrapping her arms around his waist under his suit jacket and gathering two handfuls of the back of his shirt. Seconds passed, and she stepped away from him, reaching for one of Birdie's dangerously dull kitchen knives, sawing her sandwich in half. When she didn't say anything for several moments, he reached out and touched her elbow. "You gonna be okay?"

She looked up at him, a vaguely perplexed expression on her face. "Oh, you know me."

"Yeah." He nodded, feeding into the lie because that's what they needed from each other today; the illusion of belonging.

five
tura

"I just checked the messages." Rikki leaned through the open door of Tura's office. "Bosker's been blowing up our voicemail all night."

"Seriously?" Tura gestured for her assistant to keep their voice down, waving them into her office where they could speak privately. She waited as Rikki eased the door closed between the grownups and where Honey sat in the main room, doodling on a legal pad with a black rollerball pen. Tura folded her arms. "Did you remind him that I'm not taking new clients right now?"

Rikki picked a piece of lint off the lapel of their shiny sharkskin suit jacket. "He's asking if you'd take one meeting, as a personal favor."

"Shocking," Tura murmured, folding her laptop closed and tucking it into her bag. The job was supposed to be simple: Assess the situation, find the weak spots, and instruct the client how to fix the problem. On righteous jobs, she fired entire security forces. She brought in private specialists to comb through every line of computer code for months on end, just to find the loopholes in a company's cybersecurity. Investigated corporate espionage and government moles, and trekked across continents to run down a lead, making hand-offs of obscene amounts of money to recover all manner of stolen things. While she couldn't call it a thankless job because the money was damn good, the gig had lately taken on a distinctly Sisyphean bent. There would never be a shortage of panicky clients or convoluted messes to clean up.

"So?" Rikki drew the query out, watching Tura expectantly. "You really want me to tell Bosker to screw off?"

"No." Tura closed her eyes. "But tell him this is consult *only*. And make it clear that after this, I expect to be left alone until I'm good and goddamn ready."

"You got it." Rikki nodded, scratching out a note on the spiral-bound memo pad in their hand. "In the meantime, maybe you could work on getting worse at your job."

"Cute. Very funny," Tura snarked, sliding her bag over her shoulder. Moving past her friend, she exited her office, waving for Honey to follow her. "Come on, kiddo. Time to go."

"My goodness, I've never seen this side of you before." Rikki tucked their hands into the pockets of their tailored suit pants. "You're practically *glowing* with maternal energy."

"Do please suck it." She sliced a censuring glare at her friend as Honey wrapped her tiny hand around Tura's index and middle finger, holding on tight.

"Are you sure you don't want to take a couple of spare rooms at the house?" Rikki asked. "We can set you up above the carriage house. That way you can stick close, and she won't disturb anyone if she needs a glass of warm milk, or whatever."

"Warm milk?" Tura half-turned to the door, giving her friend a quizzical stare.

"Shit...the fuck do I know about the care and feeding of children?" Rikki ran a hand through their hair, a cocky grin spreading over their face. "At least you'd both have a comfortable place to sleep."

"The couch at my place is fine." Not like she could share

her bed with a strange little girl. "Besides, all I need is for her to freak out because she hears a bunch of strangers shouting through the floor."

"That couch would qualify as cruel and unusual punishment if you put it in a prison." Rikki rolled their eyes. "Besides, just because there's never been a child at Hattie Lamont's doesn't mean we don't know how to behave like good humans. We would suspend play while she was on the premises."

"And keep her out of the gallery, the play pen, and the *dungeon*?" Tura smirked, imagining how fast Jack would wring her neck when he discovered she'd sheltered his daughter in the most notorious private social club in Providence.

"Fair enough." Rikki looked down and bestowed a genial smile on Honey, who stood between them, watching their exchange with the rapt attention of a spectator at Wimbledon. They offered her a hand to shake. "It sure was nice meeting you, lil'un."

Honey clasped their hand and held on, regarding the newcomer for a moment. Then in a clear, confident voice, she asked, "Are you a boy, or a girl?"

"Ha!" Rikki beamed, releasing her hand. "Jury's still out on that one, jellybean."

"Do you live with Tura?" Honey asked, barely phased by their equivocation.

"Used to." Rikki bobbed their head, hazel-gray eyes sparkling with merriment. "But eventually our little bird outgrew us and flew away to her own nest."

"You talk funny," Honey observed in a matter-of-fact tone, eliciting another chuckle from Rikki.

"Yeah." Rikki rocked back on the heels of their stylish wingtip shoes. "I get that a lot."

"Does Rikki really have a *dungeon* at their house?" Honey

slipped her hand into Tura's as they walked to the end of the block and started down the sharply sloping hill to downtown. "Like in a castle?"

"Yup," Tura answered, deciding this much truth would not be damaging. If Honey brought it up to Jack later, that would be his conversation to have.

"But we're going to your house?" Honey chirped, having to take three steps to every one of Tura's as she trotted along next to her. "I'm staying with you until Baba comes?"

"That's the plan."

Her building stood several blocks away, an heirloom stone high-rise just over the footbridge dividing College Hill from Downcity. Once the imposing jewel of the era with her Romanesque roofline and stunning marble foyer, she now served as a modest grande dame, standing unchanged as the concrete behemoths of the new city loomed overhead. The heels of Honey's shoes clicked on the tiled floors as Tura led her to the elevator, where Mrs. Ibrahim and her equally aged sister Mrs. Mustafa crouched in the antique brass car like half-melted exhibits in a wax museum. Each woman wore a brightly colored hijab and rested a liver-spotted hand on the handle of a rolling grocery cart.

The sisters lit up at the sight of Honey, cooing in thick Shami accents. Tura could practically hear their bones creak as they bent the additional inches their already humped shoulders would allow, peering closely at the child from behind the thick lenses of their glasses.

"What a beautiful child!" proclaimed Mrs. Ibrahim.

"She's not yours," said Mrs. Mustafa, more as a statement of fact.

"She belongs to a friend of mine." Tura took a step forward as Honey attempted to wedge her body between Tura's legs and the wall, hiding her face against her hip. The old women favored her with gummy smiles.

"She's shy!"

"How sweet!"

Straightening as much as her crooked spine would allow, Mrs. Ibrahim tidied the vividly colored fabric of her headscarf over her narrow shoulders and gave Tura a critical once over. "You look tired."

"And skinny," Mrs. Mustafa observed. "Have you eaten?"

"It's been a hectic morning," Tura explained, accustomed to the blunt style of the building aunties. Mrs. Mustafa's son served as the daytime super and had the inside track on vacancies before they posted. As a result, a large portion of the building was filled with familial offshoots from their Syrian homeland.

"I made Kunāfah last night." Mrs. Ibrahim patted her hand as the doors slid open on the eighth floor, and the old women reached for the chrome handles of their grocery carts. "I'll have Manny bring you some tonight."

"No!" Mrs. Mustafa interjected, following close behind her sister. "I'm making Barazek! I'll have Bahir drop some off."

"You really don't have to do that." Tura stepped to the side and held the door, stifling the urge to tell both women no amount of fancy phyllo-wrapped cheesecake or sesame cookies could induce her to marry their grandsons. Or anyone, for that matter.

"Bah, it's no trouble," Mrs. Ibrahim dismissed the protest, and both women shuffled off, bickering in Arabic. She gathered there was some disagreement about who had dibs on the nice girl from the ninth floor, though she had zero intention of letting them know she understood what they were saying. That would only cause them to redouble their efforts to bring her into the family.

six
tura

Tura woke to the frightful sound of someone hammering on her door. Sitting up and reaching for her discarded sweatshirt, she stumbled to the entrance and threw it open just as Jack lifted his fist to bang again. He jumped back, wild-eyed and panting, and Tura's first thought was: *It must've started raining again*. Water dripped from his sodden suit jacket, pooling on the tile under his feet. Behind him, her neighbor Faruq stood in his open door with a baseball bat gripped in his fist. Waving the man off with an apologetic smile, she moved aside. "Hey. You made good time."

"Where's Honey?" He looked frenzied, raking his hand through his damp flaxen hair. It'd gone a bit shaggy since last time she'd seen him, grown down over the tips of his ears and curling up at his collar, but it worked. He always did have the kind of hair a girl yearned to run her fingers through. He'd also grown a well trimmed stubble beard, the fur on his face coming in darker, showing the first sprinklings of gray. *When did Jack Aldridge turn into a silver fox?* He swept his eyes around her apartment. "Is she okay?"

"She's sleeping." Tura nodded, closing the door. "We watched TV. She had spaghetti for dinner, we played Go Fish, and she went to bed. I checked on her around eleven and she hasn't made a peep all night."

"She's okay," he repeated, running his palm over his face. His posture visibly relaxed, and he dragged his gaze to hers, a fierce frown creasing his forehead. "I'm sorry... I've been driving all night. I just want to see my daughter."

She led him down the hallway and pointed to her bedroom. Leaning against the open doorway, she watched him sit on the edge of the mattress and shake his little girl awake. Honey whined at first, unhappy to be woken from such a deep sleep, but when she opened her eyes and recognized her father, she flung her arms around his neck and unleashed a torrent of tears against his shoulder.

Tura felt her heart pinch, watching Jack hold his daughter. Neither of them had experienced that kind of stability, the rock-solid knowledge that the people they loved would come for them, no matter what happened. Birdie tried, but the damage was done. For Jack to choose to be a parent after the pain and betrayal of his childhood was miraculous to her.

"Okay, bug..." Jack started to gather his daughter into his arms, and Honey reached for Tura's stuffed rabbit Parsnip, hugging it to her chest. Making a cosseting clicking noise with his tongue, he started to ease the toy out of the girl's hold. Honey whimpered, clutching it harder, resting her cheek against the top of Parsnip's head. "That doesn't belong to us."

"Let her keep it," Tura said softly. She knew firsthand the rabbit was imbued with the supernatural ability to sooth fear. Jack sighed, but gave up the fight. Honey buried her face in the rabbit's fur, somehow growing smaller in his arms. Tura turned to the side as Jack carried his daughter past. "Are you okay to drive?"

"I'll be fine." Jack turned, one arm looped over his daughter's back, the other under her rear, supporting her weight against his chest. His eyes were bloodshot, but she could tell by the set of his jaw there would be no convincing him otherwise. "Thank you. But I need to take her."

"I know." She skirted around them and took hold of the doorknob, smiling when Honey turned her face out of her father's chest, watching her with those huge blue eyes. She reached out and gave the little girl's shoulder a squeeze. "Bye Honey."

"Bye," Honey whispered, reburying her face against her father's shoulder.

Jack flattened one large hand over his daughter's spine and leveled his gaze on Tura's. "We should go."

"Right." Tura opened the door and stepped back, holding it for them. Jack carried his daughter out, Honey's gaze staying on hers as they got further away. Just before they disappeared around the bend in the hallway, she lifted one little hand and gave Tura a sad wave goodbye.

seven
jack

Jack glanced at Honey's sleeping form in the rearview mirror, checking for the thousandth time to make sure she was there, buckled safely into her rented booster seat. He remembered very little about the place where he'd collected her, or the woman who'd let him in. In fact, he had very little memory of driving up to the building. His mind had been entirely focused on finding his daughter, and then once he had her, all he wanted to do was take her home. Tura could have dyed her hair hot pink and tattooed her face for all he knew.

"Baba?" His daughter whispered dreamily as he carried her up the steps and shifted her small body onto his hip, fishing his keys out of his pocket.

"Yeah baby girl?" He murmured, stroking her twiggy back as he toed the door open.

"Are we home?"

"Yup." He stepped inside and slid his garment bag off his opposite shoulder, laying it on the ground. "I'm gonna put you right to bed."

The little girl snoozed against him as he elbowed the switch to turn on the lights. He carried his daughter into her bedroom, carefully setting her down and tucking her in.

Honey wore a borrowed "Smash The Patriarchy" tee shirt, and when he'd gone to wake her, she was holding a familiar brown rabbit with floppy ears. She'd refused to relinquish the thing before they left, but he couldn't let his daughter keep it. He remembered this bunny. Birdie embroidered "Parsnip" onto the bottom of its foot in pink floss, and Tura cherished it, taking it with her everywhere until the calico ears grew threadbare and the velvet flocking on its little plastic nose rubbed off.

Fuck, he was a terrible person. He couldn't even remember stopping to thank Tura properly before they left.

The phone in his pocket rang, and when he reached for it, he was unsurprised to see Genie's name light the screen. He answered it as he mounted the stairs to the second floor, eager to undress and fall into bed. "Hey, Genie."

"Hi," Genie sounded concerned, but then she'd have to be, to have taken the time out of her long-awaited honeymoon. "Kid all right?"

"She's asleep." Jack dropped down onto the edge of his bed, loosening his tie. This whole ordeal had just about shaved a decade off the end of his life, but his daughter seemed to be doing just fine now that she'd gotten a good cry out of it. "Pretty sure I'm gonna have to find her a therapist. I don't even want to think about the call I'll get if she talks about this on the playground."

"I'll have Portia put together a list of names for you," Genie offered, not that Jack needed reminding his friend's new wife was a psychiatrist. As was typical amongst those of her profession, one of Portia's favorite, and most annoying habits, was therapizing her loved ones. Genie's voice changed then, taking on a harder edge. "What about Kathy? You talk to her yet?"

"In the car." Jack stared at the slant of morning sun feeding through the skylight and slashing down his bedroom wall. Kathleen called when he was attempting to traverse the roads of New York during a torrential downpour. She'd gotten the messages in her hotel room, after being out with her senior's group all day. Jack was too busy trying not to plow the car into an embankment to argue with her about the monumental way she'd fucked up. He couldn't bear to think about what could've happened if his daughter hadn't had the presence of mind to go for help. "I told her I would talk to Honey about going to the funeral, but otherwise, she'd better not expect to see my daughter for a long fucking time."

"Can't blame you there." A blast of feedback crackled from the other end, the sound of a garbled voice playing over an announcement system. Genie must've been calling from the airport. "I'm *wicked* sorry, but we have to get on the plane. When we get back though, I want you to bring Honey by for a sleepover with Olivia, okay? We'll take her anytime you need us to."

"Thanks." Jack smiled with genuine gratitude. "And tell Portia I'm sorry for missing the ceremony."

"Don't start with that." Genie released a jaded sigh. "She's a mom. She knows the deal."

They hung up after that, and Jack finally stripped off his suit, laying it over the back of the chair in the corner so it wouldn't wrinkle.

"She's okay," he murmured, his words like a prayer. "She's going to be okay."

He climbed into his big empty bed, grateful he'd taken the time to change the sheets before he left. They were cool and crisp against his skin as he slipped under the blankets and let out a long sigh. He fell asleep almost immediately, but the welcome bliss of rest was short-lived. He barely closed his eyes before Honey was climbing up onto the bed and tucking her little head against his shoulder. "Baba? I'm hungry."

Thirty minutes later, Jack poured Honey a glass of orange

juice and set it next to her favorite Tyrannosaurus plate, sitting down in the chair next to hers at the breakfast bar. "Honey, how'd you know to go to Tura?"

"You said she was family." Honey pointed to the fridge, where the photo from his college graduation day hung. In the picture, Noel and Jack flanked Aunt Birdie in their gowns and mortar boards. Birdie had her arms around both boys, beaming proudly as Jack held fourteen-year-old Tura in a headlock, grinding his knuckles into the apex of her skull. He remembered that moment. Birdie insisted on getting a picture with all "her kids," but Tura, forever the shrinking violet, resisted. Jack had to drag her into frame and the shutter clicked as she tried to wriggle away from him. He'd almost learned to stop seeing the damn thing after Honey hung it there a few months ago. She dug it out of a box of photos and started asking questions. He'd given her the abridged explanation, hoping she'd let it go, but she'd pitched a fit when he tried to sneak the picture back into storage. He left it up, forcing himself to live with the discomfort it caused.

Jack leaned his elbow on the counter, swiveling to study the passivity in his daughter's face as she concentrated on her scrambled eggs. "Honey I know we've had this conversation before, but it's very dangerous to go off on your own. It's a miracle Tura found you before—"

"I like her." Honey looked up suddenly. "She has a nose earring, and pictures on her arms, and her friend Rikki lives in a castle with a real dungeon!"

Deciding he wasn't in the right mindset to be having this conversation, even if he was heartened by the level of composure she'd demonstrated in the last twenty-four hours, he brought his hand to the soft curls at the side of her head and bent her toward him, dropping a kiss on her crown. Nessa's disembodied laughter echoed when he got up to return the orange juice to the fridge, her razor-sharp wit forever preserved in a quiet corner of his mind. *Our daughter is choosing people to trust by their body art. That definitely won't come back to haunt us later.*

eight
jack

Jack didn't remember Tura's building being this elegant last time he was here, but then, he hadn't been paying attention. Now he could look around without his heart hammering in blind panic, he could pick out the carved Doric colonnade holding the glass dome of the vestibule aloft, and the compass rose medallion set into the checkerwork marble floors. Boarding the polished brass elevator with Tura's folded tee shirt and childhood bunny under one arm, he felt his pulse tick upward, putting it down to his memories of that terrible day two weeks ago. He couldn't afford to acknowledge there was a part of him that was nervous to see his foster sister after years of enforced disassociation.

Finding her door without the driving need to *find Honey* providing the true north of his internal compass was more challenging. When he did, he stood in the hallway and took a deep breath, inhaling the scent of exotic cooking spices drifting from one of the apartments along the hall. Steeling himself for confrontation, he raised his hand and knocked. A beat passed before the door opened, and he felt a sudden vacuum fill the hall, unsure of where to look.

She stood in the doorway wearing nothing but a pair of

black yoga pants, sports bra and black boxer's hand wraps, eyes bright, lips open and gasping for breath. Her face was flushed with exertion, a few tendrils of hair having worked free from the disheveled bun on top of her head and stuck to the side of her face and neck.

"Wow, twice in one decade!" The arm she swept across her face sported a sleeve of intricate botanical tattoos, and she had a silver hoop in her septum, the metal glittering like a far off star. "To what do I owe the honor?"

Jack swallowed, unsticking his tongue from the roof of his mouth. "I wanted to return your things."

"Oh." She canted her head to one side, her gaze directed at his armpit. "You brought Parsnip back."

It took him a moment to remember the stuffed animal, but he handed it over. "I thought you might be missing it."

"Honey could have kept her." Tura held the bunny against her chest. "I've been lugging Parsnip around for years. I was honestly relieved she'd found a good home."

"No, you loved that thing." Jack shook his head, then remembered his task and looked down at the shirt, still folded under his arm. Once he gave it back, he'd be surrendering any remaining hope for subterfuge, and it surprised him how sad that made him feel. Taking out the shirt, he held it toward her. "Actually, I was hoping we could talk."

She accepted the proffered shirt and stepped back from the door with a subdued smile. "Did you want to come in?"

"Oh, uh…" He braced his hands on either side of the frame, physically restraining himself from entering her apartment. He'd come here to thank the woman who'd performed an extraordinary kindness for his daughter. He should accept, go inside, and talk to her like a goddamn adult, yet at this moment, the thought of crossing her threshold stopped him cold.

The door opposite hers opened, and a young woman in a

teal head covering emerged, juggling an overstuffed diaper bag and pushing a baby carriage. Tura leaned further into the hall-way, addressing the woman. "Cala! Tell your mom I still have her Tupperware and I'll get it back to her tomorrow, okay?"

"Yes, thank you," the young mother answered in a soft Middle Eastern accent, her shy smile transforming to appraisal as her gaze fell on Jack. She looked him over, her lips pursing ever so slightly, then steered the baby carriage in the direction of the elevator.

"Jack," Tura said, bringing his attention back to her. "In or out, I won't take it personally either way."

Jack couldn't help but chuckle as he dropped his hands. "All right. Sure."

He skirted a pile of luggage as he stepped inside, his eye snagging on an aluminum suitcase that looked like it was designed to take a direct hit from a ballistic missile. "Are you going somewhere?"

"Just got back," she explained. "I'm smelling a little gamey right now, but if you give me a few minutes, I can get washed up."

"Take your time." Jack nodded, checking his watch. He'd timed his visit so he wouldn't have to get Honey off the bus for another two hours, but he'd still have the ready excuse of needing to head home if the conversation went south.

"Great." She started for the hallway, unwinding her hand wraps as she went. "Make yourself comfortable, and I'll be right out."

He cut his gaze away from her ass as she walked away, closing the bathroom door behind her. The shower hissed to life, and he stood in one place for a few stilted minutes, torn between his instinct to turn tail and run and the temptation to take a look around. *You're allowed to like her, Jack.* As always, his better angel spoke in Nessa's voice, and Jack shook his head at the ground.

No. This is wrong.

But why? Hearing her advocate for Tura was disorienting.

The answer is in the question, Ness. He rolled his eyes, forcing himself to focus on his surroundings. His stomach sank. A Soviet fallout bunker was homier than this.

nine
jack

FOR ALL THE EFFORT THEY'D PUT INTO PRESERVING the downstairs, Tura's condo was a sterile corporate box with pale gray walls. There was a row of windows on one wall, the vertical blinds slicing the afternoon light into thick stripes against the laminate hardwood floors. Jack wondered if the place came furnished, because nothing about the decor suggested any sense of personal investment. Everything was done in neutral shades and right angles, without a single photo or knickknack. The only indicators a human being lived there were a potted palm in front of the window, the heavy bag suspended from the ceiling, and the folded wrestling mat leaning against the wall.

Though he knew he shouldn't, he wandered into the kitchen and opened the cabinets. She appeared to have a thing for boxed macaroni and cheese, garbanzo beans, and microwaveable stuffing mix, and she obviously didn't have a lot of guests. There was three of everything; glasses, bowls and plates, but they were all mismatched, as if she'd picked up items at random, filling holes in her collection.

The refrigerator was only slightly better, containing a pitcher of iced tea, a bouquet of asparagus in a cup of water, a wedge of Humboldt Fog goat cheese, and three dozen eggs. The freezer was stacked with at least twenty bags of frozen vegetables and a single pint of Tahitian vanilla bean ice cream.

"Get you something?" She appeared in the doorway, toweling her hair dry. Her fashion sense hadn't changed. She'd traded the workout clothes for a bulky black asymmetrical sweater and black leather moto pants.

Jack swung the freezer door closed and stepped back. He'd been so busy trying to figure how she managed to nourish herself, he'd missed the sound of the shower turning off. "Between grocery runs?"

"I travel a lot." She tossed her towel over one of the chairs next to the table and struck a pose, resting her fists on her hips. "I don't keep stuff that spoils in the house."

"Except all the eggs?"

"No." She shook her head, crossing in front of him to take out the pitcher of iced tea. She poured two glasses and carried them to the pedestal table, sitting cross-legged in a chair. "I have a friend who keeps chickens. If you don't wash them they'll keep for months."

"Where are you coming back from?" Jack sat down opposite her, and she slid the glass across the table to him, bartender style.

"Nowhere important." She raked her fingers through her hair, the damp strands brushing her shoulders in chunky rocker girl layers. "How's Honey doing?"

"As well as can be expected. I've got her set up with a therapist." He drummed his nails on the tabletop several times in rapid succession. Fuck it, might as well do what he came here to do. Leaning back in his chair, he turned over his hand on the tabletop, palm up. "Listen, I wanted to come by before now. I should've at least called when the police said they needed to talk to you. To get you mixed up with the investigation after everything you did for Honey... I feel like I owe you more than I can say. If there's ever anything I can do—"

"You don't owe me anything, Jack." She drained her glass with *shocking* speed and got up to dump the ice in the sink, giving him her back. "Helping Honey was the right thing to do. That she happened to be your daughter was immaterial."

Jack snorted under his breath. "Well, when you put it that way..."

"I'm sorry." She paused, then seemed to correct herself. "What I meant was, I didn't help Honey because I wanted to obligate you to me. She needed a safe place to stay, and I had the means to provide her one."

"And I appreciate that more than you'll ever know," he said, aware of the barbed frustration in his voice. Looking up at her for a long, tense moment, he drew a deep breath, forcing his jaw to relax. When he spoke again, he was mindful of his tone. "I feel like I'm fucking this up. I didn't come here to make it weird. I was just hoping— *Fuck*! Why is this so hard?"

Amusement flickered in her eyes. "I don't know, but I'm curious to see where it's leading."

"The thing is," Jack began, "Birdie's gone, Nessa's gone, her mother is too unreliable to be trusted, Noel's on the other side of the country with his own family, and even if I knew where the hell Gia was..." He swallowed, because speaking about the woman who brought him into the world always put a caustic taste in his mouth. "I wouldn't want her anywhere near us."

Tura's smirk faded, and she folded her arms, leaning one hip against the counter. "What are you trying to say?"

"We don't have anybody," he admitted, lifting his glass to his lips. He slugged back a mouthful of iced tea and crunched down on an ice cube, burying his other hand in his hair. "I have friends, but it's not the same."

There was a beat of silence, and he was distinctly aware of

her gaze resting on him, unyielding and dark. Taking another sip of his drink before he set it aside, he stared down at his hands, pressing his palms together. "Do you think..."

His voice trailed off, and she filled the silence with a wry remark, clearly meant to diffuse the tension and divert the conversation to lighter fare. "Frequently, yes."

Jack expelled a soft chuckle, sliding back in his chair to stare up at her. "How does someone get close to you?"

Tura shifted her stance. "What?"

"You have friends, don't you?" Jack reasoned. "I'm just wondering what those people did to get past the walls you've been throwing up since—"

"I haven't been throwing up walls," she interrupted him.

"Oh, come the fuck on," he said flatly. "I'm not an inattentive man. I want to know what gauntlet your friends had to run to earn your trust, because I haven't heard you give a straight answer in twenty years."

Tura's eyes narrowed, but she didn't respond. Jack sighed and got to his feet, reaching into his back pocket to withdraw his wallet. Closing the distance between them, he took out a business card and pressed it into her palm, standing over her. "Whether or not you think you did something special, you *saved* us, and I came here to express my gratitude. I was hoping enough time had gone by for us to set aside the past and at least be friends, because I miss us. I miss having a *family*."

"Jack." Folding her arms around herself, she spoke quietly. "Birdie made us a family. That ended when she died."

"Let's not lie to ourselves, Tura. It ended a long time before that," he retorted, the truth burning his throat like acid. Lifting one hand, he smoothed his fingers over the back of her hair and pressed his lips to her forehead. Then he turned and left without a backward glance.

ten
tura

December 25th, 2005 - 2:00 a.m.

"Psspsspss," someone hissed, as if trying to lure a cat. One of the men across the street stepped off the curb and lifted his chin, sneering at her through a patchy thicket of dark hair. "Hey baby, c'mere. I wanna talk to you."

A rumble of masculine laughter rolled through the pack of men behind him, their eyes cold and predatory as they followed her down the otherwise empty nighttime street. Clenching her jaw against the impulse to respond, Tura forced herself to keep walking, because running would only excite their chase instinct. Under normal circumstances, she might've asked the prick if his mother was too busy sucking dick to teach him any manners, but not now, after midnight, when the man had what amounted to a professional hockey team to back him up.

"Hey baby, hold up!" The men followed, laughing and jeering until she turned the corner and ducked behind the bumper of a parked car, digging into her bag for the can of mace Birdie gave her when she went off to college. A company of footsteps approached, clustering around the mouth of the street.

"Come on. Bitch isn't worth it," one voice ricocheted in the quiet, noticeably slurred.

She crouched, shivering with adrenaline and bitter winter cold as she listened to the posse scuffling down the street, laughing and kicking over trashcans as they went. Waiting for icebound minutes until she couldn't hear them anymore, she bolted to the end of the block where her car was parked. Catapulting inside, she locked the door and checked all the mirrors, scanning for any dark shapes that may be lurking. Her hands were shaking so hard it took several tries to fit her key into the ignition, then she turned it and...nothing.

"Fuck! No! Please no!" She sobbed, slapping the dashboard. This couldn't be happening. She tried again, and again, then fell back in her seat, lamenting, for the first time, never having jumped on the cellphone bandwagon with the rest of her Nokia toting peers. The yellow sign of a twenty-four hour minimart caught her eye, and she swiped her arm across her face, steeling herself. Shoving the car door open, she sprinted for the safety of the storefront, scaring the man behind the register half to death when she exploded through the door.

Jack was the one to answer the phone, voice corroded with sleep. "Mmph. Do you have any idea what time it is, asshole?"

"Jack?" She clutched the wireless handset against her ear as the cashier hovered behind her, wringing his hands. "Can you—"

"Hello? Do you know what time it is? Take me off your list," Birdie answered the upstairs phone a beat later, and for a moment there was nothing but charged silence.

"I've got it, Birdie," Jack grumbled. "You can hang up."

"Tell whoever it is not to call so late," Birdie ordered him, complaining as she dropped her end of the landline into the cradle.

There was a loud click, and Jack took a breath, sounding somewhat more conscious than he had before. "Tura? Is that you?"

"I'm really sorry, but I was at a party and these guys were chasing me and my car won't start and—"

"Okay, okay," he cut her off. "Just tell me where you are."

He came loping through the door thirty minutes later, coat flapping, the legs of his flannel pajama bottoms bunched up above the tops of his unlaced boots. He shoved her into the car and barely uttered a word, gripping the wheel with both hands for the whole drive back to Fall River. Pulling into the muddy lot next to the house, he slipped off his seatbelt and turned to her, his eyes hard as topaz. "You want to explain what the fuck you're doing, running around Providence in the middle of the night?"

"I told you. I was at a party." Feeling exposed, she tugged her coat over her legs. "I was walking back to my car and everything was fine until these guys started following me—"

"Following you?" He twisted, laying one arm over the back of the seat and pushing her hair out of her face. Grasping her chin with the other hand, he lifted her face into the meager illumination from the nearby streetlight. He looked her over, then something in his expression softened, and he let go, sinking back against the door. "No one touched you?"

She hugged her elbows, shrugging into herself. So she hadn't been hit, or raped. She wasn't going to feel "okay" for a long fucking time. "It was just scary. That's all."

He nodded to her leg, where a patch of freshly abraded skin showed through a rip in her fishnets. "What happened there?"

She frowned, flexing her knee. A thin line of blood crusted on her shin. She hadn't felt it happen. "I must've scraped it when I was trying to hide."

His nostrils flared, and he swiveled his head, staring out

the windshield. Several seconds passed, and he spoke without looking at her. "Come on. And be *quiet*. Birdie sees you like this she's gonna pop a fucking blood vessel."

They came in through the back door, kicking off their shoes and hanging up their coats in the little mudroom off the kitchen. Jack took one look at what she'd been hiding under the long winter coat and nearly choked. "Jesus *Christ*, Tura. What are you wearing?"

"I'm an angel." Tura held her hands out at her sides, displaying her leather corset and cuffed short-shorts. "Well, I *was*. I must've forgotten my wings somewhere."

"Have you checked in *Hell?*" Putting his hands on his hips, Jack regarded the wound on her knee, his humor fading. He lifted his chin, indicating the kitchen table. "Go sit down. I'll get the stuff."

Tura took a seat as Jack dipped into the downstairs bathroom. Unclasping the front of the corset, she drew a grateful breath when the thick fabric shucked away from her midsection. Hell wasn't a bad guess. It was the night of the Xmas Eve Naughty or Nice Party, when the boarding house's ballroom was transformed into the dark, glorious underworld of the Hellfire Club, the walls draped in black velvet and dancing with projector-generated flames. Rikki reigned as their own Lord Dashwood, perched atop a throne of skulls, and guests were required to pick a side, dressing as either angels or demons. The waitresses wore nun's habits with slits up the sides, high enough to show off lacy red garters. She'd come to Birdie's for the traditional Feast of the Seven Fishes dinner, believing it would be safe to sneak out after everyone else settled in for the night. Clearly, she was wrong.

eleven
jack

December 25th, 2005 - Original Sins

Walking into the room, Jack shuffled through the first aid kit in search of the extra large bandages. A movement to his right caught his attention, and he glanced up just in time to watch Tura toss her corset onto the table and stretch her arms overhead, leaving the swath of skin between the underwires of her bra and the waist of her shorts visible through the mesh of her top.

"Here we go." Tearing his gaze away from her midsection, he sat down and patted his knee. She lifted her foot, wincing at the movement, and gingerly laid it across his proffered thigh. The cuffs of her shorts rode up, and there, just below the crease of her hip, he could clearly make out the telltale shape of a monogram tattoo. Reality hit hard. Not only was she hiding a body to make the angels weep under all those kooky black clothes, but someone had *branded* her.

Hooking his fingers under the fabric of her tights, he ripped them more, providing himself a clear space to work. He unscrewed the cap on a bottle of rubbing alcohol and pressed a cotton ball to the neck, going to work cleaning the wound. He kept his eyes trained on her knee throughout, speaking in a flat, dispassionate tone. "I probably don't have to tell you how bad this could've been."

"You think I *asked* to be street harassed?" Tura's knuckles were bloodless and white where they gripped the seat of her chair.

"No." He reached for one of the big Band Aids and peeled it open, positioning it over the wound. "I'm just asking you to be careful. For all our sakes."

"I *am*." She slid her leg off his, setting her foot on the ground. "Tonight could've happened to anyone."

"True." He collected the detritus and got up to toss it in the trash. "And I'm not suggesting you deserved it, but I spent the whole time driving into the city scared shitless, thinking about what I was going to find when I got there."

"I'm sorry." She stood up carefully, testing her weight on her injured leg, then limped to the cabinet to take down a glass. "For what it's worth, I'm glad you were the one to come."

"What are you doing?" He crossed the small space, reaching up to grab a glass for her. "Just sit down. What do you want?"

"Water, please." She complied, hopping up onto the counter and tucking her hands between her knees. Waiting as he filled the glass from the faucet and handed it to her. "You don't have to fuss. I'm fully capable of taking care of myself."

"Like there's a chance in hell I'm going to sleep tonight," he spoke peevishly, opening the freezer to locate a bag of peas. After what she'd put him through tonight, he might never sleep *again*. She watched him with those disquieting eyes as he laid the bag over her knee, holding it in place. After a few seconds, he cleared his throat and took a step back, busying himself by putting together a late night snack.

"So what's up?" He skirted around her to take a box of

cereal from a high shelf. "We haven't talked in a while. Noel said something about you taking a semester off school."

"Noel said that, huh?" She directed a sardonic smile at the ground.

"You know how he can be when he gets a hair across his ass," Jack sighed, opening the silverware drawer for a spoon. "Seems like a waste, though. You're almost halfway through."

"That's because I started at sixteen. I don't think people appreciate the pressure that puts on a kid." She shrugged, unconcerned. "Also, I don't know why Noel thinks his opinion is welcome. And don't say, 'Because you're his foster sister and he loves you.' We both know he gets off on judging everyone around him. I'm not special."

"Nah, you seem to have both sides of that argument covered." Jack grinned, pleased to see time had done nothing to dull the streak of fierce tenacity that'd served her since childhood. "You're a smart kid. I'm sure you'll land on your feet no matter what."

"Yeah. That's me," she deadpanned. "I'm the smart kid."

"Shut up, you know what I mean," he said, warmed by how natural it felt, just hanging out, talking like adults. "You're gonna do you, no matter what anyone else says. I've always thought that was a pretty cool way to be, even if you never had any use for the rest of us."

"I had use for you guys," she murmured. "You were too busy."

Jack's smile faded. "Life kinda got in the way."

"Speaking of, I was sorry to hear about you and Imogen. What happened there? She seemed cool."

"God, we really *haven't* talked for a while. That was almost four years ago." He opened the fridge to retrieve the milk. "And you're right, she was cool. The problem was, we had a little *too* much in common. Like how much we both love vagina."

Jocularity gleamed in her eyes. "Could be worse, right? At least she didn't dump you for being bad in bed."

"That's what I tell myself." The tips of his ears reddened, and he laughed, somewhat chagrined. "For now, I'm just focusing on finding someone who loves my penis as much as I do."

"I've never really understood men's appreciation for their junk," she observed, earning a raised eyebrow from him. "What? It's just always struck me as terribly inefficient, carrying your genitalia on the outside."

"You know what?" He invaded her space as he reached over her head to take down a cereal bowl, the action forcing the air from his sternum and making his voice sound strained. "I'm not going to justify the utility of my dick to you."

Jack would spend years analyzing what happened next, trying to determine where the impulse came from. It probably had something to do with having shared a harrowing experience and being too emotionally fucked to see the line before they crossed it. What he *did* know was there was a clean bowl in the dish rack next to the sink, yet he chose to reach into the cabinet over her head for a new one. From there, the order of events remained perfectly ambered in his memory.

He reached up, caging her against the length of his body, accidentally pressing against her bandaged knee. She hissed, recoiling hard enough to whack the back of her skull on the cabinet pull, and slid off the counter. The bag of peas hit the ground and burst, sending them scattering like unstrung pearls.

"Shit, sorry." He caught her against him, pairing his smile with an apologetic squint. He probed her scalp with his fingers, the pad of his thumb working back and forth over the tender spot on the back of her head. "You okay?"

"I'm good." She nodded, slashing her gaze downward, a

sudden tension in her posture. "This would be hilarious if it hadn't been such a messed-up night."

"Yeah." He hucked out a sheepish laugh, but didn't release his hold, didn't back away. *Why couldn't he back away?*

The refrigerator compressor kicked on. The clock on the wall ticked, keeping time with the dull rhythm of his throbbing heartbeat. It was like a game of high-stakes chicken; they hung by a thread for the space of a few breaths, his gaze leveled on her mouth, focusing on the way her lips and teeth parted. At first he thought he'd imagined it when the hem of his shirt lifted, but then she grazed her knuckles over his hip bone and along his waist, coming dangerously close to his cock, already standing at half-mast. He closed his eyes, unable to hide the faint groan that escaped his lungs.

That was it: the moment he felt his morals leave his body.

Operating on pure muscle memory, he picked her up, clamping his hands around the back of her thighs and throwing her onto the counter as if competing in the caber toss. Sliding both hands under her ass, he hauled her closer, pressing against the crotch of those stupid tiny shorts so she could feel what she was doing to him. He wasn't thinking about shame or the alienation that would follow. The only thing in his head was sweaty skin and wet slapping noises and the way she'd feel around him when he pounded home and— *Jesus fuck what am I doing?*

His superego flung itself into frame like a secret service agent diving in front of a bullet, delivering him a hard mental slap. He backed up so fast his foot caught something and looking down, he felt a rush of heat blaze up the front of his neck, recognizing his discarded shirt. He barely remembered taking it off; just the overwhelming desire to feel her skin against his. He felt sick. What if she told someone? They'd all hate him.

"No-no-no-no-no," Jack whispered, the sound of his

heavy swallow like a handful of gravel in the barrel of a washing machine. He released a final, heartsick sigh and bent down, picking up his shirt. "I'm sorry, Tura. I'm just...sorry. "

By morning, he couldn't even bring himself to look at her. He sat on the other side of the room, stomach tied in knots. Keeping his eyes down as breakfast was consumed and Birdie passed out presents, unable to look anyone in the eye for fear it was written all over his face. *I touched Tura.* He never thought he'd be relieved to get away from that house, but he left as soon as he could, and spent the next week feeling his gut clench every time the phone rang, expecting Birdie or Noel to harangue him for being such a depraved animal. Only she never told a soul, as far as he could tell. She just let him walk away scot-free, and that's what most confused him.

Tura would be out of town a lot in the twelve years before Birdie's death, and for the times when she climbed out of whatever bolthole she was hiding in, he made excuses. Trips with friends. Spending the holiday with his girlfriend's family. Sudden, vague illnesses, just serious enough to preclude his attendance. They wouldn't see each other again until the afternoon of Birdie's funeral, and even then, they would never acknowledge what happened. One stupid mistake, and they were all but dead to each other.

twelve
tura

Skidding to a stop in front of her office, Tura hopped off her bike, her heart hammering at a brisk two hundred BPM. Rikki sat perched on the front stoop with Honey, and if it wasn't such a dire situation, Tura might've laughed at the image of her unflappable friend sitting huddled to one side as a little girl mindfully nibbled the edges of an ice cream sandwich. Tura strode toward them with her hands wide. "What the hell happened?"

"I don't know!" Rikki stood up, stricken. "She just walked right in and asked for you. Did you give her the security code?"

"Honey." Tura crouched to the little girl's eye level. "Is everything okay? Did someone bring you here?"

"Auntie Portia didn't have any appointments today, so we got to go to the library," Honey said, without looking up from her ice cream.

"You walked here?" Tura asked. Assuming Honey was talking about the Athenaeum, which laid five blocks away, it wasn't outrageous that a precocious kid might find her way here on her own. Then again, she already knew Honey was capable of walking much further, when she set her mind to it. "Where's Auntie Portia?"

Honey's shoulders leapt in a brief, guileless shrug. Taking this to mean the poor woman was back at the library climbing the walls with worry, Tura sat back on her heels, casting a troubled glance at her friend.

"Honey." Tura reached up, drawing the little girl's hands away from her mouth. "That was *very* dangerous."

Honey blinked her thick sunshine-tipped lashes. "I wanted to see you."

"Right." Tura held out her helmet to Rikki. "I'm going to need your car."

Fifteen minutes later, they pulled up in front of a dramatic Skillion roof house on a heavily wooded parcel of land outside the city. Jack was beside himself by the time Tura called, already out combing the city along with a small army of police officers. He instructed her to deliver Honey directly to his house, presumably to thwart any last minute bids for freedom during prisoner transfer.

Tura leaned forward to admire the black yakisugi and glass paneled front of the building. This wasn't what she'd pictured when she imagined Jack's home. Then again, she'd worked very hard to *not* think about Jack Aldridge for the last eighteen or so years.

Unbuckling her seatbelt and clamoring out of the back of Rikki's red Bel Air ragtop, Honey dodged onto the deck with Tura following behind. They sat with their feet up on the squat glass-topped table in the outdoor seating area, Honey keeping up an unbroken line of chatter. Tura kept her eyes trained on the gap in the trees until a sensible blue Subaru SUV came bouncing down the unpaved drive at a speed that was definitely *not* good for the suspension.

The wheels scraped to a halt and Jack came charging out

with murder in his eyes. "Honoré Elisabetta Aldridge, you are so *punished!*"

Yes daddy. Tura looked away, disturbed by her reaction. Jack stalked up the stairs in a stone gray suit and shining brown leather shoes, unlocked the front door, and glared at the little girl next to her. "Do you have any idea how *scared* your Aunt Portia was when she couldn't find you? Get your butt to your room. Right now."

Honey didn't make a peep of protest as she hopped up and scurried past him into the house. Jack slammed the door and walked to the deck railing. He dragged a shaking hand through his hair and exploded, punctuating each syllable by slamming his palm on the railing. "Fuck. Fuck. FUCK-FUCK-FUCK!"

Tura watched as he paced back and forth, fighting to get himself under control. He looked so fierce with the dying sunlight glinting off his sharp features, and she pressed her knees together, attempting to check the unwelcome thrum in her pelvis. She reminded herself he'd reached a momentary breaking point. That having horny thoughts about a man triple-naming his kid and just *barely* keeping his shit together was probably not the healthiest response, but good god*damn*...

He finally stopped and stared out at the trees, breathing hard. "What the *fuck* am I gonna do with this kid? How can she be this smart and still so fucking..."

"We both know brains are no guarantee of common sense," Tura said, noting the clench of his jaw and the tension in his shoulders. "I think she's lonely, and looking for people to relate to."

"Yeah." He dropped his head into his hands, laughing morosely. "That's what the shrink said."

"I'm glad you're getting her some help," she told him, quashing the compulsion to touch his shoulder.

Jack straightened, looking at her for the first time since he arrived. Pulling himself together, he took a big step to one side, giving her a clear path to the stairs. "I'm sorry. I could really use a glass of wine. Care to join me?"

Tura gave him an apologetic shrug. "I don't drink."

Jack let out a ragged breath. "Well, thanks for bringing her back."

"No problem." She stood up, then stopped. She'd spent the last three days beating herself up for chasing him out of her apartment when all he wanted was to be a part of her life again. The universe wasn't going to hand her another chance. "On second thought, I could use a glass of water."

"Then I'm switching to whiskey." He allowed himself a smile, opening the door. "I'm not drinking a bottle of wine alone."

thirteen
tura

Stepping inside his home for the first time, Tura took in the flood of warm red cedar and potted plants. The chic sunken seating area centered around the modern ceiling-mounted woodstove, and slatted wooden screens dividing the loft from the downstairs. "Wow. This is nice."

"Thanks." He showed her to the gleaming stainless steel kitchen tucked under the loft. "I had this place in my head for years before I finally built it."

"Wait. *You* did all this?" She slid onto a stool at the polished concrete island, taking a discreet look at the fridge door as Jack opened it to pour her a glass of water. It displayed the typical miscellany of artwork and photos one might expect from a family home. Jack in suit and tie, crouching next to his daughter on what looked to be her first day of school, a kindergarten aged Honey in denim overalls and braided pigtails, shouldering the straps of a sunshine yellow backpack. The two of them sitting on a plastic sled at the top of a hill, bundled in snowsuits and hats, rosy cheeked and red nosed. The compulsory school photo of Honey displaying a missing tooth for the camera, and *oh*, her heart gave an uncharacteristic squeeze, a closeup of Jack cradling a tiny newborn against the skin of his naked chest, beaming with elation. No photos of Vanessa, but below a sloppy finger painting of a deformed triceratops enjoying an ice cream cone, she spotted it: the graduation day photo from a million years ago. Embarrassment heated her cheeks, tempered by a sweet edge of sentimentality. She thought she'd destroyed all evidence of her steampunk phase, but there she was, preserved for all eternity in barnstormer hat, goggles and (oh, the *humanity*) corset dress, on the receiving end of a vicious noogie.

"As a matter of fact, I did." Jack passed her a glass with a lopsided smile. "I'm an architect."

"Right. I knew that." She offered him a flustered smile. Birdie kept her well abreast of everyone's progress throughout the years, even if she was actively working to not hear any of it. Casting another gaze around the open, restful home he'd built for himself, she could see her inattentiveness for what it was, an act of self defense. "Kind of a trip, when you think about it."

Taking a bottle of whiskey out of a high cabinet, he splashed a couple fingers into a glass. "Enlighten me."

"Well, space and time bend around gravity, so technically there's no such thing as a straight line." Tugging off her jacket, she laid it over the empty seat next to hers. "When you stop to consider reality itself runs on a curve, it seems almost paradoxical anyone could pursue a career based on straight lines and right angles."

"Yup. That's me. Building a life on the unattainable." He turned, sipping his drink, and did a spit take, sending a fine mist of whiskey through the air.

Tura bristled. "What?"

"Your shirt," he hacked out the words from his doubled-over position, pointing an accusing finger at her chest. He managed to right himself just as she looked down and realized she'd shown up at his house wearing the tee shirt Rikki bought her for Valentine's Day, the words BUTT STUFF printed in red script right across her tits.

"Oh." She crossed her arms over the lettering and rolled her eyes. "It was a gift from a friend."

"No, it's fine. It's just..." He wheezed, his eyes watering as the whiskey seared his sinuses. "Please don't let Honey see you wearing it. I have enough problems without having to explain *that* to her."

"Noted." She gave him another close-lipped smile, dropping her arms to her sides.

Jack sniffed and managed a pained smile. "Are you hungry? I could *murder* a pizza right now."

She lifted one shoulder. "I could eat."

"Great." Jack opened a drawer and took out a notepad and pencil. "Wait here."

He walked down the hallway, and a door opened. She heard the notepad slap onto a flat surface, and the scratch of pencil on paper. His voice echoed in the quiet. "Tura and I are going to order a pizza. You are going to sit right here and copy out the words 'Baba wants me to be safe' until you fill up the page."

Tura could just make out the soft cadence of Honey asking a question, and Jack's deep, patient intonation filled the hallway again. "One page, every other line, and then a page of your special vocabulary words. Get started, and then you can have pizza."

The door clicked closed again, and Jack reappeared, taking off his suit jacket. Tura stared, struggling to reconcile the swaggering playboy she'd watched duck responsibility at every turn with this scrupulous, dependable monument to fatherhood. She felt like they'd switched places. "How'd it go?"

"I'll take the thumbscrews off after dinner." One side of Jack's mouth hitched up in a fatigued grin as he loosened his tie and unfastened his top two buttons, his shirt falling open against his collarbones. "Let me run upstairs and change. There are menus in the drawer on the end, if you want to think about pizza."

She circled the island to retrieve the menus, listening to his footfalls on the stairs and the creak of his movements in the loft overhead. The house was quiet, but she didn't feel uneasy or hyper-vigilant, the way she often did in unfamiliar territory. It was as if he'd taken special care and built a feeling of security right into the walls of the house. A few minutes later, he reappeared, naked to the waist in well-worn jeans, pulling a Henley shirt over his head as he jogged down the stairs. She averted her eyes, consciously avoiding looking at the dusting of dark blond hair trailing below the relaxed waist of his jeans. He caught sight of her and smiled, the gold wire arms of his rimless glasses glinting at his temples.

"Wow. Glasses, huh?" she observed, forcing herself to keep her eyes above his chin.

"Only when my contacts get uncomfortable," he said, sliding up behind her. "Any decision?"

"My go-to is peppers and onions with extra black olive." She turned her head, very aware of his closeness as he leaned over her shoulder to look at the menu. His laughter rumbled against her back.

"That would be perfect for us, but good luck getting Honey to go anywhere near an olive."

"You want to get something else?" she asked, but he shook his head, holding his phone to his ear.

He ordered a large veggie double olive pizza and a small cheese for delivery, then dropped his phone onto the counter and smiled breezily. "Should be here in forty-five minutes."

"Well thank you for dinner. I was about to go home and have a peanut butter sandwich." She followed him to the sitting area, where he picked up a remote and pressed a button. A set of doors on the far wall slid open, revealing a flatscreen television.

"Nah, you're saving me from eating alone." Jack settled onto the sofa and put his bare feet up. "Honey will be having her dinner in her room tonight. Possibly breakfast, too."

"A writing assignment *and* solitary confinement?" she asked, sitting down on the tangent and leaving a good six feet between them. "You're a cruel jailer."

"The assignment is for her to think about what she did." He gave her that crooked smile again. "The time in her room is for *me*, so I can cool down after the shit she just pulled."

"You're a good dad." The words volleyed from her mouth without any forethought. She clapped her mouth closed, feeling slightly embarrassed, which again, was not in her usual repertoire.

"It's a struggle." Jack slung one arm over his head, affecting a thoroughly relaxed pose. Tura couldn't help but notice the band of flat abdominals visible beneath the hem of his shirt. Age had done nothing to wither that physique. He gave her a sanguine smile. "What are you in the mood for?"

fourteen
jack

During a commercial break, Jack stared at a seed hole in the toe of Tura's sock, his mind churning. Used to be all she had to do was exist to throw the ugliness that marked him into sharp relief, and the comparison felt unbearable. She was such a bright kid, and he'd wanted so much to preserve her from his appalling history that he'd somehow overlooked the fact she was becoming someone else.

Being with her now was like turning the page in a story and realizing someone ripped a crucial chapter out of the middle. The entire narrative skipped forward and there was no way of knowing what he'd missed. She'd grown into herself. She had stories, and secrets. He'd wager she had her heart broken once or twice, too, and all those scars created a new dimension in her.

Reaching for the remote, Jack turned down the volume and sat up, planting his feet on the ground. They'd propped their pillows at one corner of the sunken seating area, sprawling out on a ninety degree angle from each other, their heads separated by a few inches of foam. From this new position, he could admire the bridge of her nose and the way her hair fanned across the pillow. "Hey, can we talk about something?"

She shifted to look at him over the pillows. "Okay."

"What happened today won't happen again," he volunteered up front, wanting to get that part out of the way first. "I'm not saying I approve of her methods, but Honey doesn't trust a lot of people. If she had to develop an unhealthy fixation on a stranger, I'm glad it was you."

"She's one determined bad penny," she said, pushing herself to a seated position, one foot tucked under her body.

"That may be my fault." He gave her a retiring smile. "She found this shoebox of photos I'd rescued from Birdie's house and asked who the people in the pictures were. She's still too young for the whole 'we don't talk to your biological grandma because she's a neglectful drunk who allowed her shitbag husband to kick Baba in the back with crampons' conversation, and she never asked a lot of in-depth questions before. I didn't know what else to do, so I told her Birdie was a mom for kids who needed parents. I think she was just surprised to find out I came *from* somewhere, which naturally led to more questions about the other kids she took in. Then a few weeks later we were driving to the library and I pointed at your office and said 'See, that's where your Aunt Tura works.' I don't know... Maybe it was still fresh in my mind."

"I see." Tura took in this information, a gentle smile playing across her lips. "Ironic, since I never considered myself particularly child friendly."

"Okay, so you're not exactly a storybook princess," Jack admitted, earning a snort of agreement from the woman next to him. "I'm just glad she found someone that made her feel safe."

"Me too." Tura nodded, looking down. "I've been wondering how she was doing."

"It was a little touch and go there for a while." Jack pressed his hands together, his gaze fixed on the place where the wedding band used to occupy his ring finger. His daughter was too young to hear Nessa struggled with her mental health since she was a teenager, and received an official diagnosis of Bipolar Disorder in her freshman year of college. He knew he'd have to tell her when the time came, but did she have to know Nessa had managed her symptoms very well up to the day the pregnancy test came back positive? That the hormonal fluctuations and changes in medication and sleep deprivation had destroyed her well-being? A scathing laugh slipped past his lips. "I was way out of my depth *before* all this happened. Now I'm dealing with the knowledge I'm raising a very gifted stalker."

"Kids are scary stuff." She smirked. "Part of the reason I never felt tempted to go into the parenting racket myself."

"My mother-in-law tried to get Honey to kiss Nessa at the funeral." Jack closed his eyes, unsure of exactly why he felt the need to put that particular atrocity into words. "My daughter is going to spend the rest of her life with the knowledge she was sleeping in bed next to her mother when she died. She's going to have those images in her head forever, and that woman picks her up and holds her over the casket and tells her to kiss her mother."

"Jesus *Christ*, Jack." Tura reached out to touch his arm, looking suitably horrified. "Tell me you stopped her."

"Fucking right I did." Jack nodded, eyes burning. *Not now.* He hadn't cried throughout this entire ordeal. Not when Tura told him Nessa was dead. Not when he spent twelve hours on an interminable flight home, willing the plane to go faster, or seven torturous hours driving through all kinds of weather to find his child. Not when the coroner informed them the overdose was intentional, speaking over Kathy's unhinged screams from the next room. Not even at the funeral when he saw his wife laid out, looking so peaceful, yet so thoroughly changed by the years of hell she'd put her poor body through. His eyes brimmed, and a single tear broke free, tracing the side of his face. "I've never wanted to do violence to *anyone* like I wanted to do to Kathy, but I took my daughter and told her she was *done* being in our lives."

"Jack." Tura slid closer, until the sides of their knees touched. "That's awful and I'm sorry."

"I just keep thinking, what if Honey goes that way, too? What if she's already so fucked up from all this..." More tears broke free, an over-welling of emotion that poured out all at once. Not just for Nessa's death, or his fears for Honey, but the overwhelming stress of being the sole caretaker for an unthinkably vulnerable alien being for the past six years. He put so much energy into keeping her *alive,* most days he had nothing left for himself. A minute passed, maybe two, and he swiped his hands over his face, cursing himself. He laughed uneasily, casting a dolorous smile over his shoulder. "This is embarrassing."

"Jack. This is a truly shitty situation, and I don't blame you for feeling this way. I would cry, too. Anyone with a *soul* would cry." She laid one hand on the back of his shoulder, radiating benign acceptance. "But for the record, I don't think Honey will end up like Nessa. Not as long as she has you."

He turned his head to meet her steady gaze, and not for the first time, he wished he could go back to that night when lust broke the dam of his good sense and he put his hands on the girl he'd spent a lifetime promising to protect. Tell that stupid, horny kid there would come a day when all he could do was look back on those thirty or so seconds in Birdie's kitchen, aching with remorse. He never stopped to think what touching her would mean. Drawing a deep, ragged breath, he hung his head. "Fuck, Tura. I'm so sorry. For everything. I never should have let things go as far as they did."

Her hand slipped from his shoulder. "You want to do this *now?*"

"What do you want me to say?" He sighed, ready to face whatever wrath she could throw at him. "I fucked up, and I knew while it was happening. I was looking down on myself and thinking, 'You stupid asshole, you can never take this back.' But I did it anyway."

She gaped at him, her mouth dropping open for a solid three seconds before she responded. "I was there too, Jack. You act like you crawled into my bed and held me down like some dirty old man. I was an adult woman and an active participant."

"I was older. I should have known better," he reasoned. "I should have walked away, but I was too stupid and too fucked-up. Back then, sex didn't have any value because *I* didn't have any value. Things came so easily to me, but with you... I want you to know my leaving had *nothing* to do with you not being good enough."

Her brow furrowed, and unless he imagined it, he detected the slightest glimmer of amusement in her eyes. "Thank you. I appreciate your saying that."

"Good." He exhaled gratefully, a huge weight lifting off his shoulders. "I just wanted you to know. Because you were the first person to make me feel like I wanted to deserve it. Not just take what I was given."

"Jack." She put her arm around him, resting her cheek on the curve of his shoulder. "You were never unworthy to me."

Jack covered her hand with his where it rested on his bicep. "Please tell me what to say to fix this, Tura. Because I want Honey to know you. I think she needs that."

She stared into his eyes for a beat. "I only wish we could've had this conversation eighteen years ago. Things might've been different."

"Maybe," he murmured, giving her hand a final squeeze

before releasing it. She was right; if he hadn't stuck his head in the sand, things might've worked out differently. Hell, maybe they could've given it a try. He could only imagine the looks of horror on Birdie and Noel's faces when they found out, but who knows? They might've been good together. Then again, he would've done something to fuck it up eventually. He'd have lost her anyway, and he wouldn't have Honey, and he couldn't bring himself to regret any of the missteps that brought her to him. He leaned back and draped his arm around her shoulders, pulling her into his side. He propped his chin on top of her head, scuffing his hand over her arm. "We're here now."

A soft *ding* sounded, and Tura pulled away from him, reaching into her back pocket for her phone. She expelled a long-suffering sigh. "Sorry, I borrowed a friend's car to drive Honey home, and they're really needing it back."

"Oh. Yeah." He sat up, rubbing his palms together. He'd briefly registered the presence of a flashy two-tone Chevy in his drive when he got home, but once again, he'd been too focused on Honey to think about it. Tura collected her things, and he walked her to the door. "Thanks again for bringing her home."

"Meh. Forget about it." She shrugged breezily. "Not like I can keep her, right?"

Jack chuckled as he opened the door, letting her out into the cool night air. "Hey, you never know. She keeps pulling shit like this, I might be open to it."

Tura laughed as she started down the stairs to the car. Then she stopped, turning to look at him. She pushed a stray piece of hair out of her eyes. "Hey. Would you mind if I dropped Parsnip by sometime? She only takes up space at my place, and I have a feeling she'd get a lot more love living here."

Jack grinned. "Sure. Bring her by anytime."

fifteen
tura

Hattie Lamont's Boarding House was one of those notorious places that defined a neighborhood, drawing people in like the star at the center of a solar system. Originally constructed as a sea captain's private residence, the house transitioned to a brothel and rumrunner's headquarters in the early 1900s. They even had a tunnel leading from the dominatrix's dungeon in the basement to the speakeasy on the next block, which was conveniently owned by the same shadowy benefactor whose family owned the boarding house since Prohibition.

These days, few people knew what went on behind the doors of the boarding house. It was mentioned every so often in the newspapers, usually for an outrageous party thrown in its storied courtyard, or the occasional careless public figure caught coming or going in the early light of dawn. Fortunately for the players involved, all members were required to sign a nondisclosure agreement, so such rumors generally went unsubstantiated. For those on the inside, the freedom contained within was more than worth their silence.

Parties were the lifeblood of the house, the time-honored hustle that kept their hedonistic utopia in the black. Events geared toward the vanilla set, such as the disco-themed International Talk Like a Pirate Day Cannon Ball, or the Fourth of July Patriots v. Loyalists Pillow War, were open to the general public, provided attendees paid in advance. Tickets to those events invariably sold out, but as popular as they were, they were nothing compared to the members-only parties. These parties were exclusive, invitation-only events where discretion was of the highest priority, such as the Bastille Day Cake Sitting Splosh Party, or the Spring Chicks & Bunnies Cuddle Pile, or tonight's Back to School Student-Teacher Conference.

The dungeon looked very different this evening. All the usual implements of torture were moved out to make room for old hinge-top school desks and chairs, arrayed in a perfect ten by four grid facing a wall-sized blackboard. A colossal globe sat in the corner, and educational posters hung on the walls with gum paste. The only thing lacking now was a class of properly attired students, which would arrive at the stroke of ten, streaming through the doors with all the anticipation of the first day of school. Many came accompanied by paddle-wielding "private tutors," eager to mete out vigorous punishments to any pupils charged with infractions.

"It's wonderful to see you donning the Headmistress's skirt again," Rikki mused, plunking a tall canister of sturdy metal yardsticks and rubber tipped chalkboard pointers in one corner of the makeshift classroom, in case any instructors found themselves in need of a spanking implement. "It's a role you were born to play."

"Why, thank you." Tura preened, pushing the horned rimmed frames of her costume glasses up her nose before shaking out a disposable paper tablecloth printed with bright red apples and green bookworms. She laid it over the buffet table and stepped back, smoothing her hands over the hips of the aforementioned pencil skirt. "You didn't forget to order the mushroom tartlets, did you?"

"And risk getting an eyeful of your grim little puss all night?" Rikki guffawed, reminding her once again she was on *their* turf tonight. She may call the shots at the office, but under this roof, Rikki was master of ceremonies. It was a lifetime appointment, and Rikki considered it a calling, not unlike joining the priesthood. "Perish the thought. I ordered an extra tray, just for your hollow leg."

"You're so good to me." Tura started laying out cans of chafing dish fuel for the catering trays. It wouldn't do to serve cold cocktail meatballs at a Hattie Lamont's party. They had a reputation to uphold as the best orgy buffet in town.

"So." Rikki leaned against the fieldstone wall, brows arched in an expression of affectionate concern. "Is it safe to assume we'll be seeing more of Dreamboat Jackie?"

"Not sure. I'll probably be hanging out with his sidekick, at the very least." Tura put her hands on her hips, giving her friend a satirical smile. "I'm a *good influence*."

Rikki's leery snort left no space for embellishment.

"I know. That's what I said," Tura continued her musings as they started up the narrow stone stairwell to the kitchen. "It's so weird to think of Jack having a kid."

"It's definitive proof karma exists, if you ask me." Rikki chuckled, opening the door at the top of the passageway. They stepped into the kitchen, where a small army of cater waiters in plaid ties and short-brimmed uniform caps buzzed around, preparing to serve. "I can't think of a better way for the universe to balance itself out than by giving a man like that a daughter."

"And how would you know what kind of man he is? I never even introduced you!" Tura laughed, stealing one of the beloved mushroom tarts off a neatly appointed tray and earning an irate glare from the harried looking caterer.

"Which, by the way, was a huge oversight on your part. I bet Birdie is *still* turning cartwheels in her grave." Rikki fell into step behind her as they climbed the elegant front stairs to the second floor hallway. Removing a brass service bell from their corduroy professor's jacket, Rikki gave it an authoritative ring. "Twenty minutes, people!"

A flurry of movement sounded from behind the doors lining the hall, as the other residents scrambled to complete preparations for tonight's festivities. Tura knew that feeling well, the curtain call before a performance, when the butterflies took flight. They got her, every time. Rikki turned to her again, an adroit glint in their eye. "Tura milove, I didn't have to meet Jack. I was here for the aftermath of your last encounter. Or have you forgotten the way you spent weeks haunting around the house like someone boiled your bunny? What I don't get is, why go back for more? Does this man have a prehensile tongue or something?"

"Oh for fuck's sake," Tura hissed. "What would I know from his tongue? I never so much as kissed him, and you act like he was my first."

"Pssh," Rikki delivered a blithe retort. "Your 'virginity' and a hundred bucks would've bought that boy a train ride to New Haven. Lord knows that ticket was punched *long* before he got there."

Tura threw up her hands. "He never got there! There was no getting of any kind. None."

"Wait, really?" Rikki's brows shot up. "I always assumed you were lying about that."

"Why would I lie?"

"There was the whole humping on the same table where your mom fed you breakfast the next morning ick factor." Rikki's grin broadened, curling up at the corners like a mischievous cat. "Plus, the boy was the shining star of your first masturbatory fantasy, and if I'm honest, the filthy borderline incestuous wrongness of it was always the hottest part for me."

"Sometimes I worry you and I may be *too* close." Tura shook her head, trailing after them into their bedroom. "And at *no point* were we on the table."

"No, I know." Rikki flopped down onto their unmade bed, leaning back on their elbows. "That was an artistic choice on my part."

"Why am I discussing this with you? It didn't happen."

"I have no earthly idea, but that gives me another reason to dislike the guy." Rikki swept a hand in front of Tura's body. "I mean, what kind of dumb motherfucker is this man?"

"I'm paraphrasing, but from what I gathered last night, he didn't want to use me."

"Hmph." Rikki gave a resentful grunt. "That was probably the only enlightened thought to ever float through his pretty little pea brain." They sniffed, adding a pert toss of their head. "I hope it gave him a headache."

sixteen
tura

PULLING UP IN FRONT OF A CHARMING FEDERAL HILL townhouse, Tura killed the engine and checked her reflection in the window of a nearby storefront, swiping ineffectually at the mascara rings under her eyes. It was well past two a.m., and after an evening spent presiding over the punishment of dozens of students who just couldn't seem to retain the material, all she wanted was a foot rub and a good meal. The view from the headmistress's desk was entertaining, but she'd spent four straight hours in platform stilettos. No one wanted to watch the object of their unrequited lust chaw mushroom tartlets all night and there was a solid "no eating in uniform" rule at the house, which meant she was famished.

Her stomach gurgled as she let herself into Ethan's apartment. There was music playing, something unobtrusive and filled with acoustic guitar, and she smiled, dropping her bag on the table next to the door. Following the piquant scent of sofrito and spices into the kitchen, she found the man himself stirring something on the stovetop, seemingly unbothered by the lateness of the hour. "Something smells amazing!"

"Caldo verde, just like Avo used to make." He grinned at

her over his shoulder, and she slipped her arms around his waist, reaching down to caress him through the front of his slacks. Handsome in the simple, accessible way of a younger man, Ethan Silva was slim-hipped and well-dressed, with swarthy good looks passed down through an ancient Portuguese bloodline. He had the unguarded openness of a man for whom life laid down in a harmonious, abiding path. Perhaps that was why she invited his attention in the first place. She wanted something easy and uncomplicated. "You want some? I've had the strongest craving for it lately."

"Sorry. No meat," she reminded him. "I'll make a sandwich or something. Do you have any of that really good Sao Jorge cheese?"

"Check the fridge," he suggested, laying down his spoon and turning to pull her into his arms. Bending her backward over the counter, he rained kisses over her chest and neck then leaned back, his expression taking on a serious cast. "What's the matter?"

"Did I say something was wrong?" The mood effectively gone, she circled the counter to open the fridge. Ethan studied her for a moment longer, then lifted the wooden spoon again, directing a solemn gaze to the pot on the stove.

"You just have a look."

"I'm tired. It was a long day." Tura exhaled a husky laugh, unwilling to retrench her preoccupation for the benefit of yet another person. "All I want is to put something in my stomach and spend the rest of the night in bed."

"I think we can make that happen." Ethan fixed her with an equable smile, dipping himself a bowl of sausage and kale soup. "Tomorrow, we can sleep in, and then the guys were talking about heading to Newport for a pub crawl. That could be fun."

"Yeah, not really my scene." She turned her back to him, a

lance of guilt twisting between her ribs. This wasn't his fault. He couldn't have known the nightmarish heap of tragedy she lived with. A ready lie rose to her lips. "Anyway, I still have a few things to wrap up at the office."

seventeen
jack

JACK NEVER THOUGHT HE'D SEE IMOGEN VERACRUZ festooning her house with pastel balloons and streamers, let alone renting a bounce house for her backyard. Yet here he was, marooned in the controlled chaos of her stepdaughter's birthday celebration, watching the kids dashing sugared up zoomies in the yard.

The late September air was warm enough for the kids to play outside while Genie's bride Portia passed out cups of fruit punch. Cake time was over, and they'd clubbed the piñata. A few exhausted looking parents stood off to the side, but Jack didn't bother approaching. Portia's daughter Olivia and Honey both went to the same private elementary, but that was where the similarities ended. The other parents always seemed a little stiff around Jack, probably because he was well-known as the guy with the Dumpster fire personal life. Like it was *catching* or something.

"Hey!" Genie slapped his back, saluting him with the glass of California red in her hand. Petite and amber complexioned, she wore her chestnut ringlets tied back in a high, tomboyish ponytail. "Have any luck with the babysitter interviews?"

"Nope." Jack lifted his beer to his lips. Add his inability to secure competent childcare to the fact it'd somehow slipped his mind Honey's birthday was next week, and he was failing parenting on all fronts. In his defense, they'd suffered a hellish couple months, and Honey didn't really like to make a "thing" of her birthday. She'd probably be happy doing something low key and eating a slice of cake for dinner. "I'll have to figure something else out."

"Don't worry." Genie stood next to him, observing the chaos unfolding on her back lawn. "Not like it's out of the way for our sitter to pick up both girls a few days a week."

"Thanks. I appreciate that." Jack looked over at his daughter, currently having a sparkly rainbow butterfly painted on her face. "I got a call from the school councilor last week. She thinks I should enroll Honey in the summer STEM enrichment program."

"Wow." Genie leveled her cognac-colored eyes on Jack. "It's neat how your smartest sperm quit chasing its tail long enough to make something of itself."

Jack chuckled, silently watching his little girl dancing in the sunlight, swatting at bubbles. Nessa was smart like that. They'd met at a networking function shortly after he and Genie secured funding to start the firm. Nessa was there with a client they'd been hoping to land, but Jack was too smitten to care about tanking a commission. From the first moment he met the scary smart biochemist with the beauty queen smile, he'd been in awe of her. That she would spare him a moment of her time felt surreal, but she had no patience for his "I'm damaged goods, don't count on me" routine. If he wanted to be any part of her life, he'd have to start taking himself seriously. So at the ripe old age of thirty-six, Jack Aldridge finally grew up.

Fast forward a few years and Jack was coming home to find

Nessa passed out on the sofa while a pan of pasta boiled down on the stove. Honey was less than a year old then. The doctors suspected postpartum depression at first, but it soon became evident there was something much worse going on with his wife. Her moods would swing out of control, causing her to have violent outbursts that had him picking up their daughter and taking her to the neighbors' at least once a week.

After a particularly nasty episode where she threatened to stab him with a steak knife, the doctors upgraded the diagnosis to Bipolar Psychosis and admitted her for inpatient care. Medication helped, and for a while it was like having her back, but once she started to feel better, she stopped taking the meds and the problems started again. Eventually, it got so bad Jack had to take Honey and leave for good.

Without him around to help keep her straight, Nessa lost her job and fell neck-deep into drugs. Jack strung along for months, wanting to keep her on his health insurance for as long as he could. His friends begged him to see reason, labeling his inability to cut ties as enabling Nessa's behavior, but it was so much easier said than done. The final breaking point came when they lost the condo. Lacking a steady income, Nessa ran up massive credit card debt. Forced to sell their home and facing the prospect of bankruptcy, Jack had no choice but to file for divorce.

Even after that, he tried to get her into one program or another so many times he lost count. It broke his heart to see her get clean, find a cocktail of meds that worked, then relapse again. It was worse for Honey, too young to understand her mother's *illness* was the thing preventing them from having meaningful contact.

Nessa didn't attempt to contest Jack's petition for sole custody, and stopped showing up for visitations. She would call him in tears after each missed appointment, saying she couldn't stand to let her daughter see her this way. Many nights, they cried together; for the loss of their family, their home, and each other. Ultimately, the calls stopped coming, and she just *went away*. Until Nessa died, he'd been under the impression his daughter hadn't seen her mother in over two years.

eighteen
jack

"Tell us about this Auntie Tura person Honey won't shut up about." Portia appeared at her wife's side. Full-figured and garnet-lipped, with deep sepia skin and cropped natural hair, Portia didn't walk; she undulated, every movement as poised and exact as a ballroom dancer. She carried an open bottle of wine, refilling Genie's glass and fixing her incisive brown eyes on him.

"Oh, is Tura back?" Genie looked to him for confirmation. He nodded, and she pivoted to her wife, speaking with the authority of someone who'd gotten an insider's view of Jack's private life when they dated during college. "Tura was one of Birdie's kids. What, nine or ten years younger than us?"

"Eight," Jack corrected her, happy to keep his gaze trained on the activity in front of them while Genie provided the exposition. That way, no one could see the conflict knotting his brow every time he thought about Tura.

"Right," Genie said, continuing her description. "She was super smart. Started college young and then I don't know, everyone lost touch. It was always sad to me."

Up to speed, Portia looked at Jack. "And she's back now?"

"Sort of." Jack swirled his beer in its bottle, a nervous

habit he was certain Genie clocked as soon as he did it. He only prayed she'd wait until Portia rushed off to refill the onion dip before laying into him about what he wasn't saying. For now, he kept his face impassive. Nothing had changed, except his daughter had imprinted on a glamorous stranger like a baby duck, and his wife's ghost was chattering at him nonstop. "Tura's the one who took Honey when Nessa had her accident. She seems to be doing well for herself, and I thought it might be good, having a positive female role model around."

"Ah yes, as opposed to what we are," Genie teased, waving her hand between herself and her wife. "Piles of candy corn in support hose."

"Forgive me," Jack deadpanned, wondering how he and this harridan were ever romantically involved. "What I meant was *another* positive female role model."

"You really can't have too many." Portia gave him an approving smile. "Honey makes her sound so exciting, with her 'nose earring' and tattoos. And a motorcycle? Really?"

"Tura's a Riot Grrrl. Who knew?" Genie snickered into her glass. Jack tamped down the impulse to tell her Tura wasn't so little anymore, and hadn't been for a long time.

"I think Honey's starstruck by her. That's all." Jack shrugged, doing his best to hide the shudder of culpability that went through him every time his thoughts turned to Tura. Sure, they'd talked it out, but it was a hard habit to break after all these years. The motorcycle was new information, and for one hot second he was caught up in the waking reverie of watching her grip a powerful machine between her legs as she maneuvered it through traffic. Jesus, was that making him hard? *Fantastic. Let's just add that to the dung heap of complications that is my life.*

"Are you planning on getting together more?" Portia asked, earning a look of pure aggravation from him. She held up her hands, an emerald bracelet sparkling on one supple wrist. "Hey, Honey's been talking nonstop about her."

"If this whole head shrinking thing doesn't pan out, you could have a bright future as a military interrogator," Jack groused, briefly wishing Genie had settled for one of the bubble-headed sexpots she'd gone for in their younger years, rather than scoring a diamond-sharp pain-in-the-ass like Portia.

"I thought about that." Portia sipped her wine. "Didn't like the hours."

As expected, Genie waited until her wife excused herself before she swallowed a lip-puckering mouthful of wine and rounded on him again. "All right, this look you've got? I know this look. So give it up."

"Trust me, if there was anything to tell, I would." Jack forced a laugh, stonewalling as if his life depended on it. "Tura seems good, but she's grown up now. We don't really know each other anymore."

Genie looked dubious. "And you're letting her spend time with Honey?"

"Yeah." He didn't know why, but his mind went to the photo he used to keep tacked above his desk in his dorm room, the one of Birdie and Tura rolling out pie dough in the kitchen. Back when he could still think of her as Little Tura, innocuous female child. "Honey really likes her. That's gotta say something, right?"

"Sure. Tura was always a nice kid," Genie's tone remained noncommittal, in the way that usually indicated she was reserving judgement until she had more evidence. They stood in companionable silence for a few minutes, then she nudged him, a slow, evil smile spreading over her face. "Hey. You remember that time you brought me home for Thanksgiving and she almost caught us fooling around on the couch? I had your dick like, *all the way* in my mouth and you got this look on your face..."

"I remember." He laughed, chagrined. Birdie refused to let an unmarried couple share a bed under her roof, which meant Jack was relegated to sleeping on the convertible sofa. Genie sneaked downstairs and they were just getting into it when a light came on in the stairwell.

They sat petrified like lawn statues, draped in the merest camouflage of shadows, Genie's head buried in his lap. Tura shuffled through the room on her way to the kitchen for a glass of water, bleary eyed in her baggy sleep shirt. The kitchen lit up. Holding a finger to his lips, Jack quickly tucked himself away. The cabinet doors bumped open. The faucet ran. They waited for Tura to douse the kitchen light, sprinting back through the living room and up the stairs, as if the night itself pursued her. He sent Genie back upstairs before they could press their luck any further and finished himself off when she was gone, his hand shaking with adrenaline.

Their moment of shared nostalgia passed, Jack slung his arm around Genie's shoulders. "Seriously, though. How does Portia not hate me?"

"I don't have the crayons to explain a healthy relationship to you right now." She smiled, tilting her glass to her lips.

nineteen
tura

"I wasn't sure I had the right place." Avi slid into the darkened velvet booth opposite Tura, adjusting the edge of his slouchy skullcap lower on his forehead. He looked, as ever, like a perfect dirtbag in his military surplus jacket, ripped jeans, ear gauges, and collection of chunky silver rings. The type of man who flew under the radar because most people on the street avoided making eye contact, even though under the strategic layer of facial hair road grit, he was blessed with a brand of finely composed beauty usually reserved for anime characters.

Taking the seat facing the door, he left his mirrored aviator sunglasses on the table where he could keep an eye on the back hallway, both holdover habits from his time in the Marines. He swept his eyes around the green moire papered walls of the bar and nodded in acknowledgement of his own shortcomings; usually he was the one to know all the best spots.

"Good job finding it." Tura set her teacup on the table in front of her.

Avi flagged down a waitress and ordered a drink, looking sidelong at her. "Still not drinking, huh? Doesn't that get boring?"

"No, it just means I have to take responsibility for all my bad choices." She drew a tight breath. They'd gotten very good at this dance. Conduct enough clandestine meetings in nondescript bars, the conversation flows. "It's really good to see you."

"Same to you." He hunched forward, folding his elbows on the table in front of him. Slipping the spare key to her apartment off her keychain, Tura pushed it across the table. Avi chuckled, palming the key as the waitress arrived with his drink. "I guess this means we're moving on from the small talk."

He lifted his glass to his lips, the ice clinking in the quiet. "So. What've you got going these days?"

"Taking a bit of a hiatus right now," she said smoothly, sweeping her finger over the rim of the delicate china cup.

"About damn time."

"But I did have a meeting with Bosker last week. Client took a contract handling imports for a company out of Eastern Europe. Looked legit on paper, but it was a front. They've been bringing in heroin."

"Fucking hell," Avi snarled low in his throat, his lips tight with the effort of keeping his voice down. "I oughta break Bosker's arms for dragging you into something like that."

"I can take care of myself." She sighed, unaffected. "Anyway, you know how I feel about drugs."

"You and your goddamn righteous jobs." Avi smirked, once again confounded by Tura's personal code of ethics. "I assume he's already got pieces in play."

"Should be a good show." She smiled, pleased with the ingenuity of the plan. "The authorities will raid the client's offices in the next couple weeks, poke through their files, comb through the warehouse, generally make nuisances of themselves. Meanwhile, the assholes sitting on two pallets of unclaimed heroin on the other side of the Atlantic are going to see all the attention their partners are under and go looking for someone else to move their poison. As far as they know, the original importers still have no idea what they were doing."

Avi's smile faltered. "How'd Bosker get the government guys to go for that?"

"It works in their favor." Tura flipped her hair. "This gives them the opportunity to address some weak points in the organization."

"You're batshit. You know that?" Avi fixed her with a shrewd smile. He dropped a few bills on the tabletop. "Come on, walk me out."

Tura got up and followed him into the afternoon sunlight, where he surprised her by pulling her into a tight hug.

"Missed you." He breathed the words against her hair.

"Missed you too." She pressed the bridge of her nose to the soft fabric of his pretentious vintage tee shirt, soaking up as much of his presence as she could, because he was bound to vanish again. It was his way. Avi stayed on the move, always looking over his shoulder, trying to keep one step ahead of his demons. In a few more years, he'd float through town with a few more scars to mark his absence. A few more stories he couldn't tell her. That was how their lives seemed to progress, in fits and leaps of time.

twenty
jack

Jack arrived for afternoon pickup just in time to see Kathy drunkenly squaring up against one of the playground attendants. Cursing under his breath, he got out of his car and jogged across the pavement as Principal Park and the gym teacher came charging out of the school. They got there first, the principal's commanding voice booming through the courtyard. "Mrs. Berrada, you do not have permission to be here. The police have been called."

"What the fuck does that mean?" Kathleen slurred, a bead of sweat dripping down her puffy red face. Jack noticed the jaundiced orange chroma of the spray tan veiling her leathery skin with no small measure of schadenfreude. It never failed to shock him this haggard wraith had birthed his luminous wife. "She's *my* granddaughter. I have a right to see her."

"No, you do not," Principal Park said firmly, stepping between the drunk woman and the badly rattled playground aid. "Furthermore, I intend to press charges against you for trespassing."

"My baby is *dead!*" Kathleen screeched, rheumy eyes bulging. "I want to see my Honey! She's all I've got!"

"That's not going to happen." Jack took the woman's

elbow before she could do anything more to embarrass his daughter, steering her over to one of the benches. The Principal was close behind, a hard look on her face. He pushed Kathleen none too gently onto the seat and bent down to give her a warning glare. "You don't get to do this to us. You're interfering with Honey's education."

"She's *my* grandbaby," Kathleen snarled through cigarette yellowed teeth.

"And she's *my* daughter." Jack straightened without a hint of sympathy, folding his arms over his chest. "I'm not giving you anymore chances to fuck with her head."

Kathleen bounded to her feet, screaming into his face, or at least as close as she could get from her height of five-foot-nothing. Her breath reeked of alcohol, and Jack was confronted with the uncomfortable knowledge he'd left his daughter in the care of this total shitshow of a human being. "You need me!"

"*Nobody* needs you, Kathy," Jack gritted out, wishing he'd walked a little slower when he got out of the car. Principal Park looked like she could tune a bitch up. He would have enjoyed the spectacle of this lunatic taking a swing at someone and getting knocked out.

A siren chirped in the parking lot, and two uniformed officers paced onto the playground. It took both of them to wrestle the inebriated woman to the pavement, kicking and screaming. Jack was grateful they'd herded the children back into the building so they couldn't see Kathleen maced and cuffed, the stream of profanity tumbling from her lips only heightening in pitch as they dragged her out of the courtyard and shoved her into a squad car.

"Mr. Aldridge." Principal Park stood at his shoulder, a frown creasing her brow. "It's obvious Mrs. Berrada has been struggling since the death of her daughter. I feel for her loss and yours, but I want you to know I will be pursuing an order of restraint on behalf of this school."

"Good." Jack put his hands on his hips, working to slow the thundering pulse in his temples. What was another day in family court? One more stamp on his frequent plaintiff's card and he might win a prize. "I'll be your star witness. Just tell me when to show up."

"I don't think I need to remind you stability is crucial for your daughter right now." Principal Park softened, pressing her palms together. "This *cannot* happen again."

"I promise you..." Jack caught sight of one of the playground attendants leading Honey out to meet him with that guilty, kicked puppy look in her eye because as always, his daughter internalized the blame rather than being an inconvenience to others. Snapping his eyes to the principal's, he flexed his jaw, a bolt of pain shooting between his eyes, signaling an oncoming migraine. "This will *never* happen again."

And the hits just kept coming. Sitting at a stoplight in Olneyville fifteen minutes later, Jack tightened his fingers around the steering wheel, watching as some random hipster sleaze wrapped his arms around Tura. They stood that way for what felt like an eternity, holding each other and swaying. *Of all the intersections in this goddamn city.* He'd avoided seeing her for almost two decades, and now she was everywhere he looked.

He waited for Nessa's patient voice to chime in at the back of his mind, to give him some sage advice, but she chose this moment to stay silent. Of course.

"Baba? It turned green," Honey piped up from the back seat a split second before the driver of the car behind them leaned on their horn. Jack started to move up, realizing too late the light had already timed out, damning him to sit there for another round. Tura and the mystery douche finally separated, and the stranger got into a ride share going in the opposite direction. Jack watched her stand on the curb and wave him off. She turned away, and he swore he saw her wipe a tear from her eye. Was he an old lover? A friend? Had they just broken up? Jack had no idea. All he knew was he *hated* this feeling in the pit of his stomach.

"Gree-een," Honey intoned from the back seat, and Jack gratefully stepped on the gas.

By the time they arrived home, his head felt like a troupe of tiny men with pickaxes were trying to burrow out of his sinuses, and his vision was starting to blur. Honey ran up the stairs ahead of him and waited for him to unlock the door. She tugged his sleeve. "There's a present."

Jack swiveled his migraine-tunneled vision away from the door, following her eagerly pointed finger. Someone left a colorful gift bag on the deck, a pleat of tissue paper spilling out the top. After the day they'd had, he wasn't about to let her get anywhere near whatever it was until he'd had a chance to check it out. "Go on inside, baby girl."

"But what about—" She whined, gazing entreatingly toward the beckoning gift bag.

"Hey, you don't know. Maybe it's for *me*." He gave her a lenient nudge, fighting to avoid taking out his discomfort on her. "Go start on your homework or no TV tonight."

She pouted, but did as she was told. Jack paced into the bathroom and shook a couple aspirin into his palm. He swallowed the pills with a mouthful of lukewarm water from the tap, then went back out to examine the mystery gift. Lifting it off the cushions of the sofa, he pushed the tissue paper aside and smiled down at Parsnip's faded calico ears, feeling his headache subside by a fraction.

twenty-one
tura

SENSING AN INCOMING CALL, TURA'S CELLPHONE switched off the heavy metal blaring through her earbuds, leaving a sudden vacuum of sound. Tura stopped jogging, sucking in a few deep breaths before she answered. "Hello?"

"Hey, Tura?" Jack's voice fed through her earbuds, rich and comforting. "Am I interrupting something?"

"Just out for a jog," she explained, settling onto the grass to stretch. "You could have texted, you know."

"I'll try to remember that for next time." His laughter caressed her ear. "Listen, I'm sorry to call so late but I wanted to wait until Honey was down."

"It's fine, I keep weird hours anyway," she assured him, unable to hide the amusement in her voice. It couldn't be later than nine-thirty; could this really be the same Jack who used to creep in at dawn at least once a week? "So what's up?"

"I just wanted to say thank you for the stuffed animal. Believe it or not, her birthday's this Saturday, so it was timely."

"Wow." Widening her legs into a V, she twisted to the side and laid her forehead against her knee. "Couldn't have planned it better if I'd actually planned it."

"I guess not." He paused, some of the humor fading from

his tone. "I wish you'd seen her open it. It really made her night."

"Yeah, I was out running errands and figured it'd be easier to drop it off." She smiled, pleased to let Parsnip go now that she'd be in safe hands. "But I'm glad she likes it."

"So," Jack drew out the word, as if he was working up to something. "I was talking to Honey, and she wanted to ask if you'd like to join us for her birthday this weekend."

Tura paused mid-stretch, frowning to herself. She'd figured now they were on speaking terms, he might call her to babysit from time to time, when he ran out of better options, or *maybe* extend an invitation during the holidays. But a birthday party? The thought triggered flashbacks of small, sticky hands, pointy paper hats with those annoying elastics that always pinched behind the ears, and *shudder*...clowns. "I'm not sure I'm the children's party type, Jack."

"Don't worry, we have a strict no Barney Burger policy in our family." She could hear him smiling, picture the easygoing expression on his handsome face. "I asked, and all she wants to do is go to the bookstore and eat ramen."

"Wow." Tura nodded, impressed. "My kinda kid."

"I know, it's the weirdest thing. As far as I know, the only ramen she ever had was from a package. She must've seen it in a cartoon."

She got up, folding her hands over the top of her head, and pondered for a beat. She never expected to be invited to crash daddy-daughter time. On the other hand, hey, free noodles. "As long as you don't mind having me along."

"Not at all." Jack chuckled easily. "Saturday afternoon?"

"Sounds good. Meet you there?"

"We can come to you. How about noon?"

"All right, cool." A body brushed past her, and Avi stopped to stretch his hamstrings, the blade of his prosthetic clearly visible below the cuffed leg of his joggers. Tura turned her back, ignoring his quizzical expression. "I'll see you then?"

"Great." She heard him hesitate. "Have a good night."

"Goodnight, Jack."

"That was just *adorable!*" Avi called, bouncing to avoid flooding his muscles with lactic acid.

Tura pulled a face as she hung up. "How about you bite me?"

"Hey, I don't like you *that* much." Avi threw his arm around her shoulder as they started in the direction of her apartment.

"Babe?" A familiar male voice sounded through the chilly park, and they both looked up at once. Ethan approached, leading a geriatric beagle on a blue leash. He trotted across the grass, grinning like an eager puppy as his aged companion waddled along on stubby little sausage legs.

twenty-two
tura

Fan-fucking-tastic. Tura groused internally, her stomach clenching as Ethan pressed his lips to hers. A guileless smile decorated his perpetually tanned face, reminding her once again life had been kind to him. A small part of her wondered if on some subconscious level, she'd done this on purpose. She knew Ethan's office was right around the corner. She knew he jogged around the Riverwalk on nights when he worked late and had friends in the neighborhood. The odds of bumping into him while out with Avi were high. Whether this little travesty was for his benefit or Avi's was the real mystery.

"Hey, man." Ethan dropped his gaze for the briefest moment, taking note of the missing portion of Avi's left leg before he stepped up, holding out a hand. "Ethan Silva."

Avi dropped his hold on her to grasp Ethan's proffered hand, his gaze sliding in her direction. She could see the question written on his face, even if Ethan didn't know to look for it. Theirs was the wordless language of two people who'd seen hell with their own eyes. "Avi."

"Avi," Ethan repeated with an amiable grin, then looked to

Tura, pointing to the dog by way of explanation. "Dogsitting for a friend this week. This is Dexter."

Tura bent to ruffle the animal's ears, feeling the first chill on her skin as the adrenaline began to ebb. "He's cute."

Avi caught her eye, pressing his lips together in a brittle smile. The questions were gone, replaced with pure, exculpatory awareness. Ethan put his hands on his hips, his gaze moving from Tura to Avi and back. "So, how do you two know each other?"

"Friends from the neighborhood," Tura paltered, eager to supply an explanation that didn't dig too deeply into her tragic origin story. "You know how it is."

"Yeah, for sure." Ethan checked his watch. "I've gotta get him home, but maybe another night we can all grab drinks and hang out?"

"Right. Another night." She smiled stiffly, lifting a cheek for him to kiss. "Sorry, I'm all sweaty."

"You always taste good." Ethan breathed a good humored chuckle against her ear. He gave Avi a broish nod in passing, spinning to point at him. "Avi. Awesome meeting you, dude."

She stood and watched Ethan move down the walkway with the elderly beagle for another ten or so yards before she paced over to the closest park bench and sat. Tucking her hands under her thighs, she slid a guilty smile in Avi's direction. He took the seat next to hers and draped one long, muscular arm along the back of the bench, keeping his gaze directed to the water. "So, that's the guy you're seeing?"

She gnawed her lower lip, staring at the ground. "That's the guy."

"He doesn't know," Avi observed, his tone impassive. She hazarded a glance at him, expecting condemnation, but his face was blank. "You haven't told him."

"Sometimes it's nice," she admitted. "Not having to be two people at the same time."

"It certainly saves on pity." He nodded at the insight. "They don't waste a lot of time trying to make everything better. Then when it falls apart, they assume you're just an asshole."

"He'll figure it out soon." She sighed, pushing her sweaty hair away from her face.

"You deserve more than this, Tura," he said quietly, a strange look of grief clouding his eyes. Not sympathy; more akin to betrayal.

Tura swallowed, leaning into the chilly breeze coming off the water. "Maybe."

Avi didn't respond at first, instead tilting his head back and letting the autumn air move over his sweat-slicked face. At length, he reached out and tucked a strand of hair over her ear. "I'll admit I'm no expert on functional relationships, but you deserve to be *known*. All of you. Not just the parts of you that are easy to take."

"What about you?" A recalcitrant edge crept into her voice. "When are you going to stop running?"

"I don't know." He shrugged, unruffled by her defensive posturing. "Actually, I've had this feeling lately, it might be time to stop dodging ghosts and look for a more permanent situation. I kind of took your offer to put me up as a sign."

He dipped his head to catch her gaze, giving her a curious smile. The hand he'd rested on the bench closed over the back of her neck, massaging gently. "Something up?"

Inhaling a wavering breath, she slid closer to him, leaning into his side. If he'd been anyone else, she might've brushed it off. Told him she was right there with him. But Avi would always know better. "He asked me to move in with him."

"Ethan did?" His voice dropped by an octave. He angled his gaze down at her. A casual passerby might've mistaken them for lovers, engaged in an intimate conversation. "What'd you say?"

"Nothing, yet." She looked down at the palms of her hands. "I think it was more of a panic ask."

"Meaning..."

"He picked up on me holding back and overcorrected." A nighttime water taxi passed, and she lifted one hand to wave to the tourists at the railing. "It's probably just a way to force an answer to the *us* of it all."

"Or he really likes you," Avi suggested. "I saw the way he looked at you. A man can't fake that."

"You're saying I should do it?"

Avi chuckled softly, lifting his arm off her shoulders and sitting forward. He propped his elbows on his knees like a baseball player preparing to charge the field, running one thumb over the heel of the opposite hand, stretching his fingers wide. "I think you know what I'm gonna say."

"Don't ask questions you don't want answers to." She slid a mischievous smile in his direction.

"Exactly." He twisted sideways, his eyebrows shooting up. "Anyway, how are you gonna explain to your live-in boyfriend that you're hanging out with the prodigal foster brother this weekend?"

"Not that I anticipate this happening..." She gave him a portentous glare. "But on the off-chance you meet Ethan again, let's just keep that under our hats, shall we?"

Avi's smile was demonic. "What's it worth to you?"

twenty-three
jack

"Don't touch that," Jack ordered Honey when she twirled too close to a pool of something dark and sticky on the sidewalk. Her excitement at seeing Tura made her careless, and she wasn't paying attention to her surroundings. He held out a hand when she nearly stepped on what appeared to be a discarded thong, partially wedged between the curb and the pavement. "Actually, don't touch anything. Come hold my hand."

"How many books can I get?" Honey piped, skipping along next to him.

"Let's start with seven." He lifted Honey onto his hip to stop her bouncing around like a cocaine-fueled kangaroo rat as they walked through the entranceway and boarded the elevator. He set her down when they reached Tura's floor. She ran ahead and knocked, then flung herself at Tura before the door was fully open, gazing up at her with a reverence most people reserved for The Grand Canyon, or the Sistine Chapel.

"Come on." Jack reached for his daughter. "Give her some space to breathe."

"No, it's okay." Tura leaned back to get a better look at her, resting her hand on top of Honey's head. "Why don't you guys come in? I have to get my stuff."

She was wearing another monochromatic black cyberpunks a go-go ensemble today, and Jack couldn't help but grin as she shoved her feet into a pair of heavy motorcycle boots. "Looking good, Kaplan. Still fighting your way out of that simulated reality matrix, I see."

"Why is it every time you come to my home, I feel judged?" Tura stood up, tugging a knit beanie down over her ears. "You don't see me coming to your house and reminding you of the time you grew a ponytail."

Jack smirked in discomfiture. "I'm never going to live that down, am I?"

"Not while I'm alive." She rocked back on her heels, quirking an eyebrow. "I'm the one that made the 'Who Wore It Better' poster with you and Taylor Hanson."

"Which wasn't even a fair comparison, by the way. He was *thirteen* when that pic—" *Nope.* recognizing the futility of the argument, Jack put his hands on his hips. "Are you through?"

"Tay-tay was actually Birdie's idea. I wanted to use that hot Australian underwear model."

"Jesus Christ." He chuckled miserably, scrubbing both hands over his face. "Why are you *like* this?"

"Am I the only one who remembers the time you convinced me everyone has a finite amount of skin, and if they ran out they just walked around looking like raw meat for the rest of their lives?" They stared at each other for a long moment, each daring the other to break first.

"Can I pet the kitty?" Honey's tiny voice pierced the fog of nostalgia, and Jack turned to see a spindly black kitten arching its spine against his daughter's ankles.

"If you do, it'll never leave you alone again," Tura warned her, lifting her bag over her shoulder. "And don't touch its belly, even if it rolls onto its back. It's never *not* a trap."

"Is that new?" Jack asked, watching his daughter bend down to run a hand over the kitten's fur.

"It's temporary," she replied, her voice laced with perturbation. "I'm kind of holding it for someone while he looks for a place of his own."

"That's a hell of an ask," Jack observed without taking his eyes off his daughter. He'd always judged himself more of a dog person, since they generally pooped outside and seemed to appreciate human interaction, but he could see the enamored look dawning on Honey's face. He wondered how fast he could track down the world's most adorable puppy to counteract this slow-moving disaster.

"Meh. I wouldn't have agreed to keep it here, except I'm kind of hoping getting a pet means he'll stick around for a while." Tura slid a vexed look toward the offending creature. "Anyway, it's not so bad when it's not sharpening its claws on the furniture or horking up hairballs on my bathmat."

"It's so soft!" Honey exclaimed, her eyes wide and wondrous. "What's his name?"

"Hell if I know," Tura griped, starting for the door. "Come on, kid. Let's get this show on the road."

Color clung to the trees in Burnside Park, splashes of yellow, orange and red peppered in amongst the greens. Honey walked between them, clutching their hands and watching her feet the way she did when she was deep in thought. Tura lifted her face into the dappled sunlight and inhaled. "I missed this."

"Walking?"

"That air." She scuffed at the cobblestones with the heel of her boot. "It's been years since I've been home in the fall. You can't get that smell anywhere else."

"Where'd you go?"

"LA. Dubai. Seattle. Berlin." She shrugged. "Everywhere."

"You're lucky." He gave her a sideways smile, his hair

blowing in the chilly autumn breeze. "Not counting Jamaica, since I was there for less than twelve hours. So, I haven't traveled since my honeymoon in Cancun."

"Why not?"

"Work, mostly." A *shameless* lie. He had ambitions to see the world once. Nessa's late father was originally from Morocco, and when she was pregnant, they'd discussed taking Honey there to experience her North African heritage. Then everything went to hell, and the plan fell by the wayside. His thoughts cleared when Honey lifted her feet from the ground, swinging between them for a beat. Dropping his shoulder, he set his daughter on her feet and returned his attention to the conversation in progress. "Being the new guy at any firm automatically makes you the mule, so I spent the first few years after college getting established. Then Genie and her dad had a falling out. She was working at his firm in Philadelphia, but we decided to start our own after he fired her. I was already here and she wanted to get away from home, so this felt like a natural fit."

"I didn't realize you owned the business."

"It's been a slow climb," he mused, thinking back on the struggle of getting the venture off the ground. "But I wouldn't change the decision for anything."

"Wait, is this the same Genie from college?" She looked shocked. "The one who dumped you?"

"Same one." Jack chuckled. Someday when Honey understood the concept of getting dumped, she'd probably harken back to this moment and realize his relationship with Auntie Genie was more complex than she surmised.

Tura was silent for a moment, then lifted her chin and let out a breezy huff. "There are worse places to get stuck. I used to think this place was too small, but that wasn't the issue."

"What was?"

She drew a breath and let it out, a wayworn smile stretching over her face. "I had some growing to do. That's all."

twenty-four
tura

JACK UNLEASHED HONEY IN RENAISSANCE CITY
Books with a warning to stay within the bounds of the children's section, then withdrew to stand with Tura at one of the high cafe tables on the side. From there, they could observe the younger Aldridge's progress without getting underfoot, and every so often Honey trotted over to pass her father another selection, asking the same question, "How many is that?"

"We'll count later," Jack would tell her, adding the book to the stack with a pacific smile. The girl accepted this answer the same way each time, turning on her heel and marching away in a businesslike manner, curls bobbing behind her. Two hours passed. Jack checked his watch. "We'll go soon."

"Don't worry about it. Just got to the good part." Tura lifted the book in her hand. Lipping the straw of her iced lavender lemonade, she eyed the tower of books between them. "Dunno, Jack. Pretty sure that's more than seven."

"Yeah?" Leaning with his elbows braced on the table, he looked to where the stack had grown nearly to the height of his shoulder. "A few more won't hurt."

"Mmm-hmm." Tura turned the page in her book, rolling her eyes to herself. *Pushover.*

"Hey," he spoke aside to her. "Thanks for this."

"As long as I'm not watching an animatronic band, I'm cool." Tura smirked, taking another pull on her straw without lifting her eyes from her book.

"No, really." He gave her a gentle nudge. "Honey isn't the most social kid. This is a big deal."

Tura's mind went to Avi, and how little patience he had for other people. She hoped Jack didn't expect his daughter to grow out of it. "Is that weird for you? I mean, it's such a contrast from you as a kid."

"It was at first," he admitted, pushing his fingers through his hair. "I tried signing her up for stuff. Tee ball, Daisies, soccer, even ballet. She'd go for a couple weeks and lose interest, and the whole time she was coming back tired and overstimulated, having these *gigantic* meltdowns. After a while it sank in she was doing it more for me than for her. So I stopped pushing. Now she knows if she wants to do something, all she has to do is ask."

"And that worked?"

"For sure. You could feel her relax, when she knew no one expected her to be *on* all the time. And it's not like she never shows interest in *anything*," he reasoned, half-turning toward her and leaning on one elbow. "I took her to a birthday party last week, she had a nice time, and one minor meltdown in the car on the way home. It was a good day."

"Wow." Tura snickered. Who could've guessed Jack would mark success by the size of the tantrums he had to contend with from day to day? "Do they have classes for this adulting thing, or do you have to do the books on tape?"

"I mostly just panic and run to this one parent friend who happens to be a shrink."

"Sure." Tura nodded. "Whatever works."

"Baba?" Honey addressed her father from below the edge of the table, and they leaned away from each other, pivoting to look down at her. Big blue eyes pinged between them, and she cocked her head to the side. "Are you and Auntie Tura gonna do sex?"

Record scratch. Tura could feel the sudden, enthralled attention of at least a half-dozen other shoppers anchor on them. She slid a mirthful smirk in Jack's direction, admiring the crimson flush ascending from the collar of his shirt like mercury in a thermometer. Pressing her fist to her mouth, she turned her face against her shoulder. "Did you want to call that friend now, or..."

Jack cleared his throat and ducked a look at the surrounding area. Seeing the eyes on them, he ran his palm over the back of his neck, forcing a befuddled smile. "Honey, you remember that talk we had about public and private conversations?"

The little girl at least had the good sense to look mildly abashed. "But how come? Don't you think she's pretty?"

Jack looked like he'd swallowed a bug. His gaze darted to Tura's for a fraction of an instant, then flicked back to his child's innocent face. "Because Tura and I aren't that kind of friends."

"Why?"

"Because we're just *friend*-friends."

"Why?"

"Because—"

"Right," Tura interjected, leveling her attention on Honey. "For starters, your father has never asked me to do sex, and we all know that it is a very bad thing to touch someone without their permission." She paused, widening her eyes to match both daughter and daddy's stunned expressions. "And for another, that is a conversation that happens between *adults*. You do not want that kind of information about your father's life. Just trust me on this."

Honey nibbled at her lower lip for a moment, appearing to weigh the veracity of the statement. Then she nodded, placated. "Okay."

"Awesome." She gaveled the table with the side of her fist, turning to Jack. "I don't know about you, but I'm starving."

twenty-five
tura

TURA'S STOMACH GRUMBLED AS THE WAITER SET A swimming pool sized bowl of kimchi ramen on the table in front of her. Honey sat next to her in the curved booth, training chopsticks in hand, looking around at the other diners with an anxious expression on her face. Plucking a slice of fermented cabbage out of her bowl, Tura reached over and set it in Honey's, shooting her an encouraging wink. "You're *supposed* to slurp. It means you like it."

The girl brightened and dug into her child-sized portion of miso ramen, gripping her chopsticks in one determined little fist. Snaring a single noodle, she lifted it up, attempting to capture it like a fish after a worm. The noodle slipped, plummeting into her bowl and splattering broth across the front of her sweater. Honey was crestfallen.

"Hey. Here." Tura passed her a fork. "Those are tricky. Might be easier to learn chopsticks with something less slippery, like dumplings. Or chicken nuggets."

"I like chicken nuggets," Honey observed, twirling her fork overhand and shoveling a tangled gnarl of noodles into her mouth. She chewed thoughtfully, decided she liked them, and then hopped up onto her knees in the booth, attacking her food. After a few minutes, Honey leaned against Tura, tracing the tulip tattoos on her wrist. "We're going to the Trunk 'r Treat for Halloween. Do you want to come?"

"That's a while away." Jack patted the booth's cushion without taking his eyes off his food. "Come on, butt on the seat."

"Sorry weebit, but I have plans," Tura answered, allowing Honey to tuck herself under her arm. The child sighed disappointedly.

"Do you have a costume?" Honey peered up at her. "I'm going as a rhinoceros beetle."

"That's a great costume," Tura murmured, raising an eyebrow at Jack.

"She's making the mask out of paper maché." He smiled at his daughter's convoluted choice of disguise, an errant dribble of orange chili oil coloring his lips.

Ever the helpful little sprite, Honey pointed. "You have sauce on your face."

"Thank you." Jack wiped his mouth.

"So what's your costume?" Honey asked innocently, and if Tura wasn't mistaken, she'd swear she saw Jack wince. He stopped chewing, his eyes connecting with hers for the briefest moment, exactly the way they had at the bookstore.

"I'm going as ants on a log."

"Like, a celery? With peanut butter and raisins?" Honey speared a pink swirled fish cake, giving it an exploratory nibble.

"Yeah, I glued a bunch of green pool noodles together to make a celery vest, and then I wear a tan shirt and stick crumpled up trash bags to the front for the raisins."

"You should make a celery crown, too," Honey suggested, very matter-of-factly.

"That's an awesome idea. I might just do that."

Losing interest in her food, Honey crawled across her

father's lap and kneeled backwards in the booth, all of her attention taken up with watching the bright tropical fish swimming in the tank against the wall.

"Hey," Jack murmured, keeping a mindful eye trained on his daughter's back. "Sorry about before. It goes with the territory for me, but—"

"Don't mention it." She shrugged it off. "If you knew some of the shit I hear from grown ass adults, you wouldn't be sweating anything coming out of her mouth."

"I've been meaning to ask..." He chewed thoughtfully, his eyes sliding sideways to hers. "What kind of self defense do you practice?"

"Karate, Jiu Jitsu, and Krav Maga," Tura answered cautiously. She could be wrong, but something about that felt like a leading question. "Plus, you know, my personality."

Jack snorted under his breath. "I'm serious. I've been wanting to sign Honey up for karate classes, but it's tough to find any that fit with my work schedule, and even if I did, she'd only want to quit a couple weeks later. I was thinking if you were teaching her, she might be willing to stick with it, and I know you don't need the money, but I'd be willing to pay for your time."

Tura tucked a strand of hair over her ear, toying with the notion. "It's a good idea. Kids should know how to defend themselves. But you don't have to pay me. It would help me to focus on training someone else, for a change."

twenty-six
tura

CHECKING THE CLOCK AGAIN, TURA SIGHED heavily, flicking her eyes back to the television. The sun was down, and there was a freeze warning for that evening. She wanted to get home before she had to worry about ice on the roads. It was getting too cold to tool around on the Triumph everyday. It was time to roll her baby into storage for the colder months and bring out the car, especially now that she had lessons with Honey on Tuesday and Thursday afternoons. At the moment, however, her most pressing concern was the fact she and Jack had very different ideas of what constituted an "afternoon."

He'd given Tura a key so she could meet his daughter at the bus and get into the house. Bought tumbling mats so they could practice throws, as well as the child-sized strike bag which now had a home in an unused corner of the main living space. It impressed Tura how quickly Honey picked things up after only a few weeks.

What she wasn't impressed with were Jack's time management skills.

She didn't know how Honey's other sitters felt about Jack showing up three hours late to relieve them of duty, but she was tired of watching the clock. Especially because when she went out to meet the bus that afternoon, she'd gotten an odd creepy-crawly feeling that set the hairs on the back of her neck on end. She slipped her hand out of Honey's and told her to run ahead, dropping back to search the tree line, but nothing stood out. She wanted to believe she was being paranoid, that it was just her work instincts spilling over into real life, but she just couldn't shake it.

The twin beams of Jack's headlights swept through the darkened living room, and Tura felt a reflexive tightening in her jaw. She heard his footsteps on the deck, and the jingle of his keys in the lock, and sucked in a deep breath, willing the tension from her body. This would go a lot easier if she didn't begin by biting his head off and immediately put him on the defensive.

"Hey, how was she this afternoon?" Jack asked, juggling two armloads of groceries and his briefcase. Against her better judgement, she got up and went to take one of the bags, trailing him into the kitchen.

"Good." She stood to one side as he set down the things he was carrying and turned to take the bag from her, depositing it onto the counter. "I made her a grilled cheese sandwich and she's doing her homework."

"Great, thanks," he spoke over his shoulder, stashing the groceries. Eggs and milk in the fridge, pancake mix in the cabinet. Six perfect green apples in the bowl on the counter.

"It's eight o'clock, Jack." She followed him with her gaze. His hands stilled as he reached up to put away a box of assorted oatmeal packets, and she saw his shoulders slump. "If I'm going to continue doing this, I need you to respect my time."

"I know. I'm sorry." He sighed, finally looking up at her. He looked utterly defeated already, but she couldn't let it go because he said he was sorry. That's not how this worked.

"You said that last week." She wrapped her fingers around the slats on one of the kitchen stools. "And while I appreciate your apology, it means nothing if it doesn't change. In fact, it cheapens your word."

"Really, Tura, I *am* sorry." He held up his hands, attempting to delineate. "I just had a thing come up at work and I tried to get away as quick as I could, but then I realized I didn't have anything to feed Honey for breakfast tomorrow—"

"And I feel for you, I do!" Tura admitted. "I wouldn't mind if this were an occasional occurrence, like you were running late and asked if I could stay a little longer just for one night, but it cannot be a weekly thing. My time is just as valuable as yours, and I'm teaching Honey self defense for *her* safety."

"I did offer to pay you," a hard edge crept into his voice, and Tura couldn't stop herself from reacting.

"You couldn't afford my rates." Now it was Jack's turn to look surprised. "I don't know what Portia does for a living, or how she feels about covering for your open-ended schedule, but this isn't about money for me. This is about respect. Plain and simple."

He leaned forward, pressing his palms to the counter, and dragged in a capitulating breath. "As a matter of fact, Portia's just as big a ballbuster as you are."

Tura lifted her chin, unwilling to be buffaloed by the same forlorn smile he used to give Birdie when he was trying to wriggle out of trouble. "I like her already."

He stood at the counter as she stalked around gathering her things, stuffing her focus mitts and hand wraps into her backpack. After a minute, he called out to her. "So I'll see you Tuesday?"

She made for the door. "I don't know. Will you?"

"Hey. Wait a second." Jack appeared next to her, pulling

her to stop. He shifted so he was angled in front of her, his shoulder blocking the door. "I'm sorry, okay? I know I'm already on your shit list, and I've already cost you *way* too much of your evening, but I don't want you going away mad."

Seeing the entreating look in his eyes, Tura sighed. "All right, what are we doing about this?"

"Stay for dinner? It's nothing fancy, but Honey's already been fed and I just bought the stuff to make Caesar salad."

"With store-bought croutons?" She looked at him sideways, making a show of pondering the offer. "Or homemade?"

twenty-seven
tura

"Look at this one." Tura smirked, lifting another yellowing photograph out of the shoebox on the coffee table. In the picture, a shirtless, wiry muscled Jack leaned against the saddle of a well-loved dirt bike, wearing a mask of unaffected teenaged bravado. "You were a *baby*."

"Yeah?" Jack fed another log into the fire and dusted his hands together, straightening from his crouching position in front of the stove. He'd changed out of his suit, into his after work uniform of worn jeans and casual shirt, a look she preferred to his polished work persona. He settled onto the sofa next to her and slung one arm over the back of the cushions, leaning in to study the photo. "We thought we were so damn cool."

"Everyone does, at that age." Tura laughed as Jack picked up the shoebox and sat back, holding it across his lap. He took a stack of photos out and started flipping through them, stopping when he came to a trio of faded Polaroids. His smile vanished, the corners of his mouth turning down so hard that for an instant, she worried he was going to vomit. "What? What is it?"

"Nothing, I..." The pictures drooped between Jack's

fingers, and he made a strangled sound, slashing his eyes to the wall. "I guess I didn't go through this box before."

"Come on, Jack." She laughed uneasily, reaching for the pictures and feeling a riptide of repulsion crash over her head. It was a picture of young Jack standing in front of the ivy-printed wallpaper in Birdie's kitchen. The right side of his face was covered with fresh bruises, just beginning to transition from red to purple. The skin of his cheek was split. The next picture was more of the same, Jack tilting his head to display a lurid gash in his scalp, blood caking in his sun-washed hair. The final image showed a patchwork of bruises covering the back of Jack's boyish upper torso, the angry black and blue mark below his ribs neatly describing the shape of a man's boot. The date on all three read August 18th, 1993. That would've made him thirteen. Tura swallowed a wave of nausea. "*Jesus,* Jack."

"That was before you came along," he murmured, turning the photos facedown, like a poker player palming his cards. "The fucker started hitting harder after I had my first growth spurt."

"Did Birdie take these?"

"No. These were Noel." He shook his head, staring into the fire. "We thought maybe if I had proof, it might give me some kind of leverage with him. Birdie found them a few months later and freaked out. She tried going to the police a couple times after that, but Gia kept covering."

"I'm sorry. I was so young." An unbidden memory surfaced, of watching Birdie carrying a basket of folded laundry up to Noel's room. Setting one stack of shirts on the top bunk for Noel, and another on the lower, where Jack slept when he stayed over. Birdie glanced over her shoulder, announcing Jack would be living with them from now on. Tura startled them both with her reaction, bursting into tears of hysterical relief, because even a child could see the fight going out of Jack's eyes. It was only a matter of time before they killed him. *Listen to me, little gem.* Birdie had lowered herself onto the narrow bed and opened her arms, pulling Tura in for an engulfing hug, explaining that it had to stay a secret. No one could know.

Slipping one hand around the back of his neck, Tura pulled Jack toward her, resting her forehead against his ear. "All I remember is seeing you hurt and not understanding why no one was doing anything to stop it."

"No, *I'm* sorry." He closed his fingers around her other hand, giving it a squeeze. "I never wanted you to have those pictures in your head."

"It's not that, it's..." She leaned back, letting her hand slide down his arm and rest at the crook of his elbow. "When you moved in. That was the only time Birdie ever asked me to lie."

Blue eyes slid to hers, his brows gathering. "Huh?"

"There are rules. They have to vet any older kids in the household, especially when there's a little girl there. So if my caseworker ever asked about the extra boy living at the house, I was supposed to tell her you were Birdie's nephew, and you were only staying with us until your parents got home from visiting family in Italy." She smiled weakly. "Luckily, it never came up."

"Yeah, she always sent us out of the house when the social workers came to check on you." Jack blinked, as if it were only now occurring to him what a perilous tightrope Birdie walked just to keep them all safe. "I used to hate that."

"The big joke to *me* was that anyone would think you could pass for Italian." Tura released a soft scoff. Her resolve sharpened, she snatched the photos from his hand and stood up, tossing them into the stove. "I hope you didn't want to keep those."

Jack stared past her into the fire, where the pictures blistered and curled in on themselves. "I had a similar thought myself."

Picking up their empty salad bowls, he carried them into the kitchen. His voice echoed through the vaulted front room. "Can I ask you a question?"

"Sure." Tura sat down again, a pang of foreboding firing in the back of her mind.

"Were you ever going to tell me you're a vegetarian?" Jack asked. He rattled plates in the dishwasher for a few minutes, then sauntered over to the sitting area, smiling down at her. "Come on, I've eaten enough meals in your presence to notice."

He pointed over his shoulder, to the place where the chicken breast he'd grilled and sliced for her salad remained untouched on the cutting board. "What I want to know is, why wouldn't you just *say* something?"

Tura shrugged, reaching into the photo box again. "I'm not used to explaining myself."

He stared at her for a long, thoughtful moment, then heaved a resonant sigh. "Well in the future, I'd appreciate if you'd give me a head's up on things like that. It'd save me the awkwardness of putting my foot in it."

The pang of foreboding morphed into something infinitely more uncomfortable. "I'm sorry."

"I'm not mad," Jack said quietly, waiting until she finally dragged her gaze up to his. "I know you're selective about what you share with people. I'm just curious. Is it a religious thing?"

"Not really." Tura shook her head. "I was eating a salami sandwich one day and suddenly, something about the texture just *disgusted* me. So I stopped."

"Okay." Jack nodded slowly. He stepped down into the sitting area and dropped back onto the cushions next to her, propping his feet up on the coffee table. Clapping one hand over her knee, he gave her a lopsided smile. "More bacon for me, then."

Tura liked it here; thumbing through old photos as Jack watched the fire. It had all the tranquility of being by herself, but with someone else to make her food. Plus, she could steal glances at Jack's arms and shoulders when he wasn't paying attention. The firelight played across his features, chasing shadows into the hollows of his cheeks and the cupid's bow above his lips, and when he caught her looking, his mouth broadened into a gleaming white grin.

"What?" He laughed, tucking one hand behind his head.

"Nothing." She didn't really have an answer beyond liking the way he looked, and she wasn't sure she was ready to let that particular truth fly, so she turned her attention to the photos again.

His voice was rough in the quiet, his eyes gilded with fire-light. "You sure about that?"

She nodded, her attention fixed on the photo in her hand. Jack with a white rose boutonnière pinned to his tuxedo lapel, one arm around Birdie in a boxy periwinkle blue mother-of-the-groom dress and pillbox hat, the other around Vanessa, irreproachably dazzling in her champagne lace wedding dress, hair piled on top of her head in a tower of artfully formed curls, teeth pearly and white against the dusty mauve rosebuds of her lips. It was the first real proof she'd seen. Jack got married, and she wasn't there for it.

twenty-eight
jack

"Wow." Tura slid back, nestling into the overstuffed cushions as she studied the photo in her hand. It didn't seem to register with her the action caused his hand, which had perched in a casual gesture on her knee, to move up her thigh. Jack was still observing his hand where it laid, wondering if he should remove it, when she turned the picture to show him. "She was really beautiful, wasn't she?"

Jack examined the photo for a second, waiting to get the same kicked in the nuts feeling he'd had on and off for the last few months, but nothing came. "She was amazing." Taking the picture from her hand, he smiled. "Actually, you can't see it here, but she was four months pregnant."

"Oh." Tura nibbled her lip. "Is that why..."

"Yes and no," Jack admitted, thinking back to the day Nessa met him at the door of their condo, so terrified he'd leave, or demand she get rid of it. Instead, he'd opened his briefcase and produced the diamond, like that was the plan all along. "I knew I was going to propose eventually. I'd already bought the ring. It just moved up the timetable, that's all."

"I wish I could've met her."

You're allowed to like her, Jack, Nessa whispered.

"Yeah. I think you two would've gotten along. Either that, or destroyed each other in a fiery showdown that leveled the city." Jack dropped the photo into the box, forcing his eyes back to the fire. "It was a bummer you missed the wedding."

"Was it?" Tura caught him by surprise with the question, and before he could think to temper his response, he turned his head to look at her, those unfathomable black eyes reflecting the flames like mirrors.

"Yes. It was." Jack frowned, adjusting his slumped posture to look at her fully. "I sent you an invitation. Did you think I was kidding?"

"I thought Birdie did that, or maybe you were just being polite."

"No." Jack felt the muscle in his jaw tick. "I wanted my family there. I was happy with Nessa. I wish you could've been a part of it."

"I'm sorry. My mistake." Tura looked away, falling silent for a moment. She fidgeted, tucking a strand of hair behind her ear. "It's nice you still have good things to say about her. They say it's easier on the kids when parents don't tear each other down."

"Oh, I get *plenty* pissed about it, but nothing that happened was her fault. She wasn't well." He stared up at the ceiling for a moment, his thoughts a sudden whirlwind of melancholy. "This is going to sound fucking *awful*, but I still have these moments where I think, maybe if Nessa never got pregnant, she might've been fine. And I would cut off an *arm* for Honey, but sometimes I wonder if I'd been given the choice, knowing everything..." Jack blew out a breath, exhaling the darkness from his mind, and slapped on a weak smile. "File that under shit they never warn you about when you have kids."

"Jack." Tura slid closer and laid her head against his shoulder, stringing her fingers through his. She lifted his hand to her lips, and he turned his head, pressing his face into her hair. Filling his lungs with her calming scent.

Nessa was in his ear again. *You deserve your happiness, Jack.*

"Baba?" Honey's tiny coo blew the moment to smithereens. They looked up as the little girl circled the corner from the kitchen, rubbing her eyes sleepily.

"What are you doing up, baby girl?" Jack got up and walked to the doorway, lifting Honey against his chest.

She was grumpy, her bottom lip poking out. "I brushed my teeth but you didn't come to tuck me in."

"All right." He chuckled, pressing his lips to the little girl's forehead and setting her back down. "Go get in bed. I'll be right in."

Honey spared Tura a sleepy wave then pattered down the hallway, and Jack fixed her with a commanding look. "Stay put. I'll be right back."

twenty-nine
jack

Honey climbed up the ladder into her lofted bed and tugged the covers over the lower half of her face, until all Jack could see were her eyes, scrunching into sparkling crescents above the apples of her cheeks. She giggled mischievously as he tucked the blankets around her body, swaddling her like a caterpillar in a cocoon. One corner of his lips lifted. "What's so funny?"

"Nothin'." She giggled again, wriggling in her bundling.

"Uh-huh." Jack gave her a skeptical smile, casting a suspicious glance around the dimly lit space. Last time Honey looked this excited, she'd found a praying mantis egg sac and hidden it in her toy chest. A few weeks and one wholesale insect bloodbath later, he was shaking the half-eaten corpses of a hundred mantis nymphs and one fat and happy live one over the side of the porch railing and explaining to his weeping daughter some things really shouldn't be kept as pets. Folding his elbows on the edge of the mattress, he bent and dropped a kiss on her forehead. "There. You're tucked in. Now go to sleep."

"Can Auntie Tura read me a story?"

"No, Tura's leaving soon." He picked his way through the obstacle course of toys littering the floor and stood in the open door. "Don't come out again, okay?"

"Okay." The lump on the bed wriggled again.

"Goodnight, baby girl."

"G'night, Baba."

He pulled the door closed and sighed, mentally resetting from dad mode to Jack as he walked down the hallway and turned the corner. She was still there, bathed in warm orange firelight. He gave her an apologetic smile as he stepped down into the seating area and sprawled next to her. "I can't be sure, but I think she's up to something."

"If she's anything like her dad, she's a wily one." Tura's smile was directed away from him. She ruffled her fingers through her hair, the strands glinting like black glass. "I should go. It's getting late."

"Sure." Jack felt his heart sink. They'd been talking, *really* talking, and he'd glimpsed something in her that made him hope. Now the walls were back up, and the moment was gone. He tipped his head back and blew a frustrated breath toward the ceiling. The Triumph was hot as fuck. He'd nearly busted through his zipper when he'd watched her sling one leg over the flat black cafe racer the first time. It completed the picture perfectly, but it was too cold and the roads were too dicey to be riding now. "I really hate you driving that thing in this weather."

"I'll be pulling my car out of storage in the next couple days."

"Oh *will* you?" He snorted. He caught her arm as she moved to stand. "I'd feel more comfortable if you'd let me call you a ride."

"I—" Something stopped her refusing. "Okay."

"Really?" He asked, blinking in disbelief. "Tura Kaplan, are you accepting my help?"

"Well it's your fault I'm stuck here so late." She made it sound so logical, even as a wicked little smile twitched on her lips. "I can come back tomorrow to get the bike."

Whatever she had to tell herself to get home safe, Jack would take it. He reached for his phone and tapped open the ride share app. "They'll be here in twenty minutes. Sit down. Let's talk."

"All right." Tura relaxed into the sofa again. "Honey seems to be doing a lot better lately."

"Yeah. She's adjusting well with the therapy. I've been pleasantly surprised." A recent memory surfaced, something he'd put out of his mind since that afternoon. "The head of the PTA called today. The school's taking Honey's class to the zoo next week, and apparently I need to get more involved. Either I step up and chaperone, or 'it will be noticed.'"

She slashed an acerbic grin in his direction. "If you don't go, will they send someone to break your legs?"

"You're underestimating the brutality of PTA moms." Jack exhaled an exasperated chuckle.

"Thoughts and prayers, dude."

"Ouch!" He barked out a laugh. "I should've known better than to come to you for sympathy."

"Hey, you're the one who wanted to be a dad." Her laughter was bright and unapologetic. She fell back against the cushions next to him. "See, what you should be thinking about is, what happens when she doesn't need you every minute of the day. When you send her off to sleep-away camp and you have more than a few hours to yourself. Because those days are coming. Then what are you going to do?"

Spend a month getting worked over between those thighs. Jack wavered, stunned at the sudden clarity of the instinct when his head was unclouded by guilt or anxiety. Was this growth, or was his brain playing a greatest hits marathon of his most fucked-up moments? What were they talking about again? Gazing at the adumbral mirage next to him, he shook his head. "I'll have to figure something out."

thirty
tura

Halloween, 1996

YEAR OF THE CHARLIE CHAPLIN COSTUME. BIRDIE probably had to mug a ventriloquist's dummy to find a set of coattails small enough to fit her, but Tura was the perfect image of the Little Tramp, right down to the toothbrush mustache and cane. The Trick-Or-Treating was good those days, when parents still let their kids out for Halloween. Kayla Costa's mother dropped her off with her pillowcase of candy, and she was walking up the drive when a sound from the garage caught her attention. Creeping over to the door, she pushed back the brim of her bowler hat and peered through the dirty glass pane, feeling her breath catch.

Jack stood against the side of Birdie's old Rambler station wagon, his tee shirt hitched up above his lean midsection as a girl in a gingham dirndl dress and red capelet knelt on the dusty cement floor in front of him, her ruffled red petticoats puffing out above the curve of her backside. Jack was staring at her with his mouth open and panting, seemingly transfixed by whatever she was doing. He commanded, his voice low and raspy. "Harder."

The girl appeared to hold onto one leg of his jeans, the other hand hovering somewhere in front of her as she moved her head in a slow, even rhythm that made her shoulders flex. To Tura's childish mind, it looked like she was doing pushups while balancing her weight on her nose. Jack combed his fingers through the girl's shiny brown hair and started thrusting his hips against her face. His head lolled back, and he moaned again. He dipped his chin again, raking the girl's hair back, his voice a gravelly whisper in the quiet. "Look at me. Yeah. That's right."

He let out a long, low moan, the sound tapering off to a strangled growl. He clamped his hand around the back of her skull and held on for dear life, his head rolling back, eyes closed, mouth agape. The girl at his feet made a wet slurping noise and pulled away from him, wiping an arm across her mouth. "I told you I was good."

Now the part that so confused her; Jack seemed to respond with startling brutality, eradicating any trace of the genial cartoon prince she'd always believed him to be. He lifted the girl to her feet by her hair and spun her, opening the back door of the car and pushing her inside. The girl yelped out a laugh, tumbling onto the bench seat in a froth of short red petticoats before Jack crawled in on top of her. Tura couldn't see much beyond his forearms disappearing under the girl's fluffy skirts and peeling a pair of white panties down her legs, tossing them out of the car. Her knees fell open on either side of his hips, the open top of his jeans falling down over the waist of his boxer shorts. The girl's patent leather shoes hooked around his back, and he reached into his pocket. There was a crinkling sound, like tinfoil or plastic, and then he lowered his hips, shoving against her hard enough to draw a gasp of surprise from the girl under him. Tura heard him shush her, whispering something sharp and urgent, and a muffled feminine giggle answered.

They started moving together, hard enough to rock the car under them. The air filled with grunts and moans, and the girl's hands slid under his shirt as if she were trying to claw herself free.

Her stomach twisted, and Tura turned away, walking fast toward the house, her bag of candy feeling somehow heavier slung over her small shoulder.

It took her a long time to decipher what she saw that night. She knew what sex was, at least on an intellectual level. Birdie caught her watching a soap opera one day and tried in her own chaste, well-meaning fashion to explain sex was natural and quite pleasant when done properly, but it was an activity reserved for grown-ups. What Jack and the girl in the garage were doing looked painful, nothing like the loving exchange Birdie described. What was more, Tura couldn't fathom the strange sense of exhilaration it gave her to watch. It wasn't until she'd done some growing and had her own experiences that she realized it wasn't lovemaking. It was *fucking*.

thirty-one
jack

Jack's Halloweens were looking radically different from the bad old days of pregaming, pranks, and girls in trashy lingerie. These days, he had to help Honey put on her costume before the sun went down and drive her to the school for the Trunk 'r Treat, where the teachers gave out candy and firefighters let the kids play on the ladder truck. There were games, with gift certificates for Newport Creamery and Build-A-Bear handed out as prizes, and he was relegated to spectator, standing off to the side and holding Honey's impressive but ungainly mask.

"Hello, Mr. Aldridge." Shannon Brady materialized next to him, dressed in pink taffeta and sequins, looking every bit the good witch of MILFkinland.

"Hey, Shannon." He inched away, keeping his eyes trained on the spot where Honey was competing in the beanbag toss.

She followed his gaze. "Is that your little girl? She's beautiful."

"I know," he responded, folding his arms. Jack and Shannon connected three years ago, when he made the mistake of allowing Portia to set him up with one of the receptionists from her practice. They met for coffee, and he'd known within the space of time it took her to order a ridiculously complicated white mocha latte frappe monstrosity with six pumps of various syrups, whipped cream and chocolate curls that as gorgeous as she was, they weren't going to work out. It wasn't the blended dessert she was sucking down, or even the way he couldn't stop staring at the scarily sharp square ends of her french tips, wondering how she didn't accidentally lacerate a cornea when putting in her contacts. It was something about the negative energy she gave off. He'd walked away sure they'd end up feeding off each other's bad moods and make themselves miserable in the longterm. That didn't stop him from taking her call when she reached out a week later, asking if he'd like to work out some no strings attached frustrations.

Things were fun in the beginning. She didn't ask for dates, or gifts, or any of the other intimacies that came with an actual relationship, and he felt disinclined to give them to her. It made a refreshing change of pace for a man used to leading with his heart, but the arrangement proved to be unsustainable.

It got so bad he started to actively hate the sound of her voice, and every encounter would end with him sitting on the edge of her bed as the post-coital depression set in, trying to work up the will to put on his clothes. He wondered if his tendency toward self sabotage was becoming an impediment to finding something worthwhile, and though he knew he should look for someone else to take his base urges out on, the idea of going through all the same steps to end up in the spot again was just exhausting. He made the decision to go cold turkey on romantic entanglements, comforting himself with the knowledge that at least this way, he'd hate himself a little less.

"Morgan's dad moved out of state to get married, so I have

her full time now," Shannon purred, a hopeful glint in her eye. "Maybe we can get the girls together some night?"

Jack clamped down on the instinct to tell her to get the fuck away from him, because like *hell* was he using his daughter as an excuse for more poor choices. He actually felt grateful when Honey dashed out of nowhere and wrapped herself around his leg. He lifted her up against his chest just in time for her to projectile vomit a stomach full of gummy fish and fun-sized candy bars down the front of his shirt. He flinched, feeling the wetness soaking through his clothing, and rubbed her back as she started to cry.

"I think it's time for us to head out." Seizing the opportunity to depart, he carried his daughter back to the car before Shannon could press for an answer.

"My tummy hurts," Honey whimpered as he knelt to help her take off her shiny black costume wings and clean off her mouth with a wet wipe.

"I don't blame you." He buckled her into her car seat and stood outside, peeling off his button down and balling it up into an empty shopping bag, leaving him in his vomit-dampened undershirt. Climbing behind the wheel, he glanced at her in the rearview. She rubbed her eyes tearfully. "You're supposed to make the candy *last,* bug. Not eat it all in one sitting."

Pulling out of the parking lot, he heard her retch again, turning just in time to see her spew the last of her stomach contents onto the lap of her costume leotard. He winced, cursing under his breath. "It's okay. At least you threw up on yourself and not on the seat."

One tense ride home, an unscheduled bath and some children's Pepto Bismol later, and Honey was settled into bed as Jack deposited his vomit-soaked clothes into the laundry machine and went to finish the dinner dishes and wipe down the counter. He checked his watch as he climbed the stairs to his bedroom an hour later, killing a bottle of beer as he went. He'd folded the laundry, unloaded the dishwasher, mopped the kitchen floor and taken out the garbage and it was not yet ten p.m. Seemed about right.

The stairs to the loft led directly into his office space. A short hallway divided the bathroom and closet, providing a certain level of soundproofing from the rest of the house, which was handy on nights when his imagination wasn't cutting it and he had to cue up a little internet porn to get him to the finish line. The hall opened into the master suite, an eight-foot square section of the ceiling above the bed enclosed by a double-paned skylight allowing a spacious view of the night sky.

"I know, it's my fault," he murmured, setting the beer bottle on the bathroom counter and staring into the mirror, stretching the skin under his eyes to assess how bloodshot they were. Resting both hands on the edge of the sink, he hung his head, wondering what Tura would think if she saw him wandering around his house, talking to his dead wife. Probably nothing good. Then he realized thoughts of her were starting to intrude on thoughts of his wife, and here came the guilt chaser.

Bending to rest his elbows on the counter, he scrubbed his hands over his face. Nessa's voice was in his ear again. *You don't have to live this way, Jack.*

"I know, I know," he complained, straightening to stare at himself in the mirror again. "*Fuck.* You don't have to keep telling me."

Walking into the bedroom, he stripped off his sweatshirt and ran his hand over his stomach. He'd been hard up before, so he had to remind himself it wasn't just Tura causing these distractions. It'd gotten so bad lately he was taking two hour lunches so he could stay at the gym and work off his excess energy. Sometimes he'd be sitting in a meeting thinking about the curve of her ass, or her gorgeous mouth, someone would ask him a question, and he'd realize he'd been zoned out for twenty minutes.

Lying back in bed, he stared up at the stars through the skylight, musing over the unexpected changes that came with age. Women in past fantasies were fleeting characters that drifted through his thoughts at an opportune moment, the legal assistant from the firm downstairs pinned to the elevator wall, or the two cute baristas at The Fiendish Bean taking turns sucking him off in the back room of the store. Lately though, it didn't matter where he started. When he reached the point of no return, his brain always served up Tura, as if to say, *There ya go guy, have fun living with yourself now.*

His phone bleated, momentarily rescuing him from his recriminations. He dug it out of his pocket and sat up fast as Tura's message lit up the display:

i need you to call me right now

thirty-two
jack

IF HIS FRIENDSHIP WITH GENIE HAD PREPARED HIM for anything, it was never to ignore such requests. More often than not, it was a bad date, but sometimes a guy at a bar wouldn't take no for an answer and a girl needed an excuse to walk away without looking like she was blowing him off. Because it was seriously fucked that women had to employ such tactics, and he hoped his daughter would always have someone willing to call her with an out, he shoved aside the nagging little voice telling him the last thing he needed was to talk to Tura and did as she asked. Lifting his phone to his ear, he frowned at the sudden detonation of pounding bass and static. "Hello?"

"Hold on!" she shouted above the din. "Let me get somewhere quiet!"

The maelstrom in the background ceased as abruptly as it began, followed by a relieved sigh from the other end. Her voice sounded scratchy, no doubt from shouting over that god awful music all night. "Thanks."

"Will you be needing any bad news this evening? For specials tonight, we have 'Grandma fell down the stairs, ' or 'the dog ran away,'" he offered, enjoying the wave of warm, throaty laughter that rolled down the line. "The 'I have a flat tire, can you come pick me up' is also very nice."

"Can I get the 'I need bail money' with the sauce on the side?"

"Oooh, sorry. No substitutions." He laughed low in his throat, hearing the distinct sound of footsteps on creaky wood stairs from her end. "What's up? Everything okay?"

"Yeah, I was standing there thinking, I would rather be anywhere else right now." She sighed, sounding wrung out. "Then it hit me, I bet Jack doesn't have anything better to do, I'll text him!"

Jack barked out a laugh, instinctively cupping his free hand over the bulge in his jeans. *Jesus, what's wrong with me?* He released his hold, letting his hand fall to the bedspread. "Then I'm glad to be of service. That music sounded like someone trying to play a synthesizer with a chainsaw."

"It's not so bad. I'm just not in the right headspace for a party, and these shoes were *not* helping." She let out a deep, relieved groan, and he heard the offending footwear clatter to the floor. "Hey, can I tell you something? It's probably hideously inappropriate, but it always hits me around this time of year, and it's about you."

He grinned, matching her conspiratorial tenor. "Absolutely."

"Once on Halloween, I saw you in the garage with a girl," she told him, a secretive smile in her voice. "I never actually saw tab A going into slot B, but you were definitely getting it on."

"Oh Christ!" He covered his face with one hand, doing his best to hide the mortification in his voice. The things he'd done in that garage could've scarred a child for life. "You're going to have to be more specific."

"If memory serves, she was dressed like Little Red Riding Hood in a red tutu."

"Ah." Daphne Barbosa. That was one of his better nights, back in the first bloom of youth, when he could get up, get off, wait less than five minutes, and do it all over again. He still stroked it to that one on occasion. He ran his fingers through his hair, laughing in embarrassment. "Well, I hope it wasn't too traumatic for you."

"Not at all. Except I think about it every time I see a woman in a red tutu," she mused. "I don't know why I brought it up."

"See a lot of red tutus tonight?"

"A few." She fell silent for a beat. "How about you?"

"No, no red tutus."

She laughed. "Ha, no. I meant, how was your evening?"

"Halloween is very different when you have kids." He sighed, replaying the events of the night. "The high point for me was getting thrown up on."

"Hey, I held a girl's hair back in the bathroom."

Jack laughed, feeling marginally better about his whole miserable evening. "Ah, Tura..." He drew a deep breath. "I really needed to hear your voice tonight."

"Me t—" she cut off the statement as another voice sounded in the background, the same one he recognized from the first morning, at her office. She took the phone away from her mouth and addressed the newcomer, and when she spoke to him again, there was a snide edge in her tone. "Apparently, they sent out the bloodhounds."

Her companion let out an indignant squawk, and Jack covered an unexpected bolt of disappointment with a chuckle. "You have to go?"

"I probably should, but I'll see you Tuesday?"

"Five-thirty sharp." His smile widened. "Have a good night."

Hanging up the phone, Jack took a deep, chest expanding breath, stunned to realize he was still smiling. The air felt less oppressive. He waited for the guilt to descend again, but all he heard was Nessa's forgiving tone in his ear. *It's time to let go, Jack.*

thirty-three
tura

Tura looked away for an instant, just long enough to start the oven preheating, and when she turned around, Honey had raw egg oozing through her fingers. Her little lip quivered as she offered up a fistful of mangled shell. "It didn't break right."

"Oh." Tura reached for a tea towel, sopping up the puddle of egg that wasn't caught by the front of Honey's child-sized apron. "That's my fault. I should've helped you."

She held open the towel, allowing Honey to deposit the remnants of the shell in it, then broke a fresh egg into the bowl and handed the spatula to Honey. "You stir that and I'll take care of this."

Tura shook the smashed shell into the garbage disposal, watching the intense look of concentration on Honey's face as she mixed the batter. It was an improvement from the pitifully shattered expression she'd been wearing when she got off the bus that afternoon. Wiping her hands on her apron, Tura licked her lips, choosing her words carefully. "So how's school?"

"Okay, I guess," Honey muttered, keeping her eyes on her work.

"That's good to hear." Tura took a step closer, eyeing the bowl. "That looks done. Here, let me do this part."

Tura lifted the bowl over the baking dish, scraping the sides. "You know, I had a lot of trouble making friends when I was little."

"Really?" The little girl's eyes widened. "People were mean to you?"

"Maybe a little, but my brother was at the same school. We mostly stuck together, so I never felt lonely. Kind of like you and Olivia." Setting aside the bowl, she tapped the pan to level out the batter. "But then I changed schools and couldn't be near him anymore."

"That's sad," Honey said, using her finger to doodle in the dusting of spilled brownie mix on the counter.

"Yeah." Tura nodded, thinking back to childhood. "I was younger than everyone else, so one or two kids tried to make friends because they were hoping I'd let them copy my homework, but most of them just ignored me. I ate lunch alone everyday."

"Older kids *suck*," Honey interjected, showing an impressive level of vehemence for such a tiny person.

"They can, for sure." Tura slid the pan into the oven and turned, facing the girl over the cement island. "But I was lucky, because if anyone *really* hurt my feelings, I could talk to Aunt Birdie."

"Did she make people be nice to you?" Honey asked, kneeling on the stool and leaning the top half of her small body on the edge of the counter.

"She would talk to my teachers." Tura nodded. "But most of the time, she'd just listen, and it made me feel better to talk about it."

"Like when I go to Ms. Tracy?"

"She's your counselor?" Tura asked. Honey nodded. "Then yes. Exactly like when you go to Ms. Tracy. Or, you can talk to your dad. Or me. Or your Auntie Portia. We all care about you."

"I don't want Baba to worry." Honey stared at the counter, looking forlorn. Tura paused, wondering if Jack was even aware of just how truly like him his daughter was.

"Look at me, weebit." Tura pressed both hands to the countertop and tipped her head to one side. Honey's eyes darted up to meet hers. "That is your father's *job*. He's the grown-up. He's supposed to take care of *you*. Not the other way around."

Honey didn't respond. She seemed mostly engrossed in licking the tip of her finger and dabbing at the spilled brownie mix. Tura grabbed the sponge and shooed her away to start her homework, preparing to clean up the last of the mess.

thirty-four
jack

WALKING IN THE DOOR, JACK DETECTED THE SCENT of warm chocolate in the air and looked over his shoulder, momentarily wondering if he had the wrong house. Aside from the sleek black car parked in his driveway, it *looked* like his yard.

"It smells great in here!" He grinned, loosening his tie. "I didn't know Krav Maga had a baking component."

"We decided to bag practice tonight and make brownies instead." Tura twisted to give him an oddly apprehensive smile. "Listen—"

"Baba!" Honey tore into the room, racing for him at top speed. He bent to catch her just in time, before she could head-butt him in the crotch. "We made brownies! I picked one out for you!"

"That sounds *great,* baby girl." He chuckled, kissing one round cheek and lowering her to the floor again. "How about I eat it after dinner?"

"Let's have dinner now!"

"In a few minutes, okay?" Jack looked to Tura, who appeared even more troubled than she had before. "Just let me change and I'll get it started."

"Honey, did you finish your homework?" Tura asked, drawing the child's attention away from him.

"Yes!" Honey crowed, her register unchanged. If he wasn't mistaken, Tura flinched.

"Good job." Jack put his hand on the girl's shoulder, turning her so she was looking up at him. "How about half an hour of TV before dinner?"

"Yeah, come sit down, kiddo." Tura turned on the TV, patting the spot next to her. Honey was so engrossed in the program when he came back, she didn't notice as Tura followed him into the kitchen.

"Are you staying for dinner?" he asked, assembling the ingredients for Thai peanut curry on the counter between them.

"Oh. Uh..." She surveyed the vegetables spread out in front of him. "Sure. That's definitely healthier than what I was planning."

Jack chuckled softly. "Dare I ask what you were planning to eat at home?"

"Cold leftover tater tot poutine with mushroom gravy."

Jack grinned at the cutting board, crunching down on a strip of red bell pepper. He cast a watchful look in the direction of the sitting room and dropped his voice. "Something up?"

"Yeah," she said, creeping around to his side of the island. "Honey got off the bus today looking like someone capped Santa. I think she might be having trouble with the other kids."

Drawing a breath, Jack squashed his first instinct, which was to march into the next room and demand the names and addresses of every one of the little shits tormenting his daughter. "Did she tell you that?"

Tura folded her arms. "She alluded to it."

"And what did you say?"

"I told her it helps to talk about things, and if she's feeling bad she should tell someone who cares about her." She sighed, shrugging into herself. "And she shouldn't be trying to protect you from her hurt feelings."

Jack's next impulse came upon him so powerfully it stole his breath away. He laid down his knife and took hold of her elbow. "Come here."

She leaned away, her dark eyes flicking over him. "Why?"

"Just shut up and come here." He chuckled, pulling her in. She collided with his chest, her spine going rail straight as he put his arms around her. Bending his head to press his cheek against her temple, he inhaled the last traces of woodsy, herbaceous cologne clinging to her skin. She still smelled the same, even after all these years, and try as he might, he still couldn't decipher the scent. His breath moved in her hair, the strands ruffling against the tip of his nose as he spoke. "You know we love you, right?"

She softened after a beat, and he felt her hands alight on his back, resting gently, hesitantly, in the neutral space just below his ribs. She leaned her weight into his chest and laid her cheek against his shoulder, allowing him to hold her. Jack felt his breath catch in his throat. He felt like he hadn't been hugged in *years*. Unable to resist the urge, he turned his head and brushed his mouth against the side of her face, breathlessly aware of how easy it would be to kiss her. All she'd have to do was look up.

"Baba?" Honey spoke, and Jack felt a sharp jab of yearning as he took a step back and turned to look at his daughter. She stood in the open space between the sitting area and the kitchen, her eyes volleying between them. "Can I have a snack?"

"Dinner'll be ready in a couple minutes." He picked up the knife and started chopping again, his voice gravelly in his throat. "You want to work the can opener?"

All meals in the Aldridge household were consumed at the kitchen island, and on evenings when Tura stayed to eat with them, she and Honey sat on the stools while Jack ate standing up, leaning against the counter. That evening, as he watched the girls spooning coconut curried vegetables and rice from their bowls, keeping up a lively conversation between themselves, he resolved to buy another stool. They needed to make space for her.

thirty-five
jack

AFTER DINNER, THEY MADE BROWNIE SUNDAES WITH tin roof ice cream and watched a movie. Honey pouted when he announced it was time for bed, insisting she wasn't tired, even though she was already nodding off when he lifted her from the sofa. He tucked her in and stood next to her, rubbing soft circles on her back as he waited for her breathing to slow, then he crept back to the living room, offering Tura an apologetic smile. "I think she's done for the night."

"I guess that's the other side of that unstoppable kid energy, huh?" Tura said quietly, shifting sideways as he collapsed onto the cushions next to her, finally able to relax. "I wish I could sleep like that."

"Me too." Jack chuckled. "You're good with her, though."

"Hey, no one's more surprised by that than me." Tura tilted her head, looking pensive. "Did she mention anything about school?"

"Nah, let her have a good night." He propped his hands behind his head, thinking out loud. "I'll ask her about it tomorrow, then I'll talk to her teacher, and her therapist. And then I'll find the little fuckers that've been picking on her and break my foot off in their asses."

"Sounds like a full day." She gave him a sophic smile. "Hey, I told Honey we could take a ride in my car sometime soon. Why don't I surprise her and pick her up tomorrow? If she points out the kids giving her a hard time, I could save you that last step."

"I think she'd love that, but we're already on shaky ground with the principal, so it's probably best if you didn't go mad-dogging any children." He dragged both hands over his face, his rough groan transforming to a weary laugh. "This is what I get for being such an asshole as a kid."

"It's funny you put it that way." Tura snickered.

Jack narrowed his eyes at her, feigning indignation. "What's that supposed to mean?"

"Nothing, that just happens to be *exactly* what my friend Rikki said when I told them you had a kid now." She ran her hand over the knee of her yoga pants. "Actually, I believe their exact words were 'It's definitive proof karma exists.'"

"And how the hell would they know?" He barked out a disconcerted laugh. "Have I ever met this person before?"

"No," she admitted. "But they've known *me* for the last nineteen years. They came with me to Birdie's funeral."

"Ah." He nodded, dredging up a fuzzy memory of an ambiguous stranger in a gangsterish double-breasted suit. At least now, he could finally comprehend where this Rikki person's animosity stemmed from. He'd have wished a beautiful, sensitive daughter on him, too. "Rikki knows where the bodies are buried."

"Mine, yours, and everyone else's." She leaned closer, a spark of devilry lighting her dark eyes. "But don't worry. They're a vault. Secrets are their business."

"That's a relief." They let the scripted action on the television fill the gap in conversation for several minutes. Then during a commercial break, she turned her head and caught him looking at her.

She raised her eyebrows questioningly. "What?"

Jack watched her for a beat longer, weighing the wisdom of asking. They'd talked about everything else. "Why are you single?"

She smiled suspiciously. "Who says I am?"

"If I'm wrong, set me straight." He grinned, giving her a prompting nudge. "I just assumed, since you have a lot of free time."

She shrugged, breaking eye contact. "I'm sort of seeing someone, but there hasn't been anyone serious since my last major breakup."

He chuckled. How could any man spend more than five minutes with her without wanting to lock her down for the rest of her life? "And what stupid shit did he pull to lose you?"

"He asked me to marry him."

His smile vanished. "And you said no?"

"I had to." She fixed him with an unflinching stare.

He proceeded with caution, choosing his words like a man picking his way through a minefield. "Why's that?"

"We wanted different things." She answered, tousling her hands through her hair. "I heard he has a kid now, so I like to think everything worked out the way it was supposed to."

Lifting one hand, he skimmed his thumb over the curve of her knee. "You never wanted kids of your own?"

Something hardened in her expression, and she turned her eyes to the wood stove, clearing her throat. "No. And I had my tubes tied when I was twenty-five, just to make sure."

Jack let out a subdued guffaw. "Really?"

"You must've missed the newspaper announcement." She huffed with humorless laughter, fidgeting uncomfortably when she saw the assessing frown on his face. "What? I was one hundred percent sure I didn't want to have a baby, and hormonal birth control has all sorts of side effects. I didn't want to risk it. "

"Hey, it's not for everyone." Jack's experience had taught him that no one should attempt parenthood unless they wanted it more than anything. The knowledge he went into it with his eyes wide open was the only thing keeping him sane. He exhaled a world-weary laugh. "I'm just impressed you knew what you wanted at that age. I didn't even know how to use an iron when I was twenty-five."

"How about you?" Tura loosened, hazarding a droll smile. "Things working out how you planned?"

Jack chuckled, reaching for the remote. "Well, I sure as shit didn't anticipate having to do it alone."

thirty-six
jack

JACK CAME TO AS ANOTHER SCI-FI RERUN STARTED IN the background. Tura was spooned up against his side, her legs tangled with his, the weight of her head on his shoulder making his arm tingle with pins and needles. She had her arms wrapped tight around him, one hand resting over his heart, and when he twisted to give his arm a break, she cooed softly, nuzzling her face into the side of his chest.

Relaxing sideways against the pillows, he pushed a strand of hair away from her face, admiring the celestial being coiled against his chest. He'd been sleeping alone for so long he'd forgotten how good it felt to hold a woman at night. How comforting it was to wake up with the warmth of another body against his.

Tura's face at rest showed the slightest hint of a smile, all the intensity stripped away to reveal a softness he knew she worked very hard to hide in her waking hours. He lifted his hand, hovering so close to that plump bottom lip he could almost feel the softness against the pads of his fingers. A blast of laser fire from the television snapped him back to his senses.

Snatching his hand away, Jack located the remote and killed the television, checking his watch. It would be so easy to give in and fall asleep again, but Honey would be up in a few hours. If she found them like this... He gave Tura's arm a feeble shake. "Tura? Wake up."

"Shh," she murmured, nestling into him. "Jus' a lil' longer."

He swept his hand down his face, resolving to keep his eyes pointed at the ceiling. He'd give her five more minutes, and then he'd wake her. Any longer than that, and he'd run the risk of passing out again.

It didn't make sense to leave his arm dangling off the side of the couch, so he circled it around her, allowing her to use him as her body pillow. His mind drifted, undone by her scent and the way she held onto him *so tight,* drawing him back to the blighted hinterland of that night so long ago, when they'd put a toe across the line.

In a former life, that shitty little hatchback might've been a shade of metallic beige, but by the time Tura came into possession of the beaten-down junker, a good portion of the body was rust-eaten and Bondo gray. Everyone offered to help her buy something new, but she refused. She loved that car.

Birdie was standing watch at the living room window, fretting that Tura's crummy car finally kicked it and she was stranded somewhere. The high-pitched clangor of a perforated exhaust system rattled in the drive, and Birdie flapped her hands at the boys, ordering them to do the gentlemanly thing and help their sister with her bags.

Snow wafted on the wind as he jogged down the front steps behind Noel, looking forward to seeing Tura after an absence of two years. The first season, he missed the family holiday to go skiing with friends, and the next, Tura was mysteriously out of the country, but sent a box of intricately sculpted marzipan fruit and woodland animals for Birdie to serve at dessert.

He remembered watching her climb out of that shitty

little car with crystalline lucidity. Noel opened the rear hatch and hauled out her bags, and Jack caught the driver's side door as she shouldered it open. She stood up from the driver's seat, and a single perfect snowflake landed in her hair, all six dendrites visible to the naked eye. Jack gulped, *gut-punched* by the sudden realization that Little Tura was gone forever.

"Oh thank fuck, you cut your hair!" Her first words were characteristically acerbic, but he barely heard her. He didn't *recognize* her anymore. She was so changed. So different.

"Tura. Wow." A breathless chuckle slipped out, and he opened his arms to give her a careful sideways hug.

"I know, right?" She laughed, walking arm-in-arm with him up the steps. Flipping her hair to one side, she tucked a finger behind one ear, making it poke out. "I grew most of the way into the ears!"

"Come let me look at you," Birdie crowed as they walked through the door. She wiped her square nonna's hands on her apron, all steel wool hair and zaftig body, as if she'd been formed with two generous scoops of cafeteria mashed potatoes. She reached up to pat Tura's cheek with her right hand and Jack's with her left, her eyes shining with pride as she looked between them. "Ah, my loves. What a beautiful picture you make!"

That was the last night they were all together, Birdie and her final crop of foundlings, a small selection of her friends from church, and her priest, Father Bernadino, clustered around the table in the formal dining room. It was one of those warm memories Jack tried not to let in, the sweetness double-edged, traveling hand-in-hand with the splenic shame of what happened later.

He could still hear the terrified quaver of Tura's voice on the phone, like being shocked to wakefulness with jumper cables. Feel the frigid air washing around his ankles as he dashed out into the darkness, pulling on his boots as he went.

He could still picture the look of sheer, worshipful ardor on her face when he sprinted through the doors of the minimart and found her sheltering behind the counter, being served tea by the cashier. He didn't know if he'd ever felt truly wanted before that moment, or been so paralyzed with rage when he saw the blood trickling down her leg. But above all, he remembered the *dread*. Slavering, bone-deep dread pursued him like a deranged beast of prey the whole way to Providence and sank it's teeth into his dick when he saw what she was wearing.

On second thought, maybe he wouldn't wake her. If she woke up, she'd see the intimate position they'd inadvertently found themselves in. They didn't need anymore awkwardness. He lifted her carefully, moving at a snail's pace, until he fully disentangled himself. Covering her with an extra blanket, he retreated to the safety of his bedroom.

When he woke in the morning, she was already gone. She left a note on the front of the fridge, including a doodle of herself slinking out the door in a long trench coat, a fedora pulled down over her eyes. He laughed as he pressed the button on the front of the coffee maker, his brain chasing amusement with an unexpectedly hollow ache.

thirty-seven
tura

SITTING IN THE BOARDING HOUSE KITCHEN, TURA slicked another coat of pearlescent blue polish over Rikki's right pinkie toenail, listening to her friend detail yet another strained phone call from home. "And I said, 'Mother, I'm happy Lawrence got into college. Lord knows he has exceeded everyone's expectations, considering what an unabashed *donkey schlong* he's been since infancy, and while I'm sure Aunt Clarissa is relieved he managed to gain entry to an institution so fortuitously close to someone he shares blood with, there is no way on God's green earth that child is moving in with me.' Which of course set her off again."

"Maybe her objection laid more with your liberal use of the phrase 'donkey schlong,'" Tura suggested in a carefully modulated tone. The sepulchral hush in the kitchen seemed to necessitate quietude. Nobody else was awake at this hour, save terminally flaky plant biologist Fenton, currently working to cultivate a potent new genus of cannabis indica for a local vertical farm startup. Tura suspected he sampled the product a little too frequently; it made him paranoid and destroyed his circadian rhythms.

"Who, Abigail?" Rikki muttered, directing a saturnine

snicker at the tabletop. Few in Providence knew it, but Rikki was born into one of the richest families in Savannah, proper old money folks who could trace their lineage all the way back to French nobility. To that end, Rikki's hardboiled socialite mother never let anyone in her circle of acquaintance forget the elevated company they were keeping. "I've heard her use language that'd have a Baptist minister summoning a Catholic exorcist, but *nevah* in public." They heaved a sigh, their accent thickened with ennui. "No, the only thing that matters in public is how things *look*. And it just wouldn't look right for one of *her* babies to let down the family. As if it were my job to play host to every son of an uncle who ventures above the Mason-Dixon Line."

"I don't suppose she knows where you live," Tura asked, casting an illustrative glance around the room. As safe as it was, the boarding house could be a dangerous environment for an intemperate greenhorn experiencing life outside their privileged, insular upbringing for the first time.

Rikki rolled their eyes. "Oh, but if she knew, she couldn't tell everyone in the ladies auxiliary I was a securities executive, could she?"

"Is that what she thinks you do?"

"I'm not sure." Rikki smirked. "I put that one down to selective hearing. Like she heard 'executive assistant' and 'security consulting firm' and autocorrect took over." They pursed their lips, gathering wool for a long moment before abandoning the subject entirely. They forced a moot smile. "At any rate, I think it's time to drop Sophie from the roster."

Tura gave her friend an arch look. "Pray tell."

"She and her husband are going through some shit." Rikki sighed again, and Tura cringed. It would be accurate to say Rikki's freewheeling attitude toward romance bordered on relationship anarchism, but contrary to what their critics might've said, they did care about the people with whom they shared their bed. They saw their partners at their most vulnerable and believed people's predilections were the things that made them the same, not what drew them apart. Still, rule number one in the playbook: Rikki had no interest in partnership, especially at the cost of another person's marriage.

"I'm sorry," Tura said, reflecting on what little she'd gleaned from her limited interactions with Rikki's latest paramour. Difficult to get a sense of someone when they were trussed up in red silk rope and dangling naked from a hook on the ceiling. "She seemed like she had excellent breath control."

Rikki's lips curved into a wistful smile. "She really did."

"Oof. Already speaking in the past tense."

"Yes, well. Spilt milk and all that." Rikki clicked their tongue, selecting a cruller from the box of assorted doughnuts on the table. "I have to say, I'm a little surprised. Usually I'm the last one sneaking through the door in the morning. Classy of you to stop for treats on your walk of shame, though."

"I refuse to be baited," Tura murmured, keeping her eyes on what she was doing. "I neither work, nor live here. Therefore, it is not a legitimate shame walk. And for the record, I snuck in from Ethan's last week and you said *nothing*. Had my shoes in my purse and everything."

"Oh, that didn't count and you know it, button," Rikki said crisply, rapping on the top of Tura's head with a cuticle pusher. "You can't do a walk of shame if you're dating the guy. Spending the night in the throes of a forbidden tryst with a handsome older man, though..."

"How many times do I have to tell you, if you cannot consume gothic novels responsibly, you shouldn't keep them in the house." She screwed the cap onto the nail polish bottle and fanned her hand over her friend's toes in an ineffectual effort to speed up the drying process. "I fell asleep on his couch. There was nothing sexy about it."

"Oh, wasn't there?" Rikki smiled in that melting way that

made the rubes go all moony-eyed and free with the cash. "Seriously, Tura. What is your life? You have achieved levels of drama a professional such as myself can only aspire to."

"And I'm so proud," she deadpanned, peeling back the lid on her raspberry hibiscus tea.

"This is what I've been saying," Rikki expounded around a mouthful of pastry. "Complicated history aside, this man comes with a veritable mountain of baggage. You really want to take that on?"

Tura rolled her eyes. "I'm not sure if you've noticed this, but I have at least a foothill's worth of baggage myself."

"Lord knows." Pausing to stretch their arms toward the ceiling, Rikki yawned. "Aaaah, goodness! I'm sorry, but either I catch a wave right now, or I'm gonna hit the floor. Are you staying?"

"No, I should head home." Tura shrugged on her coat. "I said I'd pick up Honey from school today."

"Uh-huh." Rikki shambled to the door, pouring their last reserves of strength into an astute grin. "You have fun with that, sugar bumps."

thirty-eight
tura

"Picking up Honoré Aldridge." Tura informed the playground bouncer, sliding her sunglasses onto the top of her head. The woman looked dubious, but took her ID and swiped it through a handheld scanner. A moment later, the machine trilled out a cheerful tone, confirming Tura was on the list of adults approved to pick up Jack's daughter from school. The woman passed her ID back to her and made a mark on the clipboard in her hand. "You're good. Through the doors to the right."

"I'm sorry." A vivacious strawberry blond sped up behind her in the hallway. "Did you say Aldridge? Are you picking up Jack's daughter?"

Tura squelched her knee-jerk response of, "What's your need to know?" and instead paused to inspect the overeager arch of the woman's otherwise flawless brows. From an empirical standpoint, she was undeniably beautiful, with her dusky blue eyes and bee stung lips. In fact, she looked like exactly the type of annoyingly perfect woman she'd imagined Jack dating. *I bet she could carve a radish rose in under a minute.* Tura nodded, deciding it wasn't unreasonable for a person to ask what brought her here, especially since between the two of them, she was the one who was out of place. "I am."

"Oh, you must be the new sitter! I'm Shannon Brady, an old friend of Jack's. I work at Dr. Winthrop's office, so I was privy to the after school pickup drama." The woman affected an exaggerated pout. "It's such a shame what they've been through, but I'm so glad he finally found someone to help out."

"Auntie Tura!" Evading the posted sentry, Honey dashed out of the doorway on the right, attaching herself to the lower half of Tura's body like a love-starved octopus.

"Whoa, kid." Tura stumbled back, unwinding the girl's arms from around her hips. "We need to talk to your dad about getting you signed up for peewee football, because that tackle was on point."

"Hello, sweetie!" Shannon bent down in the universal posture of adults addressing children, all smiles and hands on knees. "I'm Shannon! I know your daddy!"

Honey shrunk away from the other woman, casting a questioning stare up at Tura. The full picture clicked into focus. *Knows the daddy, not the daughter.* Tura put her hand on the girl's shoulder, pulling her against her hip. "We should be going."

"Oh, okay." Shannon straightened, giving her a more thorough sizing-up as Tura turned to take Honey's insanely heavy backpack off her birdlike shoulders. Whatever Jack had going with this woman, he hadn't deemed her important enough to introduce her to his daughter himself. As for the woman, Tura took out her phone and dashed off a quick missive.

fyi, i think the woman you've been putting it to just tried to introduce herself to honey

She shoved the phone into her pocket, considering her duty done. Let him explain to his girlfriend why he had a stranger picking up his precious little girl at school.

Her phone beeped just as they stepped out the door. Tura smirked at his reply. *I'm not putting it to anyone.* Another message popped onscreen before she finished rolling her eyes. *What did she look like?*

Tura handed Honey her bag as they approached her car, directing her to get in back and buckle herself into her booster seat. Standing outside the open car door, she composed a quick brief. *5'5", strawberry blond, blue eyes, 130 lbs. said her name was shannon brady. wasn't sure how you'd want it handled so I didn't tell her anything*

He took his time messaging back. Sitting at the outlet of the parking lot, waiting to merge into traffic, Tura looked down at the dash when the car announced a new communication in her stolid electronic voice. "Incoming message from, DILF: 'Okay. Thanks.'"

She laughed under her breath. If she was going to be driving Honey around, she needed to change his name in her phone, ASAP. The car spoke again, "Incoming message from, DILF: 'We were hooking up for a while, but it's been over for a couple years.'"

Tura pushed the 'talk' button on her steering wheel before he could send anything more incriminating. "Did I mention my car has this nifty feature where it reads all my texts out loud?"

A beat passed after it sent, and then the car returned a flat reply, "Incoming message from, DILF: 'Shit.'"

thirty-nine
jack

THE ROOM ECHOED WITH A DOZEN ABRUPTLY stopped conversations as Jack pushed through the revolving door of Tura's building. A convocation of sharp-eyed matriarchs tracked his progress from the second floor mezzanine, their rapacious silence following him down the hallway before ending in a chorus of quarrelsome feminine shouting, everyone picking up their previous topics at the same time. Jack boarded the elevator with a wary glance over his shoulder, half-expecting to see an elderly woman bolting after him with a sharpened knitting needle.

The ninth floor hallway was empty as Jack stopped in front of Tura's door and knocked. He kept his eyes trained on the elevator, cracking a farsighted smile as the door opened. "I think your neighbors may be plotting my death."

"Mine too," the stranger at the door greeted him from behind a pointed ducktail beard. He was tall, easily a few inches taller than Jack's very respectable six-two, built like he juggled steel girders for fun, and concealing his nakedness with a bath towel. His hair was bound up in a damp topknot, and every inch of exposed skin below his chin was covered in biomechanical tattoos, save the bizarre white plastic prosthetic replacing his shin and foot. Giving Jack an assessing once over, he lifted his chin, his lips curving into a baneful sneer. "Looking for Tura?"

"Damn it, Avi!" Enter the lady in question, stomping out of the rear hallway with murder in her eyes. "Your emotional support goblin puked on my bed again."

"Aww!" Time slowed to an excruciating crawl, an operatic requiem playing at thunderous decibels in Jack's head as the interloper slung an arm around the back of her neck and hauled her in, swabbing the flat of his tongue up the side of her face like a panther bathing its young. "That means she *likes* you!"

"Oh, blow me, you cretinous sack of protein powder!" she raged, gouging an elbow into his ribs. Spinning to face Jack, she swiped at her cheek with the sleeve of her sweater, the deep-set aggravation draining from her tone. "Jack! Hey! What's up?"

Jack glanced between them. "Should I have called first?"

"What?" Her confused expression transformed to horror. "Oh my god, *no!*" She waved a dismissive hand at the stranger. "This is just my asshole brother."

"Oh. *This* is Jack." The other man held out a hand, his expression transforming into another malevolent smile. "She told me about you."

"Don't worry." She slashed a glower at her brother, her voice flat and vindictive. "He's not dangerous. That's just his *face*."

forty
jack

Five hours P.A. (Pre-Avi), Jack escorted Honey across the manicured green lawn in the cemetery, combing the headstones for Nessa's name. They located the granite marker in the open ground, away from the shaded areas with established trees. Just a simple, flat stone laying flush with the ground, providing the bare minimum of information: *Vanessa Serafina Berrada, 1976-2024.*

No epitaph was included, probably because engraving was paid for by the letter, and for once, Kathleen refused to take his money. He'd gotten a good sense of the mental gymnastics she had to perform in order to lay the blame at his feet, and the last name was no doubt a final fuck you. As far as he knew, Nessa never went back to using her maiden name. Maybe it should have bothered him more, but standing over the sad remnants of her life, he didn't have room for anything other than heartbreak and volcanic, gut-wrenching anger. At her, the universe, the doctors, the shitbag drug dealers, and yes, he reserved a fair amount of enmity for himself, too. Maybe if he'd gotten her help sooner, or demanded the doctors pay more attention...

He choked down a meteor-sized lump of shame as Honey

bent to place the flowers on the stone. Just when he thought he was done mourning, this shit knocked him down out of nowhere. According to Portia, this was totally normal.

"The five stages of grief aren't a checklist, Jack. You'll go through them multiple times, and sometimes you'll feel all of them at once," she'd explained in her maddeningly discursive shrink's tone more times than he could count. "One of the biggest fallacies about grieving is that the pain lessens over time. The truth is, we just learn to cope with it differently."

Well, fuck her for being right. He set his jaw as his daughter came to stand next to him, taking his hand and leaning her weight against his leg. "Baba?"

He had to clear the knot of emotion from his throat before he could answer. "Yeah, baby girl?"

"Do you think we can bring Tura for Thanksgiving?"

He knew he shouldn't be surprised her thoughts were engaged elsewhere. Honey couldn't remember a time when Nessa was a dedicated presence in her life, so this loss wouldn't affect her as strongly. Another excellent point made by Portia and repeated ad nauseam, Honey was taking her cues from him. What she'd remember most about this time was how sad he was. Still, Jack caught himself frowning at the implication.

The last couple months had seen Tura around enough that he'd started planning at least one meatless meal a week for all three of them. She'd stopped rushing out the door as soon as Honey was down for the night. Including her in Thanksgiving, however, traditionally spent with his friends and several members of Portia's extended brood at the family compound in Maine, was a prospect that hadn't even occurred to him.

He wondered what Genie would say to such a request. Hell, he wondered what Portia would say. She'd surely have some biting observations about enmeshing an outsider in his daughter's life at such a critical time. Then again, maybe this was an opportunity to gain some much needed insight on the matter. He waited, trying to summon Nessa's voice from the ether, but she was conspicuously silent, as she'd remained since Halloween. Coincidence? He didn't want to speculate. The situation was fraught enough as it was. He squeezed Honey's hand. "I'll talk to Genie and Portia and see what they say. Okay?"

"They'll say yes," Honey said, her certitude enough to give him pause.

"You think so, huh?" he asked as they turned and walked back to the car, Honey skipping along next to him as if it were just another day at the park.

"Uh-huh." She nodded, her face a mask of wisdom extending far beyond her years. "I need stability and consistency."

"Did Ms. Tracy tell you that?" He chuckled, referring to the mild-mannered therapist Honey saw every Wednesday afternoon.

"No, Auntie Portia."

"And did Auntie Portia know you were listening when she said it?" Jack asked, able to deduce from the guilty expression on her face that his daughter was as gifted an eavesdropper as she was a stalker. Unlocking the car door, he lifted into her booster seat. "I'll talk to them, but I want you to think about how you'd feel if someone spied on you when you were having a private conversation. Am I being clear?"

She nodded, falling silent as he got in the car and navigated them to the frozen custard stand around the corner, where they bought peanut butter cookie ice cream sandwiches. He set her up with a movie when they got home, carrying his phone upstairs to make the call.

Genie didn't miss a beat. As soon as the request was out of his mouth, she passed the phone to her wife, who proceeded to give him the third degree in her most clinical voice. "Of course we would be happy to have her, provided you're comfortable with her being there."

"Sure." He took a seat behind the desk in his office. "Why wouldn't I be?"

Portia's insinuating silence from the other end made him grumble. He tilted his head back and stared up at the ceiling for a beat. Somehow, he'd failed to put together that taking her with them would mean waking up and seeing her for several consecutive days. "All right, I admit I was unprepared for Honey to ask, but that doesn't make it a bad thing. Tura's great. I think she'd fit in well, and she'll be alone otherwise. So if no one has any objections, I'd like to invite her."

"We'll have to make some tweaks to the sleeping arrangements," Portia answered smoothly. "Anthony's flying in from Seattle, and it's Cameron's year with the boys. Steve and Declan are coming, and Sigrid and Sarah are both bringing their boyfriends. Plus Kris, Lydia and Aaron were going to drive up the day of and Lydia's bringing the kids. They'll probably crash overnight before driving back."

Jack snorted under his breath. Portia's father made several savvy tech stock purchases in the eighties, which meant the "house" was in actuality a rustic ten-room Gilded Age lodge on a semi-private lake in Maine. It was true most of the kids chose to sleep in the communal bunk room in the basement, but that was because it was fun, like camp.

"I haven't asked her yet, but I can do that today. If space is limited, I'll take the couch or the guys and I can draw straws to see who bunks together."

"If you're sure." Portia laughed, sounding thoroughly unconvinced. Bunking with either Cameron or Anthony came with the added risk of waking up spooning one of Portia's brothers. "How about you talk to her and let us know?"

Which is how he found himself being led like a fatted calf into Tura's kitchen as her gargantuan brother pulled on a pair of jeans under his towel, tossed the damp length of terrycloth over the end of the sofa, and set about swapping out the plastic prosthetic with a jointed titanium model.

Jack had a hazy memory of Birdie asking a small, scabby kneed Tura if she wanted to call her brother one morning. It stuck out in his mind mostly because the kid had lived there for almost a year, and this was the first he'd heard about the existence of another Kaplan child. They'd been sitting at the breakfast table, and Tura had shaken her head without looking up, a closed book even at that age. She shoved another spoonful of Farina into her mouth, and the subject was permanently abandoned. At the time, Jack assumed this unknown sibling had reached adulthood; a satellite who'd served her enough disappointment and gotten himself written off.

Looking at Avi now, Jack was almost embarrassed he hadn't seen the similarities before. They were both taller than average, with unusually pale skin, inky hair, and penetrating black eyes framed by boldly defined brows. The section of Avi's face not obscured by beard had the same knife-edge cheekbones and distinctive nose. Factor in the tattoos, and there was no doubt they shared DNA. "So. That's what you'd look like as a guy."

"Yeah." Avi slid past him barefoot, jeans left unfastened at the waist to display his dark happy trail. Taking a beer out of the fridge, he hopped up onto the counter and took a long pull from the bottle, fixing Jack with a sinister grin. "Whatever john paid extra to ride without a raincoat was shooting some high caliber shit, huh?"

Tura glared at her brother for an instant. "Someday, a cleansing fire will come and take these troubles beyond me."

"What? I thought he knew!" Avi chuckled sadistically, reveling in his sister's fury. "All those years I spent hearing about—"

"Avi, I *will* have you gelded," Tura enunciated darkly. "You think I don't have that power, but I can make it happen."

"Whatever. I've got business to take care of anyway." Avi shoved off the counter and grinned, satisfied he'd done a sufficient amount to embarrass her for one day.

He spared Jack a passing shoulder slap, dropping his voice to a deep, secretive rumble. "You sure you wanna fox with this one? She can be a real beast."

"Avi I swear to God!" she barked, and Avi raised an eyebrow, as if to say, *Case in point.*

"Don't say I didn't warn you, bruh," Avi muttered. Moving into the living room, he pulled a shirt and a pair of socks out of the overstuffed duffle against the wall, then headed for the door, grabbing his boots and coat on the way. "Love you!"

"Go buy me a new comforter!" she shouted, folding her arms as Avi ambled into the hall and slammed the door without bothering to put on his shirt or shoes, or even pausing to close his fly.

forty-one
tura

Setting a cup of decaffeinated jasmine tea in front of Jack, Tura took the seat opposite his at the kitchen table, cradling her mug between her hands. "Where should I start?"

"How about, when did the two of you get in touch?" She didn't fault Jack for feeling wronged, especially after weeks of intimate conversations, sitting on the sofa in the hours between Honey's bedtime and the moment she had to leave.

"Easy answer would be birth, I guess." She shrugged. "Avi and I were born seven minutes apart."

"Twins?" Jack canted his head, his brow furrowing. "I don't understand. Why—"

"Wasn't he with me at Birdie's?" she finished the thought for him, leaning back in her seat. "You know how foster care can fuck a kid up. They tried to place us together at first, but our last home was..." She let her voice trail off, unable to continue. This was the way it always was. She hated to think about the terrible things he'd suffered. Could barely conceive of them, which was saying something, facing Jack across this table and knowing everything he'd endured. "*Not* ideal, and Avi being Avi, he always put himself in the way. So here's this kid with major ADHD back when the diagnosis wasn't well understood, dealing with a whole bunch of shit he was afraid to tell anybody about. He was struggling all the time and no one was paying attention, so he started running away. Getting into fights. Fell in with some older kids and got caught with stolen property. The 'special needs' label is pretty much the kiss of death when you're in the system, but add 'behavioral issues,' and you might as well be radioactive. They had to split us up."

"Ah." He nodded. "So you went to Birdie's, and he..."

"Pediatric group home." She blew out a gloomy sigh. "The fucked up part is, he is *so* smart, but no one cared enough to ask *why* he was acting out. He was a child, but they'd already dismissed him as an unmanageable defective. Birdie tried, but they kept telling her she didn't have the right experience or some shit. She was good about making play dates with the social workers, but they thinned out as we got older. It was tough for him, knowing he got the shit end of everything, and it made me sad, so we never talked about it at home."

Jack's voice was quiet and laced with compassion. "But you're still friends now. How'd that happen?"

"He joined the Marines the day we aged out, and you've seen the results. I was his only next of kin, so I visited a lot while he was in recovery. I helped with his physical therapy. Since then, he's mostly stayed on the move. We don't see each other much."

Jack tilted his head. "What's he doing here now?"

Tura cleared her throat, her foot bobbing under the table as she mentally sifted through all the available lies. Anyone else, she might've given him one of a dozen canned answers designed to stop further inquiries. But looking at him now, she couldn't bring herself to rattle off another half-truth. "He comes through town every so often. Sometimes I float him a little work to keep him on the line, but this time I asked him to stay."

He shifted in his seat. "And the work you float him. What does that entail?"

"I'm a security consultant. I fix things. Avi's freelance asset recovery."

"And this is legal?"

"Of course it is. The whole point of what I do is to keep the client on the right side of the law. People, usually corporations, pay me to evaluate their security. Sometimes when they have a problem, I help make it go away."

His brows knitted together, and he nodded. "I bet you're good at that."

"When I do it right, it looks like nothing was wrong in the first place."

He pressed his lips together, swirling the liquid in his mug for a few seconds. "What's in this tea, anyway? If it nets these kind of results, I may start keeping it around the house."

"You could always hook me up to a lie detector."

"You wouldn't offer to take one if you weren't confident you could beat it." Jack shrugged, and she coughed, setting her mug down fast. Having finally found even footing, his grin renewed itself. "I think you're forgetting, I've played enough Monopoly with you to know that it's not the winning you love. It's the *strategy*. You want me to be surprised you made a career out of working the angles? I got nothing for you."

His level of insight was becoming irksome. And why did he have to keep *looking* at her like that? Folding her arms on the table, she dropped her head and pushed her hand through her hair, exhaling a huff of exasperated laughter. "I'm sorry, did you need something? Or were you in the neighborhood and thought you'd pop by for a friendly interrogation?"

Jack's smile widened. "Now that you mention it, we spend Thanksgiving at a friend's place in Maine every year, and we'd like you to come. We drive up Wednesday night and everyone stays at the house for the weekend. We commune with nature and everyone takes turns cooking. It's a lot of fun. You'd be more than welcome." He paused, frowning thoughtfully. "Of course, that was before I found out about Avi, so I completely understand if you were planning on spending it with him instead. On the other hand, if you didn't mind, I could probably prevail on Genie and Portia to let us bring him too. Provided you keep him muzzled."

Looking away, she weighed the unanticipated kindness of the invitation against the unwanted pinch of resentment in her chest. "I have to ask you something, and I'm not sure how you'll take it."

"I think we've known each other long enough to be frank."

"How are you friends with Imogen?" The urgency with which the words seemed to erupt from her mouth made them sound harder than she'd intended, and the amusement died in his eyes. She dipped her chin, smoothing her hair over her ear. "What I mean is, nothing even happened between us and you couldn't stand to be in the same room with me. She breaks your heart and gets a pass. How is that fair?"

"Genie never broke my heart." Jack set his mug on the tabletop with a *tump*, a bewildered laugh slipping past his lips. "We weren't in love. We both knew it, and it took us an embarrassingly long time to come to terms with that fact. I'm not saying it was like flipping a switch. There was a good three months there where I didn't want to talk to her either, but after the dust settled, we still had a solid friendship. It's going to sound weird, but I can't even remember what it was like to want her that way, and I love her more now than I did when we were together."

"Which brings me back to my original question," Tura reiterated. "How did she skate with three months when I—"

"Because she and I were *friends*, Tura." He scoffed, shaking his head. "You and I barely *saw* each other. This is going to sound so fucking juvenile, but I was young and bulletproof and dumb enough to believe everyone was expendable, even the ones I should be *trying* to hold onto. By the time I realized how wrong I was, it was too late. I thought if I tried to reach out, you'd tell me to go to hell."

"You're right," she admitted. "I probably would have."

He sat forward and set his elbows on the table. Staring into her eyes for a long, grave moment, he ran his tongue over his lip. "Here's how it is. I feel like I have this room in my head. I can be surrounded by people and feel completely alone, because I live in a place no one, not even the people I *want* to let in, can get to. Genie's my best friend and I love her, but you and Noel? You know where I live. It's as simple as that."

Tura stared into her mug for a few seconds, lost for words. He'd described it so perfectly, the sense of isolation that dogged her steps for as long as she could remember, and knowing she wasn't the only inmate in that sad prison block made the loneliness recede by an infinitesimal degree.

forty-two
jack

"WHAT HAPPENED TO YOUR LEG?" HONEY CRANED her neck, gazing out the open car window to where Avi stood on the curb, one leg of his sweatpants cuffed above the curved composite of his prosthetic.

"Honey," Jack warned, leaning around the open rear hatch of the Subaru. There was a frigid crapehanger's brume wafting off the river, fog preceding the blizzard predicted for that evening. He was in a hurry to get on the road.

The other man ignored Jack's fatherly chastisement and folded his arms, betraying nothing by his expression. "Got hit with an IED."

Honey blinked owlishly, undeterred by his unsmiling demeanor. "What's an Eye-Eee-Dee?"

One corner of Avi's mouth turned up. "Kinda bomb."

"Your foot got blown up?" Honey asked with childlike directness.

"It went with the leg."

"Come on, man." Jack stepped up onto the curb and glowered, pointing to the spot where his daughter sat belted into her booster seat. "She's a fucking kid!"

"Baba said a bad word," Honey sang from the back seat,

and Avi turned away, suppressing a grin. If he hadn't been relieved before, Jack was suddenly overjoyed Tura's brother declined the invitation to join the trip. He could only imagine the negative effect four days in his presence could have on Honey.

"Guys. Don't make me be the adult here. I'm so bad at it." Tura deposited her rolling carryon in the rear cargo space of the car and slammed the door, positioning herself between the two men. She pointed at Avi. "You: Ix-nay on the war stories. The world is scary enough." She pivoted to Jack. "And you: Some things cannot be sugarcoated. Give him credit for answering the question with respect and honesty."

Watching Tura put her arms around her brother's neck and seeing the way the cynicism vanished from his demeanor when he lifted her off her feet was a little bittersweet. Even if she threatened him with bodily harm every five minutes, and he seemed to take perverse pleasure in pissing her off, they had love for one another. Jack was man enough to acknowledge there was a part of him that felt a little envious of that.

Jack started for the car when he heard her asking Avi if he was sure he didn't want to come with them.

"C'mon, kid." Avi lowered her to the sidewalk, giving her a remarkably genuine smile. "I'd rather down a shot of gasoline and chase it with a match than take a bite of that shit sandwich."

"Cute." Tura laughed, stepping away from her brother. "Very classy."

She climbed into the passenger side and reached for her seatbelt as Avi leaned into the open window, fixing Jack with a sinister grin. "Good luck, brother." He glanced into the back seat and lifted two fingers, saluting Honey. "Take it easy, short stack."

Honey's mouth opened into a wide grin, and she flapped her fingers. "Bye!"

"Don't make eye contact, weebit. That's how he steals your soul," Tura spoke over her shoulder. Then to Avi, she said, "I left the car keys on the counter. Just try to keep it on the ground, okay?"

"No promises." He ruffled her hair, and she batted his hand away. Setting a canvas overnight bag across her knees, he gave her a blackhearted grin. "By the way, Rikki brought by a little care package from the crew at the boarding house. Just some road snacks, in case the adults get peckish."

"Great," Tura sniped, shoving the bag into the footwell next to her feet. "Love you."

"Yeah, whatever. Love you too." He turned his head as a pretty girl strutted past, his grin taking on a deerstalker gleam. She pirouetted to walk backwards, her eyes sliding down his body and lingering near his feet. Avi winked. "Relax, baby. I've got an extra one."

"Right. Thanks for making it weird." Tura sat back and waved Jack on. She seemed to remember something at the last second and leaned out the window as they pulled away from the curb. "The kitchen table can *not* take the weight of a full grown adult!"

She had a funny look on her face as she pressed the button to close the window, something between irritation, begrudging affection and deep, consuming guilt. Jack's brows gathered into a frown. "You sure you don't want to stay? Spend the holiday with your brother?"

"No." Her smile wobbled as she deflated into her seat. "Avi doesn't care about the holidays, anyway. And Rikki said they'd check in on him. He won't be hurting for company."

"Evidently not." Jack smirked, casting a glance into the rearview mirror, where the girl was already scrawling her number on Avi's palm. Tura swatted his arm.

forty-three
jack

Honey fell asleep almost as soon as they hit the highway and started traveling at a constant rate of speed. He watched her little head roll to the side in the rearview and then glanced at the woman next to him. She sat watching the darkened world blur past her window, their headlights bouncing off the trees like static on a television screen. Now seemed as good a time as any to ask the question that'd been weighing on his mind for days, since they'd be spending the next five hours trapped in the car together. Jack laid one hand on top of the steering wheel and leaned toward Tura, mindful to keep his voice low. "Hey. The way Avi talks... Have either of you ever thought about finding your parents?"

"No. Our mother tried to sell us for drugs when we were still in diapers." Her clipped, dispassionate tone left no space for further inquiry on the subject. "Our father could've been any one of a thousand men."

Behind them, Honey jolted in her sleep, her foot shooting out and connecting with the back of Tura's seat. Jack brought his eyes to the rearview, watching her little head pop up as she briefly regained consciousness, then dozed off again. He returned his attention to Tura. "Sorry. I didn't know."

"I got out. I have a good life, and I'm grateful." She shrugged, unruffled. "How about you? You ever think about looking for your dad?"

"He died before I was born," Jack reasoned, checking Honey in the rearview, relieved to see her still snoozing away.

"Car accident?"

"Wind sprints." He slid a subdued smile in Tura's direction. "Captain of the high school football team. Had some kind of freak cardiac event and died on the field."

"It wasn't anything hereditary, was it?" she asked, then looked away, shaking her head. "Never mind. Sorry."

"Nothing to apologize for." He reached over to give her knee a placating squeeze. "Canceling out his defective genes is the one decent thing Gia ever did for me."

Tura didn't challenge the fact he still refused to allow Gia the title of mother. To the uninitiated, it might've appeared callous, but if anyone could appreciate how it removed the sting from his memories, he knew she would. Jack released his hold after a beat, and a weighty silence filled the car for the next forty-five or so miles, until Tura's stomach rumbled loud enough to be heard over the music on the radio. Jack leaned in again, setting his elbow on the center console. "I told you we should've stopped for something before we left Massachusetts."

"Right now I'd settle for just about anything." She sighed, flicking on the overhead light and retrieving the care package from the floor of the car. She pawed through the contents, her lips curving into an enigmatic smile.

Jack lifted his chin, eyeing the bag. "You holding out on me, Kaplan?"

"Not sure. Road snacks from the crew could just as easily mean—" She stopped and draped her arms over the top of the bag, giving him a sheepish smile. "Nothing."

Jack cocked an eyebrow and leaned closer, trying to steal a look inside. "Oh come on. Now you *have* to tell me."

"Uh…" She twisted in her seat, checking on his slumbering daughter before she pushed around the contents of the bag again, taking stock. Her voice got more quiet as she started listing items inside. "Looks like fuzzy handcuffs, a vegan edible thong, passion fruit-flavored, a lipstick vibe, condoms, and a glow in the dark butt plug shaped like— You know what? There's no reason to make this political. Let's just say he's not universally loved. And, oh! Brownies!" She fished a plastic container from the bag and opened the top. Giving the contents an exploratory sniff, she put them back. "Newp. Those are from Fenton. Best to save them for when we're not in a moving vehicle."

"You attract some very odd people."

"A self-own, if ever I heard one." She returned the bag to the floor of the car. "But hey, at least they thought enough of you to get the extra *large* condoms."

He laughed, reaching up to kill the overhead light. "We can stop somewhere if you want, but if you can hold out for another couple hours, they should have dinner ready when we get to the house."

forty-four
tura

THE FINAL STRETCH OF THE JOURNEY SENT THEM crawling down a long, winding drive through a tract of dense forest. The darkness appeared to consume any illumination granted by the car's headlights, and Tura lost track of how many twists and turns their route took. Just as she was beginning to wonder if the scenery would ever change, the blackness gave way as if someone had drawn the trees apart like the curtains on a stage.

The house appeared, perched on a rocky outcropping above the motionless expanse of a frozen lake. It was lit up like the star atop a Christmas tree, brassy light spilling down the embankment and giving them a perfect view into the ground level bunk room, where several children were walloping each other with pillows. Climbing out of the car, Tura inhaled the scent of wood smoke and frosty pine wafting through the air and gave a low whistle. "Some *house*."

"You'll get the full effect tomorrow." Jack chuckled, lifting his sleeping daughter out of the car. "Just leave the bags for now. I'll get them later."

They had to climb the stairs onto the wraparound deck to enter the main level, greeted by a wave of savory warm air and a chorus of hellos from the dozen or so people congregating around the kitchen island. A flurry of introductions followed, each person lifting a hand or nodding in acknowledgment as Jack said their name.

They were a relatively young group. With the exception of Steve and Declan, two handsome retirement aged men standing on the opposite end of the kitchen island, she saw no one above their mid-forties. She recognized Imogen as she charged out of the center of the gathering and went straight for Honey, resting in her father's arms. She put her hand on Honey's back and leaned in to give the groggy girl a bright smile that made Honey burrow deeper into her father's chest and rub her eyes.

"I'm going to put her down." Jack pivoted to Tura, speaking quietly. "You'll be okay?"

"We'll take care of her." Imogen's wife Portia put a glass of merlot in Tura's hand, waving him off. One of her brick-bodied brothers, either Cameron or Anthony, took a tray of lasagna out of the oven, and Tura felt her stomach gurgle with insistence at the sight of all that bubbling tomato sauce and cheese. Portia leaned in and put a hand on her arm. "There's meat in the lasagna, but don't worry. Sigrid's vegan—" she pointed to a willowy woman with a disheveled ice-blond fish-tail braid, "—so we have eggplant manicotti with sun-dried tomato pesto, and salad."

"And focaccia bread!" A bespectacled pixie interjected. Sarah? "We've got carbs for *days*."

Jack appeared at Tura's side and plucked the glass from her hand, downing the contents in one gulp. Portia scoffed at the impudent gesture. "Wouldn't you rather get your *own* drink, Jack?"

He exhaled a loud, satisfied *ahhh*. "Tastes better when it's stolen."

"I think he's trying to avoid announcing that I don't

drink," Tura informed their hostess, earning an apologetic frown from the woman next to her.

"Oh, I'm sorry. Would you prefer—"

"The fridge is the big square thing over there." Jack pointed, selecting an olive from the charcuterie tray on the counter. "Help yourself."

"Really?" Portia demanded, leaning around Tura to widen her eyes at him. "If this is how you treat guests, it's no wonder you never have any."

There was a long table in the great room, framed by the starless black sky beyond the windows. The conversation flowed, lubricated by many bottles of wine. Tura enjoyed Jack's friends, but she was very aware of her status as an outsider. They'd known each other long enough to have inside jokes and shared stories, and when the dishes were cleared and the dinner mess was cleaned up, the adults retired to the firepit on the deck.

Bundled in cashmere blankets, they lounged in Adirondack chairs and deck chaises, sipping hot mulled cider while the children watched movies and ate toffee popcorn in the rec room downstairs. No one looked at the clock or fretted that the kids were up past bedtime. They were granted special dispensation to stay up at the lake house, a formality according to Jack, since there would be no hope of getting any of them to sleep with the four-day sleepover going on in the bunk room. They would be dead to the world by midnight anyway, and letting them get away with flouting bedtime allowed the grownups to sleep in.

Someone brought out a guitar, and they took turns choosing songs, singing along when they knew the words. One by one, people headed up for the night, until only a handful remained to gaze into the dying embers of the fire in contemplative silence. Finally, Portia got up and kissed Imogen goodnight, announcing she'd check on the kids, and Jack leaned over, resting his weight on the arm of his chair. "Tired?"

Tura nodded, smothering a grateful yawn against the back of her hand. Jack smiled. "All right, come on. I'll take you up."

"Portia has her in the Egret Room," Imogen volunteered, sinking deeper into the fuzzy blanket around her shoulders. "You're in Osprey."

"Great." Jack led her through the french doors at the back of the house and up the stairs to the second floor, explaining as they went. "All the bedrooms in the main house have bird names. The Egret Room has one of the nicer views but it's too small for two people." He stopped at the end of the hallway and opened a door to a steep tunnel of stairs. "You go up. I'll get the bags out of the car."

forty-five
tura

THE ROOM OCCUPIED ONE OF THE HEXAGONAL turrets at the top of the house, allowing no space for furniture. The economy of square footage was dealt with by building a high berthing into the bay windows, providing its occupant a panoramic view of the lake. It was a cozy space, but not claustrophobic, with its high knotty pine ceiling coming to a point in the center. There were geometric black bears and trees on the quilted coverlet, and she was just testing the mattress for firmness when her phone chirped. Retrieving it from her coat pocket, she felt her mood falter as Ethan's name lit the screen. He'd gotten tickets for a show downtown that evening. She sighed and sent a quick reply. *that sounds amazing but i'm out of town this weekend*

Ethan's response rolled in a moment later, sounding understandably disappointed. *I wouldn't have wasted the money if you'd said something.*

i'm sorry. this thing came up and we didn't have any plans so i didn't think it'd be an issue

It rang a moment later. Hopping off the bed, she tiptoed down the treacherous stairwell and pulled the door closed, holding the phone to her ear. "Hey, what's up?"

"I thought this might be easier than texting." She heard the smile in his voice. "So what's this thing that came up?"

"Just a family thing," she said quietly. "It was kind of last minute, but we ended up driving to Maine."

"We?" *Damn.* She pinched her eyes shut, clenching her teeth. How could she have made such an idiotic slip?

"Uh, yeah." She climbed the stairs, but lacking the territory to pace on the landing, she was reduced to a linear waltz. Step, step, turn. Step, step, turn. "My foster brother and his little girl invited me."

Ethan's good humor fled. "You never said you had a foster brother."

"You never asked." It was a pitiful excuse, she knew, but it was all she had to offer.

It stunned her how quickly the anger overtook him. She heard a loud *bang* in the background, as if he'd punched a hard surface, and the shuddering reverb of him dragging in a deep breath, tenuous control in his voice. "If we're going to be *anything* to each other, I need you to start telling me shit. You have a *goddamn foster brother!* That shit is relevant!"

"Okay, I get that you're angry, but if you're going to scream at me, I'm hanging up," she said in a tight voice, forgetting to be quiet. There was an arctic snort from the other end of the line.

"Wait, are you adopted?" he asked suddenly.

"Does it matter?"

"No, but it would explain some shit," he ground out, an accusing edge in his voice. "I can't believe it never occurred to me that we've been seeing each other for almost five months, and I know nothing about you. I don't even know where you live. You really don't give a *fuck* about me, do you?"

And no matter how many times I told you, it never sank in that I didn't eat meat or drink alcohol. Tura pressed her thumb and forefinger into her eye sockets. "That's not fair."

"Wow. Way wrong answer, kid."

The line went dead, and Tura tossed her phone onto the bed, the dreamy feeling of a night well spent thoroughly dispelled. The door opened at the bottom of the stairs, and she turned away from the sound of Jack's footsteps, breathing through the twinge of defeat.

forty-six
jack

JACK LUGGED HER BAG UP THE STAIRS, STEELING himself for what he might find, but as he crested the top, she was staring out the windows, obdurate as a statue. She pivoted, giving him an insincere smile over her shoulder. "Great. Thanks."

Jack stood to the side as she took the bag from his hand and set it on the bed, unzipping the top. He watched her search for a few seconds, her posture rigid. Not the scene he'd expected. He felt a stab of guilt, knowing he should give her space to handle her personal business. "Everything okay?"

"You heard that, huh?" Her profile was a glacial mask of composure. "Oh well. It was bound to happen eventually. Always does."

Jack stepped closer, dropping his voice to a low rumble. "Was he really screaming at you?"

"Jack , I swear..." She exhaled an elegiac little laugh, raking her fingers through her hair. "I would rather talk about *anything* other than this right now. Ask me about the time I accidentally threw up while giving Todd Lewis a blowjob, or—"

"*Jesus!*" Jack cringed, a horrified laugh exploding from his lips. "Forget I asked!"

"I'm not saying it's a persistent problem or anything." She held up her hands. "My technique has improved quite a bit since."

"Stop!" More laughter racked his body, until he had to sit down on the bed and cough into his fist. Sucking in a ragged breath, he stifled another wave of chuckles. "I don't care if I have to sleep in the car and die of exposure. I will leave this house."

"Fine. You win." She located her toiletries case, dropping it onto the bedspread next to him. When she looked up, all the laughter had gone out of her eyes. "I'm honestly a little relieved."

Jack ran his hands over his legs, his mind spinning. If she'd been crying, if she'd looked the least bit overwrought, he wasn't sure what he'd have done. Maybe if he were a better friend, he would've said she deserved better than some asshole who would scream at her, or offered to kick the guy's ass, but the truth was, he was relieved, too. He took her hand, pulling her toward him so she stood between his knees. He looked down, matching his palm and the length of his fingers against hers, comparing the difference in size. "Will you be able to sleep tonight? Do you need anything?"

She gave him a sober smile. "I'll survive."

"That's not what I asked."

Her smile widened, and she laid a hand on his shoulder, giving it a good natured squeeze. "I'll be *fine*, Jack."

One person remained awake when he went back downstairs. Genie had switched from cider to scotch, but she was sitting in the exact spot where she was before, bundled into a fuzzy blanket with her feet propped up near the fire. Catching sight of him opening the door, she shot him a sly grin, her voice carrying the first traces of a slur. "She grew up *nice*, didn't she?"

"Please don't start," Jack pleaded, lifting a blanket from a nearby chair and settling next to her. Nothing about this turn in conversation surprised him. He'd been preparing for it from the first moment Genie laid eyes on Tura, and he'd seen the subtle jump of her brows.

"No, I just want you to acknowledge I knew something was up months ago." She waggled a finger at him. "After years of us flinging women at you, literally exhausting the supply of male-attracted single women in our acquaintance, hoping and praying someone would finally strike your fancy and drag you out of your post divorce-trauma funk, I *knew* I recognized that dumbass look on your face."

"I don't know what you're talking about."

"Oh, fuck you!" She kicked out at his ankle. "Now tell me what the hell is going on, because I can either run interference, or let Portia set you up with another one of her dull-as-dirt work friends."

"Please don't ask." He sighed, staring deep into the fire. "I can't afford to lose more people. *We* can't."

"Are you threatening to cut me off if I don't shut up, or are you suggesting catching feelings for Tura could only end in disaster?"

Jack pondered for an instant. "Yes."

Genie cackled. "Well get cutting, because this is happening."

Jack sighed, looking up at the stars for a long, restive moment. "Okay, listen. I never told you this because at the time it was really bad."

Genie grinned into her glass. "This sounds promising."

Jack closed his eyes, preparing himself for her reaction. "About eighteen years back, we had a near miss. Nothing actually *happened*, but if we didn't stop when we did..."

Genie looked thunderstruck. Slowly extending the index finger on the hand holding her drink, she gave him a portentous stare, all the humor gone from her expression. "Imma need you to fill in some of the more pertinent details. Like, how old was she when this happened?"

"She was legal." He rolled his eyes. "Jesus, what do you take me for?"

"I'm sorry, have we met?" She offered him a hand. "I'm Imogen. I've seen you cry, throw up, and come."

"Don't start with that shit right now. I'm pouring out my soul here." He glared at his trusted friend and confidant. "She was *eighteen*, we were all at Birdie's for Christmas. She snuck out for a party and called me for a ride when her car wouldn't start."

"Sure, I've seen this porno. The guy threatens to tell her parents unless she—"

"Again. What do you take me for?"

"*Algarete.*" Genie reined in her giggles. "I'm assuming the 'bad' part is this happened under Birdie's roof, and you were thinking she'd be *horrified* if she found out two of her kids were playing doctor."

Jack folded his arms and tucked his chin, his expression darkening. "Exactly. Kinda difficult to be around someone after that."

"Which is when you lost contact," Genie concluded, finally understanding. "So when you say, you can't lose more people, you mean, you can't lose her *again*."

"After Birdie and Nessa, no. I don't think I could take it. Plus, the timing on all this sucks. Between losing Nessa, and all the upheaval around Kathleen, Honey doesn't need—"

"Okay, firstly? Fuck you for using your kid as an excuse for getting in your own way. You do her a real disservice." Genie dismissed his equivocations with a flick of her hand. "There's no good time for *anything* in life, and *nothing* is promised.

Fate is an opportunistic twat waffle, just waiting until you let your guard down so she can sneak up and slap you with one of those jumbo comedy powder puffs. Just look at me. Married with a stepchild was no part of my plan." She drained the last of her drink, setting the glass on the deck next to her chair. "Can I give you my honest opinion?"

Jack laughed, always thrown off guard by Genie's habit of becoming the voice of the sage after a couple drinks. "What kind of bullshit question is that?"

"Sorry, forgot who I was talking to." She grinned at the oversight. "You know why Portia and I work? Because underneath it all, we're too fucking cynical to buy into all the hearts and flowers bullshit. She's a realist, and that's why I fell for her. Candlelit dinners are nice, but I'd rather have someone make me a Denver omelette on nights when I'm too tired to cook."

Jack smirked, curious to see where this meandering left turn would lead. "What does that make me?"

"You play at being hard, but deep down, you are an honest-to-God, dyed in the wool true believer." Genie added a decisive purse of her lips to the pronouncement, the corners of her lips quirking up. "You never stopped loving Nessa, and no one could hope to compete as long as you were carrying a torch for the woman who dealt you that first round heart-break. So when the time came to move on, it makes perfect sense you would go for the most inappropriate woman you could find. On some level, you think it gives you a failsafe. You can't possibly get hurt if you can't get close, right?" Genie tilted her head to the side, giving him a sad, world-weary smile. "Only it turns out all those old reasons don't matter anymore. Now you've got a real problem, because you don't trust your-self. You're scared shitless and searching for any wedge you can drive between you and the first woman to show potential for a long time."

Jack shifted uncomfortably, blistering under the close lens

of her scrutiny. Why'd she have to be so damn *right* all the time? "You've been spending way too much time around shrinks."

"Or maybe Portia came along because I needed the motivation to pull my head out of my ass," Genie suggested, plowing on. "Look, the way I see it, you and Tura aren't blood. Even the age thing isn't that big a deal anymore. I mean, eight years is chump change at this stage in life. So if this is something you really want, I say wear those legs for earmuffs and apologize for nothing. If it doesn't work out, at least Honey will have learned the very valuable lesson that there are worse things in life than losing in love. Because the way you're going, you're only setting her up to be afraid of things that are pretty much inevitable anyway." She paused there, stifled a burp against the back of her hand, and continued. "And as far as Birdie is concerned, I'd be willing to bet money the only hope that sainted lady ever expressed for your future was that you be happy. I see no reason not to take the instruction at face value."

Jack blinked at her, his eyes narrowing. "You're fucking *scary*. You know that?"

forty-seven
tura

Tura opened her eyes to watch a gyre of fat snowflakes scatter past the windows of her lended room. The sky grew light beyond the tops of the trees, fading from dark indigo to hoary sterling as she sat up and looked out at the lake, the water choppy and dark, the shore crusted with dull gray ice. She dressed and padded down the stairs in sock feet, the smell of woodsmoke hanging in the air as she caught sight of the bodies moving around the kitchen, already hard at work. Apparently, sleeping in was reserved for mornings when they didn't have to get Thanksgiving dinner on the table.

"Morning!" Portia warbled, her voice abrasively cheerful so early in the day. She sautéd celery and onions as Declan and Steve bustled around behind her, intent on their own tasks. Portia pointed to the coffee maker with the spatula in her hand. "Coffee? There's half n' half in the fridge."

"Not on an empty stomach, thanks," Tura said, her voice a little rusty on first use. "I have a pitiful tolerance. One cup of coffee and I start to wonder how anyone does cocaine."

"God love her," Declan spoke in a spine melting Belfast brogue, lifting a twenty pound bird from a contractor's bucket of brine and arranging it in a roasting pan. "Don't you just want to carry her around in your pocket?"

"Yes, dear," Steve gave her a stealthy wink, mindfully snapping green beans. "She's an Adam Ant song in shorthand."

"That's one I haven't been before." Tura smirked, pouring herself a glass of orange juice from the pitcher on the counter.

A devilish smile curved over Steve's lips. "Sleep well?"

"No complaints." Tura hoped no one was waiting for her to be shocked by the unremitting refrain of banging headboards and jungle noises in the night. After a decade spent in Hattie Lamont's, this den of robust monogamous sexuality looked positively tame by comparison. She did, however, understand why they put the kids downstairs. "Is there a plan for today? Anything I can help with?"

"I think we've got this part handled." Portia transferred the vegetables to a bowl of bread cubes, nodding to the void of swirling white outside. "This mess wasn't supposed to start until after one and they already bumped the projected accumulation to over a foot, so anyone who was supposed to be driving up today had to cancel."

"I prefer a smaller party, myself," Declan said, the smile unmoved from his stylishly stubbled face. "Maybe tomorrow we can take out the snowmobiles."

"I'd be up for that." Tura grinned at the mention of speedy recreational vehicles.

"So Tura," Portia began, cracking several eggs into the stuffing mix and stirring. "We're so happy you were able to join us this weekend. I hope we're not depriving anyone of your company."

"I usually do a very informal Friendsgiving with my old roommates." Tura took a seat at the island, gathering her hair up in a ponytail. To call it informal was an overstatement. Thanksgiving was one of the few days a year when people stayed home with their families, allowing the boarding house residents a few hours free of the nonstop hustle that took up the rest of the year. Most of them got as far away from Providence as they could, together or alone, and whatever small faction of roommates remained in the city would share a pumpkin pie and watch pulpy monster movies. "But it's cool. My brother's in town so they can slot him in."

"Oh, I'm sorry." Portia frowned. "I didn't realize you had a brother. We would have invited him, rather than breaking up your family."

"Don't worry about it. Avi isn't a huge fan of social gatherings. Or holidays. Or people." Tura waved off the suggestion. "I'm sure he's happy for the alone time. It'll give him a chance to work on his manifesto."

"And we've all seen enough movies to know nothing good happens when the creepy twins show up." Jack shuffled into the room in glasses, pajama bottoms and a ratty UIC shirt. He opened a cabinet and took down a mug, pouring himself a cup of coffee. He took it unadulterated, leaning against the counter with one hand tucked in his pocket.

Steve glanced up and grimaced with comedic displeasure. "That mug is false advertising and I resent it deeply."

Jack turned the mug to read the side and snorted under his breath, then went back to drinking, happy enough to put off apologizing until he'd had his first infusion of caffeine. His eyes glittered at her above the rim as Tura tilted her head, reading it aloud. "I'm so gay I can't even think straight."

"This world is so damn unfair," Steve sniped, giving Jack a prankish smirk.

"Relax, love," Declan said. "We have to leave some for the straight girls."

More people drifted downstairs, and soon, the coffee maker began giving off a continuous hiss, infusing the air with the scent of fresh brew as it was emptied and refilled. Preparations for dinner were set aside so breakfast could be made, and someone turned on the television, tuning to the morning news and leaving the sound muted.

A headline caught her eye, and Tura paused, a glass of orange juice halfway to her lips. *Investigation Halted Against Embattled New Jersey Import Company*. B roll of a row of baleful FBI agents carrying evidence boxes out of a nondescript office building filled the screen. A beat later, the film flipped to footage of a feckless salt and pepper type addressing a mob of reporters, a lightning storm of flashbulbs going off around him.

"How about you, Tura?" someone asked. She looked away from the television, smothering an effusion of adamantine satisfaction.

"Please repeat the question." A yawning silence followed, glances exchanged around her. It took a moment to realize she'd spoken while still in work headspace, which made the request sound like an order. She schooled her flat expression, trying to manifest something akin to humor. "Sorry. I didn't hear."

"Everything okay?" Jack lowered the forkful of vegetable frittata in his hand, his brow furrowing.

"Just some work stuff," she explained, earning a round of laughing groans from the others.

Jack dropped his fork on his plate, sweeping his hand over his face. "This one doesn't count. She didn't know."

"That's your fault, not ours," an amused male voice called from the other end of the table. "You're both liable!"

"Did I miss something?" Tura searched the smiling faces around her.

"We have a rule. Anyone who uses the W word has to do penance," Portia told her, turning an evil grin on Jack. "I think Cameron's right, though. It's your fault for not warning her, so you should share the same punishment."

forty-eight
jack

"You know, if I'd stayed home, the worst I would've had to worry about was forgetting the whipped cream for the pie. And that's saying something, because my friends are off their *gourds*." Tura's laughter vibrated with cold as she trudged up the hill behind him, carrying the inflatable body of a snow tube over one shoulder. It was late. Thanksgiving dinner was over and the dishes were done. The kids had long ago crashed, having ridden the carb-high of the meal all the way to the bitter end. The only thing left was to mete out Tura and Jack's punishment, which the adults decided to put off until they could enjoy the spectacle from the comfort of the twelve person hot tub on the deck.

"This'll teach you to underestimate the malfeasance of bored preppies." Jack exhaled a rueful chuckle, feeling a trickle of melted snow dribble down his naked leg and into the insulated padding of his boot. The wind was blowing hard enough to go right through the thick cotton terrycloth of his robe and shrink his balls to birdshot. He stopped, turning to stare down the steep hill running alongside the house, the moonlight glittering like diamonds on the snow. "But yeah, we're so glad you're here."

She laughed again, the sound rippling on the wind as she climbed the final handful of feet, having to lift her knees high to get through the heavy snow. "Once, I got stranded out in the middle of south nowhere Cameroon. This was way back in the day, before I started my own storefront and had to take the jobs I was given. So it's me, two shady-ass hired German bodyguards, and our client, this weasely idiot who'd managed to get himself snatched right out of a hotel lobby in Lagos, and I'm trying to negotiate for the purchase of a beat up shitbox truck with a rural chieftain. We're going back and forth in pidgin English and French and I have maybe *six* words of Ewondo, so I already know we're gonna take a bath on this deal, and someone hands me a dish of wood larvae the size of my *thumb*. I'm looking down at these big, fat, squirmy bugs, and the guys around me are grinning like assholes because they know if I back down, I'll be walking back to Douala with the client riding piggyback."

"Okay." Jack grinned, half-turning to glance over his shoulder at her. "And why are you telling me this?"

"Because embarrassment is the price of admission. Sometimes, you just have to eat the damn grubs." She stepped up to face him, giving him a confident, if shivery, smile. "Now let's get this done. In twenty minutes, it'll be another funny story we tell on holidays."

He started working the knot lose on his robe. "I hope you're right."

They stripped down in a gale of quietly uttered curses and laughter, standing to face each other. The others had allowed him to keep his boxers and Jack was grateful, because despite the sight of Tura's body in her black hiphugger panties and tiny tank top, he was pretty sure the cold had shrunk his dick to an innie. They turned and crouched like racers at the starting line, and Jack grinned. "What are the odds we make it to the bottom without going in the lake?"

"Better the water than splattering on the back of the house," she spoke through gritted teeth. "Hey, Jack?"

"Yeah?"

"If I die, I want my bike to go to Honey. Don't let Avi fuck you around about it." She didn't wait for a response before bellyflopping onto her snow tube, sailing down the hill like a superhero in flight, one fist raised. "I regret *nothing!*"

What am I doing? I have a child! The thought flickered through his mind as his chest connected with cold PVC. It was too late to take it back though, and he shot down the hill in her wake, screaming like a kamikaze pilot.

A chorus of hoots and whistles greeted them as they approached the bottom of the hill. By some slim margin of fate, they did not go in the lake, instead plowing into the snowdrift accumulated against the driveway retaining wall. The sudden upward movement tipped him off onto the ground, his back prickling in direct contact with the hard, ice-glazed top layer of snow. He lunged to his feet and raced after Tura, already sprinting up the stairs onto the deck. She cannonballed into the center of the hot tub, where the rest of the party was enjoying a nice, leisurely soak.

"Someone call the Postmaster General and have my mail forwarded." Tura slicked her hair back, sinking onto the bench between Declan and Sigrid. "Because I live here now."

Someone handed him a beer, and he slugged down a mouthful, sitting between Steve and Sigrid's boyfriend in the twelve person tub. The water was hot enough to sting, but he welcomed the pain, knowing much needed warmth waited on the other side.

"And have we learned our lesson?" Declan put his arm around Tura's shoulder, giving her a playful jostle.

"It won't happen again," Tura promised, dipping her head to secure her hair in a ponytail. She looked up and leveled her eyes on his, her cheeks flushed with the heat of the tub. "Hey. When did you get a tattoo?"

"Oh, uh... Seven years ago." Jack turned his head to contemplate the ink on his right shoulder, seeing it for the first time in years. From this angle, he could only look at it upside down; the talons and beak of the great horned owl covering his left pectoral, the body and wings captured in mid-flight, wrapping over his shoulder and bicep and terminating above his shoulder blade. Giving the thing an affectionate smile, he lifted up and twisted to afford her a better view. "Right after Birdie got the diagnosis."

She nodded, her eyes continuing to trace the ink over his shoulder for a few seconds more, her smile tempered with sadness. Of the people present, only she would appreciate the subject matter, and the fact the owl's wings covered the constellation of scars on his back, where his stepfather's snow cleats had torn through his flesh. Not even Genie knew the full story behind those scars, or that Birdie collected owl figurines. "I bet she loved it."

"She sat with me for all three sessions." He sunk into the water again, keeping his eyes on her. She wouldn't look directly at him, her gaze pointing down and away, her lips compressed in a flat line. Guilt hammered through him, but he refused to make her cry in front of all these people.

Silence reigned. That his past was a sensitive subject was well-understood amongst his friends, and even the newcomers must've felt the heaviness in the air. Genie released an farcical sigh. "You ever get the feeling there just isn't enough wine in the *world*?"

A round of subdued laughter ruffled through the group, and Tura's expression brightened. "Hey. Does anyone wanna get weird?"

forty-nine
jack

"ALL RIGHT, EVERYONE." TURA SLIPPED INTO THE tub a few minutes later, carefully holding the container of brownies above the water. "These are from my friend Fenton, and unless you plan on flying home without a plane, you only need *one*."

"Sweet Jay-sus, I knew I loved this girl." Declan grinned, leaning in to make his selection. The others hovered like trash birds as he took a bite and hummed his approval. "Fenton does good work."

"So I'm told," she said, passing the container to the right. It made its way around, bypassing Sigrid, whose veganism precluded her indulging in the butter and egg ladened treats, and Portia's youngest brother Anthony, whose work in the defense industry required sporadic drug testing, coming to Portia last. She reached into the almost empty container and hesitated, glancing between Tura and Jack.

"Did either of you get one?"

"Help yourself." Jack nodded for her to go ahead. He'd avoided drugs ever since he tried mushrooms in college and ended up lying face down on the floor of his dorm room, afraid to leave the protective perimeter of the ugly orange area rug for nine hours.

"I keep telling you, man." Genie smirked, licking chocolate frosting from her fingers. "That shit had to be spiked with something."

"I'm not contesting that," Jack returned, then just to show her it could go both ways, he offered, "You want some tequila to wash that down with?"

Genie's face twisted. "Don't be a dick."

"What about you?" Portia asked Tura.

Tura shook her head. "They're a hostess gift. You're the hostess."

"Thank you." Portia took the final brownie without protest and settled back into her seat. "You'll have to thank your friend for us."

"I'm sure he'll be pleased to know his work was appreciated." Tura set the empty container on the edge of the tub. Conversation resumed for some time, the snow-muffled quiet of the landscape carrying their laughter further, making it echo out over the lake. He knew the moment the brownies started to take effect, the people around them growing quiet, their faraway gazes directed at the sky.

"You are a source of continual entertainment, Miss Tura." Declan grinned, as slow as molasses. "In fact, Steve and I have been trying to place you since you got here. We feel almost certain we know you from somewhere."

Tura's smile was cryptic. "Spend much time in College Hill?"

"I *knew* it," Steve murmured, wagging a lazy finger at his husband. "You owe me chicken vindaloo for New Year's."

Portia lifted her head, squinting at Declan. "Are we missing something?"

"You remember that club I tol' you about?" Steve slurred. "That very *exclusive* club?"

Portia's mouth formed a perfectly round O, and she snapped her fingers a few times, unable to get much sound out of it with her fingers already wet and pruned. "Hattie...*something's*."

"Lamont's," Sigrid spoke, drawing their attention. She lifted one shoulder, a clandestine smile painting her lips. "I've heard things."

"So have I." Jack stared across the steamy surface of the water at Tura. Tales of Hattie Lamont's circulated like vintage girlie magazines among the people of Providence. Everyone had a story, usually related to the elaborate public parties they threw several times a year. But people with insider's knowledge were as rare as Sasquatch sightings. "I've been there."

Tura's eyes met his. "What event?"

"The Arabian Nights party." He floated into the center of the tub as if drawn there by magnets, his gaze locked on hers. To this day, that party remained one of the most visually fantastic nights of his life. The perimeter of the courtyard was framed by Bedouin tents. Jewel toned Persian rugs covered the cobblestones. Guests sat on silk pillows smoking hookahs and sipping mint tea. Belly dancers and contortionists wandered between the tables, moving their bodies in ways that boggled the mind. There was an enormous genie's bottle on the roof, and at midnight, an aerialist floated out of the top with nothing but a thin layer of strategically applied gold leaf to cover her skin, her blue silks wafting like magic smoke. "But that would've been—"

"Twenty-twelve." Her smile was serene, unbothered by her association with a place most people only spoke of in hushed tones. "I was out of town for that one."

"Spend a lot of time there?" He stared at her mouth, wondering what kind of trouble a girl like her could stir up, set loose in a place like that.

"Less since I moved out. But yes, a fair amount."

Genie reacted first. She flubbed her lips, her head bobbing in a slow, dopey nod. "Little Tura lives in a sex cluuub."

Steve let out a high-pitched chortle. "S'not a sex club. Sex jus' happens there. S'different."

"Dude, they're so *baked*." Anthony looked around, dimples pitting his fleshy cheeks. "This is *embarrassing*."

fifty
tura

One, two, three, four... Tura watched Sarah measuring scoops of coffee into the machine, hearing Birdie's voice in her mind, her diction precise, one generation removed from the Sicilian motherland. It didn't matter that she didn't touch stimulants, she'd observed this ritual every morning for ten years, watching her foster mother spoon coffee into her dented Moka percolator and set it on the gas stovetop. Birdie would always add an extra tablespoon and wink, whispering, *And for the angel's share...* It sent a soft pang through her heart to watch someone leave the angels out. She leaned her chin in her upturned palm and mouthed the words, setting the moment aside for herself.

Declan passed her a spatula and deputized her for pancake duty, and a minute later a pint-sized ball of moxie came barreling up the basement stairs and wrapped itself around her hips. "Baba says I can come to town, but only if I ride with you because Auntie Genie is a bad driver and he doesn't know Steve and Brent is riding with Uncle Cameron."

"No offense taken, I'm sure," Steve scoffed, stepping around them with a platter of bacon and hash browns.

"Excuse me?" Imogen sputtered, pointing to the child

wrapped around Tura's waist. "Apparently, I'm the *bad driver*. You're just *new*."

"I'll have you know I was stationed at Fort Wainwright in Alaska for three years." Steve sniffed with decorous indignity. "I could perform *surgery* on the back of a snow mobile."

"You heard him, Honey." Tura patted the little girl's shoulder. "Run and tell your daddy Steve says he'll remove your wisdom teeth on the way to Nipawset Harbor."

"But I want to ride with you!" Honey howled, jumping up and down hard enough to jostle Tura sideways.

"Slow your roll, kiddo." Tura lifted the spatula out of the way and hugged the little girl's head against her side, shielding her from the heat of the griddle. "You get burned and Baba won't trust me, either."

"I would appreciate if you didn't light my child on fire." Jack came bounding down the stairs and bent to press a kiss to his daughter's head, pivoting to pour himself a cup of coffee. "She ask if she could ride with you?"

"She did." Tura nodded, directing her attention to the griddle. "I thought you were coming too. You don't want to take her?"

He leaned against the counter and crossed his legs at the ankle, taking a sip from his mug. "She wanted to go with you. I told her to ask."

"Does that mean you *didn't* insult my ability to operate a motor vehicle?" Imogen snarked, fixing him with a viperous glare.

"You think they're driving *paddle boats* in Alaska?" Steve muttered under his breath, setting out jars of wild blueberry jam and orange marmalade.

Jack gave her an unabashed grin above the rim of his coffee cup, clearly accustomed to playing the pigeon under this roof. "You don't want to do it, I can take her with me."

"*No!*" Honey tightened her hold and poked out a lip, her eyes growing huge and shiny.

"All right, you little con artist." Jack peeled his daughter off Tura's legs, steering her out of the kitchen with a hand on top of her head. "Go sit down at the table." He turned to Tura. "It's up to you. Just as long as she wears a helmet and you keep it under thirty-five."

fifty-one
tura

THE VILLAGE OF NIPAWSET HARBOR WAS TYPICAL OF many towns in this corner of the state, a charming, slightly touristy row of shaker-sided shops and cottages hugging an antique fishing port. A lighthouse stood watch on the bluffs to the north, and the docks extended long fingers out into the deep green waters of the crescent-shaped bay, the rotund bodies of fishing boats swaying in their berthings. The scene would be picturesque under any circumstances, but under a thick covering of winter white, it was a Thomas Kincaide canvas come to life.

I wouldn't last for five minutes in this place. Tura thought, looking around at the charming scene.

"What are you smiling at?" Jack asked quietly. He was wearing a parka and beanie borrowed from the cache of sporting goods back at the house, carrying his helmet and Honey's in one hand and holding his daughter's mittened paw in the other. They'd saddled up the snowmobiles after breakfast, with Honey riding in front of her for the thirty-minute journey to town. She could feel Jack's presence behind them the whole way, her desire to take the machine off a jump battling with the awareness he was trusting her with his child.

"Just wondering how long it'd take me to get burned at the stake in a town like this."

"Baba!" Honey pointed at the mammoth victorian gingerbread house displayed in a bakery window, complete with poured sugar glazing and licorice widow's walk. She gave him a hopeful smile. "Can we go there?"

"After we get groceries," Jack told her without slowing his pace. It was "their" night to make dinner. Tura didn't know how she got automatically lumped into the Jack/Honey unit, but she supposed it was because he'd been the one to invite her.

"But..." Honey's hand hung in the air, still pointing.

"She can come with us." Imogen offered Honey a gloved hand. "Come on, mija. You can help us pick out something for dessert."

Jack reached to the inside pocket of his coat and counted a few bills from his wallet, passing them to his friend with a communicative look. Imogen grinned and led Honey away, no doubt scheming to pump the kid up on enough sugar to shoot her to the moon.

They walked to the grocery store in silence, picking their way along the frozen walkway and stumbling through a time warp sixty years into the past. It was the type of place that still had handprinted signs in the window and required the staff to wear cotton soda jerk hats, cheerful green suspenders and bow ties while on duty. Tura pulled the shopping list out of her pocket, gnawing her lip. "Are we sure about the samosa pie?"

"You want to make something else, now's the time." Jack leaned on the handlebar of the shopping cart, giving her an amused smirk. "That lentil shepherd's pie sounded good."

"Okay we'll do that." She crumpled the list and continued through the produce section, grabbing things off shelves. She turned to drop them in the basket, suddenly struck by the placid way Jack paused to examine a bin of celery root. Grocery shopping together felt so domestic.

He glanced obliquely at her. "How are you liking it so far?"

"Everyone seems nice." She started filling a produce bag with potatoes. "I definitely slept better last night, with everyone knocked out."

"I probably should've warned you, the turkey wouldn't be the only thing getting stuffed this weekend." He took the bag out of her hand and knotted it, a reflective smile hitching up one corner of his mouth. "Actually, now that I think about it, I'm pretty sure Honey was conceived up here."

Tura snorted. "Man, if I wasn't already sterile, I'd be *real* nervous about spending a weekend at the baby makin' house. Especially getting in that hot tub."

"I don't know how to tell you this Tura..." Jack brushed past her to grab a package of carrots. "But if that's how you think babies are made, you might be doing sex wrong."

"Works for shellfish."

"Yeah, but shellfish don't have genitals."

She shot him a sly grin. "I thought we agreed not to talk about my exes."

His laughter was gratifyingly open, forming crinkles at the corners of his eyes and bracketing his lips, and for a few seconds they stood shoulder to shoulder, sorting through a mound of papery Chinese garlic. Selecting a good-sized bulb, he turned to pass it to her, his voice dropping to a serious timbre. "Listen, there's something I wanted to talk to you about last night, but I figured I'd wait until I could catch you in private."

"I'm listening." She took the bulb from his hand and dropped it in the basket, moving on to a bin of loose green beans.

"Honey said something a while ago, about your friend

having a dungeon in their house." He stood behind her, leaning on the cart as she stuffed handfuls of beans in a bag. "I brushed it off, but then I heard the thing about the boarding house last night and I'm not judging anything you do in your personal life, but I need you to be more careful about the things you say around her. She hears *everything*."

"I will, sorry." She cleared her throat, grappling with the burdensome notion she had somehow stumbled headfirst into the job of role model. "I've always taken it for granted, how unconducive my lifestyle is to having kids. I never imagined I'd be in a position to exert influence over one."

"Best laid plans, I guess. Anyway, she thinks you're a rockstar."

Tura sniffed. "She hasn't met a lot of people."

"There aren't a lot of people *I* know who hang out at Hattie Lamont's on the regular. Let alone people who've lived there."

"If that's what qualifies." She hazarded a glance over her shoulder as they looped into the next aisle. "I feel like you're working up to something. You want to know if I take my clothes off? Have sex for money?"

An elderly woman in a puffy blue coat and rubber galoshes sent a scandalized scowl in her direction. Jack's eyebrows arched with amusement. "Actually no. But since you offered…"

"I wear what I'm comfortable in, and what the occasion calls for. Always in that order." She reached for a bag of lentils and tossed it to him, seeing no reason to lie. "As far as the other thing, no. I don't see anything *wrong* with sex work, but for me personally, I require more emotional investment from my partners."

"And you've never…" He waved a prompting hand.

"Gone to bed with someone from the club?" She leaned to the side, addressing the woman in the puffy coat as she trailed behind them, pretending to shop for canned vegetables. "You getting everything you need, or would you care to join us? How's your shorthand? You can take minutes."

The old woman huffed and wheeled her cart in a circle, marching in the opposite direction. Jack dropped his head, his shoulders shaking with silent laughter. "I can't believe you did that."

"And I can't believe *you* can't believe I did that." She watched the busybody's retreating back, continuing her previous thought. "Anyway, what do you want me to say? It's a highly sexualized atmosphere. I defy anyone to remain unaffected all the time." She looked at him askance. "As if you've been a monk all your life."

"Not all my life, no." He gave her a wry grin. "Birdie had to know, right? I can't imagine her letting you move someplace she didn't see first."

"She wasn't so hot on the idea, but after she got to know everyone, she used to come by and cook family dinner at least once a week. Her marinara recipe is still the house standard." Tura laughed, seeing his eyebrows leap in surprise. "What? Underneath it all, she was actually cool."

"Hey—" He broke off on a stunned chuckle. "There's cool, and then there's letting you move to Hattie Lamont's."

"Come on, she didn't *let* me do anything." She fell into step next to him, nudging him with her shoulder. "I was going to move out no matter what. At least this way, she could be reasonably sure I'd be in a secure place with people looking out for me. No one would dare lay a finger on me in a place like that. Not without risking grievous bodily harm."

"Oh man, I was not prepared for this." Jack shook his head. "I mean, I thought I knew Birdie."

"You knew her better than I did." Repudiation contorted in her gut. She lifted one shoulder. "At least she *told* you."

"It wasn't like that." He stopped pushing the cart and

took hold of her arm. "She didn't tell *anyone*. I was at the house dropping something off, and I found the letter from the doctor. I begged her to tell everyone, but she made me promise not to say anything. She said she wanted to spend whatever time she had left as normally as possible, and she didn't want to be treated any differently."

"That's so her, isn't it?" Tura sighed, unable to hide the hard edge of bitterness in her voice. "No children, go about your business, it's just a *malignant tumor*. And you wonder why we all grew up to be such self-involved assholes. She's lucky she didn't tell me. I would have hogtied her and dragged her ass to chemo."

"I had the same thought." He let out a somber chuckle.

"Then why didn't you?"

Jack's smile was dismal. "You think you have a monopoly on stubbornness?"

fifty-two
jack

A SCANT FIVE MINUTES FROM THE LAKE HOUSE, A trio of teenagers on stupid-fast snocross racers blasted past their convoy without slowing down. Something small and brown darted across the path ahead, and Steve slammed on his brakes as one of the racers cut him off. A plume of snow went up, and the dark body of a snocross machine went cartwheeling into the trees. The air filled with screaming engines and the deafening crash of metal against wood, like gunshots echoing above the melee.

A horrendous chain reaction followed. Genie slid into Steve, stopping just short of jackknifing through her windscreen. Cameron and his son slid into Genie. Tura, reflexes honed after years of defensive motorcycle driving, jerked the handlebars of her snowmobile to the right, sending them fishtailing sideways. Jack felt his heart leap into his larynx as the low body of Tura's snowmobile coasted along the drop off on the edge of the trail. His daughter's head swiveled, eyes wide behind the visor of her helmet, searching him out. The ass end of the machine slammed down hard as equilibrium returned, leaving the nose dangling over the side, and Jack skidded to a stop *inches* from toppling them over the embankment and into the lake. The groceries secured to the seat behind him broke loose and pelted his back, scattering forgotten over the ground as he leapt off his machine, snatching Honey up in his arms. Meanwhile, Tura swung off her snowmobile and went sprinting hell for leather down the trail.

At first, he thought she intended to chase the kids down and crack their heads together. He might've had the same thought himself, if his heart wasn't pounding so hard it made him lightheaded. Then he saw Steve and Genie running ahead of her, and the twisted, disarticulated body of an animal pouring its lifeblood into the snow.

Carrying his daughter against his side, he pulled his helmet off one handed, a flux of scalding terror sending the helmet battering against the trunk of a nearby tree when he flung it away. He pulled hers off too, checking her over as he walked. "All right, baby girl?"

"Uh-huh." Honey nuzzled into him, wrapping her arms around his neck.

"Good. Okay." He scanned their surroundings, noting the shards of black plastic and fiberglass scattered across the snow. They were in a heavily forested area. It was a miracle no one appeared seriously injured, because it could take hours for emergency services to arrive. He rubbed her back through the layers of long underwear and insulated snowsuit, speaking more to himself than to her. "We're fine. We're gonna be fine."

"You guys okay?" Cameron stood holding his ten-year-old son's hand in the center of the wreckage. He didn't wait for Jack to answer as he whipped off his hat and turned to survey the confusion, running a hand over his hair. "If I ever find those little fuckers..."

"*Ah, shit!*" Jack muttered as he drew closer to the scene. He spun away and clapped his hand over Honey's eyes, shielding her from the sight of the injured deer lying on the side of the trail. It was disoriented; its eyes rolling around like white marbles in their sockets. One of its legs was badly broken, the other was already off and laying a few feet away next to a length of intestine, but it was still trying to drag itself into the woods. Thick black blood burbled from a tear in its chest, a flap of tattered fur hanging open.

He clenched his jaw, following the shouts to the edge of the trail, where a line of saplings was snapped off just above the ground, the jagged ends poking through the snow like fence pikes. Halfway down the ravine, Steve worked to lift the broken body of the snocross machine off a sobbing kid, the boy's lower half pinned against a boulder. Genie stood next to him, throwing the weight of her body against the machine, holding one arm cradled against her chest. Tura laid face down, reaching under the perilously leaning debris.

"Here." Jack shoved his daughter into Cameron's arms and ripped the zipper of his parka down, glissading along the side of the hill. "Take my machine and get the kids to the house. Send Portia back!"

"Portia's not that kind of doctor," Cameron called, struggling to maintain control of Honey as she fought to follow her father down the side of the hill.

"No, he's right!" Steve shouted back, his voice strained. "She has more medical training than any of us. Right now any doctor is better than none."

Cameron disappeared from the top of the hill, and Jack heard the sound of Honey's screeching carrying through the air. He shoved the sick feeling down as he flung his coat onto the ground and shouldered up next to Steve, searching for a handhold on the machine. What could he do? Let this kid die while he tried to reason with a distraught six year old? He couldn't have her here for this. Up above, the snowmobile roared to life, buzzing into the distance.

"It's wedged," Tura said, a frustrated edge in her voice. "I don't think we can move it without dislocating the joint."

"Please don't," the kid blubbered, his face crumbling. Jack felt a jab of sympathy worm its way through his anger, because the boy was only fifteen or sixteen, suspended in that delicate stage of life when he had the body of a man and the mindset of a child.

"What's your name?" Tura demanded from her place under the machine.

"Tyler." The boy sniffled.

"Well Tyler," Tura said. "Do you want to die? Because those are your choices."

The boy gulped back his tears, and Jack stifled the instinct to tell her to go easy. She crawled out again, crouching on her heels. There was blood on her hands, and Jack recognized the look of resolutely bridled determination on her face. Swinging her gaze to Steve's, she gave him a stern shake of her head.

"*Fuck.* Okay, save it," Steve barked.

"I got the tourniquet on there, but we can't afford to wait." Tura's tone was grim. She pointed to the lake. "It'd be easier to roll it that way and let gravity do the work. But it'll have to be one clean motion. This thing moves the wrong way, it could crush him."

"Right." Any trace of the unassuming older gentleman was gone from Steve's demeanor. He nodded to Genie. "Find something to jam under there. Maybe we can lever it off."

Genie was off like a shot, coming back with a thick tree branch a few moments later. She jabbed it under the side and waited as Tura slid underneath, flattening her back against the sharply slanted rock and bracing her legs against the wreckage. The men got into position, their hands grasping the cold metal flanks of the machine. Steve gritted his teeth, counting off. "One, two, three. *Go!*"

There was a metallic creak, followed by a revolting popping sound. The boy let out an agonized scream. Jack felt a bolt of jubilation go through him as the machine finally gave way, then something snagged his leg and he was falling, sliding, rolling end over end in the wake of something much heavier. The air was knocked from his lungs, and the last thing he registered before he hit the water was the sharp whine of an approaching snowmobile.

Airless freeze closed around him, instantly flooding his nose and ear canals. Bubbles filled his field of vision, stirring up a fine slush of mud and rotted leaves from the lakebed. The water *sounded* cold, high pitched and friable, like slivers of ice clinking together. Gooseflesh turned to razor blades as his muscles contracted, and he swung his arms, fighting to counteract the weight dragging him down.

Distant shouts. Splashes. Hands closed around his biceps, hauling him up. He felt the leg of his snow pants rend, and he was free; gasping for air as Steve and Tura dragged him up the shore, slogging through the sludgy water. Footsteps struck the swampy ground, and firm, warm hands touched his face, compressed his sides, feeling for injuries. Portia's governing voice cut through the turmoil. "Jack? Jack. Can you move? Are you hurt?"

He hacked out a miserable laugh, speaking through chattering teeth. "I'll never be warm again."

"Yeah, he's making jokes." Portia's voice hovered above him, sweetened with breathless amusement. "Get him back to the house."

Somewhere in the periphery, a newly arrived Anthony dispatched the deer with a rifle taken from the gun safe at the house, and Tura doubled over, coughing up a spray of vomit onto the snow.

fifty-three
tura

GRIPPING HER TOOTHBRUSH IN HER FIST, TURA tipped her head back and captured a mouthful of hot water from the shower nozzle, swished, spat, and watched the foam swirl down the drain. Reaching for the mini tube of tooth-paste in the soap dish, she doctored the bristles with another bead of mint stripe paste and brushed again, until she stopped tasting bile at the back of her throat. Resting her head against the wall, she closed her eyes, letting the water run down her face. She didn't understand this. She'd managed countless casualties throughout her career and never felt like she'd gargled with drain opener.

She couldn't stop seeing the look of undisguised fear on Jack's face. When he realized something was terribly wrong, but didn't yet know how it would play out. That instant when the momentum took him off his feet, the snowmobile drag-ging him down the hill in a crocodilian death roll. It was a miracle his leg wasn't ripped off.

She thought about pulling him out of the water, and the cadaverous purple-blue of his lips. The relief that clawed through her when he took that first breath and *laughed*. When she knew it was going to be okay, and all she wanted was to fling herself on top of him and kiss every inch of his body.

The overhanging mood in the house was funereal when she ventured downstairs. A small party had elected to go on a snowshoeing excursion around the lake, and the remaining folks seemed satisfied to stay apart, amusing themselves with whatever small tasks they could accomplish alone. Having lived communally for long enough to know sometimes it was best to just ride out the funk, Tura settled for making herself a cup of tea as Imogen sat at the counter playing solitaire.

"How's the stomach?" Imogen asked as Tura filled the electric kettle from the faucet and put it on to boil.

"I'm not dead." Tura shrugged, setting out a mug and selecting a teabag from the bamboo box on the counter. She eyed the ice pack strapped to the other woman's wrist with an Ace Bandage. "How's the arm?"

"Just a bad sprain." Imogen looked down at the bandage for an instant. "Portia wants to go to the clinic in town and get some X-rays done tomorrow. Just to be safe."

"Not the worst idea."

"Yeah." Imogen turned to look out at the deck, where Declan, Steve and Jack were taking a soak in the hot tub, the scene reminiscent of a family of macaques in a Japanese hot spring. Jack had Honey in his arms, bobbing from one end of the tub to the other as his daughter clung to his chest. "He was worried about you."

"Don't know why." Tura crossed her arms. "He's the one who got dunked."

"Because that's what Jack *does*." Imogen's gaze swung to hers, her ordinarily warm eyes filled with reproach. "He's like a street dog. Spent half his life getting kicked around, has no reason to trust humans, but he'll roll over and ask for a belly rub if you feed him."

Tura was relieved to hear the kettle starting to hiss.

"You never saw him after the divorce, did you?" Imogen probed, her tone laconic.

Tura gave her a wooden smile. "No."

"Well, it was bad." Imogen stole another look out the window. "He wasn't coming to work, barely left the house. There were nights we were afraid to leave him alone." She nodded to the place where Jack was making funny faces, trying to coax a giggle out of his frightened daughter. "He had two things going for him. That little girl, and this — I don't know if I'd call it a will to survive — it was more like he just checked out and kept moving." She shifted in her seat, folding her arms on the edge of the counter. "I knew his childhood was fucked. He'd let details slip here and there, but you don't develop a talent like that without enduring a lifetime of pain. When I saw him disassociate like that, walking around like a zombie for months on end, that was the first time I realized he'd been straight up tortured."

"I'd say that's a fair valuation," Tura acknowledged, following the other woman's gaze.

"And you were around for all of it?" Imogen asked, her expression inscrutable. "You know what was done to him?"

"Toward the end, at least." Tura nodded, thinking about the night he crawled up to Birdie's door with bloody ligature marks around his neck. His stepfather tried to garrote him with an extension cord. Birdie ordered her to her room, but she'd sat at the top of the stairs listening to him recount the entire ordeal, his throat so sore he could barely get the words out. His mother was sitting right there, he said. Never even got up. The queasy feeling renewed itself. This conversation was not helping her stomach.

"Maybe that's why." Imogen drew a deep breath and slid her elbows off the counter, awkwardly shuffling the cards in her hands.

Tura paused, unable to parse her meaning. "Why what?"

"He's different with you." Imogen watched her reach for the kettle and pour water into her mug. "I don't know. Maybe it's because you were around before all those scars healed over, when he was still soft."

"I hadn't noticed." Tura swirled the tea bag in her cup, watching the color bleed into the water.

"You wouldn't, though," Imogen reasoned. "Because that's the Jack you've always known."

Tura could feel Imogen watching her, seemingly weighing something behind those big doe eyes. Finally, Imogen cleared her throat and looked down, setting the cards on the counter. "Listen. I know I've been a little standoffish this weekend, but I think we can at least be up front with each other."

"I did pick up a bit of a vibe," Tura said. Imogen hadn't addressed her directly since they'd arrived, but there was a lot going on. In a crowd that large, it was very easy for two people to miss out on face time. "But I didn't take it personally."

"Good, because I want you to know, I've got nothing against you."

"That's a relief." Tura couldn't hide the sardonic edge in her laughter. "I was really eating myself up about that."

"No, I mean it." Imogen squared her shoulders. "I know how this is going to sound coming from me, but he's been through too much already. None of us could stand to see him get flattened again."

"You're right. He has." Tura turned to face her, selecting her words with a deft hand. She could lie and say she hadn't thought about what it would be like, but the truth was she was already coming apart at the seams. It didn't matter if she was willing to admit it or not. "If it makes you feel any better, I have no intention of doing anything to hurt them. Frankly, we've been out of each other's lives for so long I'm just trying to figure out where I fit in."

"If that's how you want to play it." Imogen snorted,

resuming her game now the hard part was over. She laid another card on the counter. "But just so we're clear, it doesn't matter who it is or what kind of crazy commando skills they have, if someone hurts that boy? Te lo juro. I'll steal a fucking tank and run their ass down."

Tura cast a surreptitious glance at the window. Jack was climbing out of the hot tub, steam rising off his broad shoulders in the wintery air. He turned to wrap Honey in a plush towel, and Tura flicked her gaze back to the woman at the counter. "Entendida."

Imogen's eyebrows arched, and she gave her a slow up and down perusal. "Bien."

fifty-four
jack

THE ACCIDENT CAST A PALL OVER THE REST OF THE weekend. Cameron ended up taking the boys home after Brent wouldn't shut up about the way the deer's entrails looked spilling out of its body. With the dinner groceries destroyed, Sarah and her boyfriend Ivan moved up their night and made a beautiful venison stew, an unfortunate choice after the events of the day. The venison went largely ignored as thirteen people attempted to make a meal out of the chickpea, pumpkin and herb stuffed shells intended for Sigrid and Tura to share. As a second course, they picked enough meat off the leftover Turkey carcass to make sandwiches while Tura and Sigrid enjoyed peanut butter and jelly on vegan flatbread. Everyone went to bed early.

Honey refused to sleep anywhere but in his bed. He wasn't mad. It provided balm to his rattled nerves, and he knew he only had a few years to bask in his daughter's unconditional love before she got old enough to recognize he was making shit up as he went. Unfortunately, it also precluded any chance of talking to Tura, who was still noticeably affected.

The next morning saw no improvement. Now the roads were clear, a handful of folks peeled off to go sightseeing, leaving the rest of the residents to enjoy their collective solitude. Steve strained a muscle lifting the snocross machine and spent most of the day alternating between the hot tub and lying flat on his back on the living room floor. Portia and Genie went straight to the clinic in town, then came home and took Olivia and Honey to tour a nearby goat farm. Jack stayed behind to catch up on his reading, keeping a surreptitious eye out for Tura. He wanted to talk to her, to see how she was doing after the excitement of the previous day, but she was being extra elusive, skulking around like a hunted animal, always with a look of jittery consternation.

The rest of the household started to trickle in by late afternoon, loaded down with farm fresh cheese and maple syrup candy. They cobbled together an evening meal of leftovers, the omnivores choking down some of the stew, which he had to admit, was delicious.

Spooked by the size and emptiness of the bunk room with the other children gone, Honey and Olivia fought sleep until nine, then passed out on the living room sofa, curled together like two puppies from the same litter. The adults left them to snooze and gathered around the fire pit, making one last valiant effort to enjoy each other's company.

Jack slouched in his chair with his temple resting against his fist, flicking covert glances in Tura's direction. She sat in one of the chaises on the far side of the circle, bundled in an oversized cardigan and moccasin socks, perfectly content to sip hot cocoa as the others told stories and jokes, laughing and talking across one another.

Portia stood up to ask if anyone had any preferences on the next bottle and a self-elected quorum of bodies filed into the kitchen to make a selection. Someone brought out a dessert grazing board. The guitars appeared, and everyone was singing along to an old Roberta Flack tune when Honey pushed open the doors and shuffled out onto the deck. She climbed into his lap and curled against his chest, rubbing her eyes. Jack put his arms around her. "You ready for bed?"

She made a soft, crabby noise in response, and he started to stand up, eager to get his daughter tucked in before the overtired stage, when persuading her to go to sleep would become impossible. "All right. I should put her down."

"Hey, where do you think you're going? Come on. Pay the toll." Portia hopped out of her chair, cutting them off in front of the french doors. She pressed a kiss to the top of Honey's head, speaking to Jack. "I changed the sheets in the Robin Room this afternoon. Olivia won't stay in the bunk room alone, so if you want to put Honey in there, they can share the big bed when I bring her up later."

"Baba?" Honey peeped as he climbed the stairs.

"Yeah, bug?"

"Does Auntie Tura have to go home tomorrow?"

"Yup. We all do." The room was dark, save the maple leaf nightlight plugged into the socket next to the bed. It bathed the room in warm orange light and saved him from bashing his shins on the pine bed frame when he tucked Honey in and stretched out on top of the coverlet next to her.

"No, I mean..." Exhaling a quiet huff of vexation, Honey rolled onto her belly. "I wish she could come home to our house."

"I know, baby girl. Me too," he admitted, petting her back in slow circles. "It's time for sleep."

"M' not tired," Honey murmured, her eyes already beginning to droop. This was the fragile time between dozing and sleep, when the slightest sound or movement could wake her and start the whole process over again. Lifting his hand from Honey's back, he pushed his fingers through his hair and stared up at the ceiling, listening for the change in breathing that signaled her final descent into dreamland. He was usually careful not to respond when Honey made those suggestions, because he didn't want to encourage any false hopes. At the same time, he had to wonder if she said similar things to Tura, and what Tura's rejoinder might be.

fifty-five
jack

JACK RETURNED SOMEWHERE BETWEEN THE SECOND and third verses of a woeful breakup ballad, stepping between two chairs and sitting down on the end of Tura's chaise. He clasped one hand over the toes of her fuzzy sock. "Hey. I'm sorry I haven't been able to check in with you."

She looked marginally nonplussed by his sudden closeness, but easily shrugged it off. A serene smile bent her lips, the firelight playing across her features. "That's okay. Honey needed you."

"Mind if I sit with you?" He asked, earning another accommodating smile as she folded back the blanket, making space for him to recline into the curve of her body. Arranging the blanket over himself, he laid his elbows on her splayed legs, letting his head fall against her shoulder. "You make an excellent chair."

"And you make an excellent blanket." She slipped her arms under his and around his chest. "Did you get bored, sitting over there navel gazing all night?"

"Yeah." He smiled contentedly. He'd missed this; the security of being wrapped up in someone, of not feeling like the loneliest person in every room. It felt good. Maybe *too* good. "You don't mind, do you?"

"Not at all." She shifted slightly. He felt her touch his hair, absently twiddling with the strands at his temple. Her breath tickled the side of his neck. "I could use the extra body heat."

He tilted his head back to smile up at her. "Happy to help."

Eventually the circle grew quiet, the crackling of the fire filling the gap. A light snow began to fall, giving the moonglade shimmering across the surface of the lake a particularly dreamlike quality. Jack dozed, feeling the occasional feathery prickle of a snowflake alighting on his skin. Out there, beyond the tiny shared world of this chaise lounge, Monday and all the vagaries of real life lurked, but not now. Right now, he was warm and safe, and a beautiful woman was running her fingers through his hair.

Portia let out a irenic sigh. "Every time I come here, I wish we didn't have to leave."

There was a whist of acknowledging hums, then everyone fell silent again, engrossed in the stillness of the night. Lacing his fingers through hers where they laid against his sternum, Jack opened his eyes, staring up at the snowflakes fluttering from the velvety sky. Portia was right. He wished they could stay this way, curled up in the safe envelope of space and time between right and wrong, where these transgressions didn't even bear commenting on.

"All right. We have a long drive tomorrow. I'm heading up," Genie announced, standing up to gather empty wine bottles into the crook of her injured arm. Stepping over and around knees, she stopped next to their chaise. "Hey ugly. Gimme kiss." She bent to peck him on the cheek, then straightened, directing a smile over his head to Tura. "Dulces suenos, gata."

"Mmhmm. Que descanses." Tura surprised him with the

easiness of her response, but then, he reasoned, he probably shouldn't be. Genie returned an unfazed grin and reached for his empty wine glass, adding it to the collection of items to be brought inside.

"She's right, I think I'm ready for bed." Portia stood up and clapped her hands over her wife's shoulders, the two forming a truncated conga line into the house.

Combing her fingers through his hair again, Tura spoke in a mellow murmur. "It's getting late."

Jack closed his eyes, lingering for a few precious moments. "Shh. Not yet."

Her fingers were chilled when she stroked them over his forehead. "Jack. Please."

Exhaling a melancholy sigh, he pushed himself to his feet, holding out a hand. "Come on."

Jack slipped his arm around her shoulders as they mounted the stairs. Tura wrapped her arm around his waist in turn. He could feel the boundaries eroding, every step closer to the top bringing a fresh fear closer to the foreground: That this new latitude between them was temporary, existing only in the here and now. Approaching his room, he slowed his steps, trying to come up with the correct combination of words to tell her he didn't want to wake up in the morning and find nothing had changed. He pointed to the Osprey placard on the door. "This is me."

"I know." She gave him a puzzled smile.

He surprised himself by pulling her to a stop and sweeping his thumb across her forehead, pushing her hair out of her eyes. "You could stay."

Her smile vanished. She cocked her head in an unintelligible avian gesture, like a bird of prey watching a house cat through a window, and stepped out from under his arm. For one awful moment, he damned himself for ruining everything all over again, but she only moved closer. An eternity ticked by as she searched his face, the wheels turning behind those nebu-lous eyes. "And in the morning? Will you freeze me out?"

Ouch. That stung. She looked away, and understanding splintered through him. She was scared, too. Reaching for her, he threaded both hands through her hair, forcing her to look at him. Heart juddering in his chest, he shook his head, his voice uncommonly rough. "I don't think I can take another night without you, Tura."

fifty-six
tura

Jack ushered her into the room and drew the door closed, the action sucking all the air out of her lungs like a bell jar. They'd spent a lifetime with the specter of taboo standing between them. Now they were completely alone, and it was hard not to feel put on the spot.

Turning to inspect the room, Tura hugged her elbows, working to conjure up some semblance of nonchalance. The windows overlooked the barren slope of the backyard, but the designer had compensated for the lackluster view by providing a gas fireplace and enough space for a small sitting area to one side. Two wing back chairs upholstered in nubby green plaid faced the mantel, each with a matching footrest. She flexed her fingers, suddenly aware of how cold her hands were. They'd been outside for hours, yet she hadn't felt the chill seeping into her joints, making them stiff and creaky.

Divining her thoughts, Jack stepped around her and picked up a remote. The fire roared to life with the press of a button, bathing the space in soothing saffron light. He sat down on the arm of the closest chair and took her hands in his, blowing on them the way he used to when he and Noel took her sledding, buffing them between his palms to get the blood flowing. Struck by the implausibility of the situation, she let out a nervous laugh. "So. We're really doing this, huh?"

"Only if you want to," Jack said, puffing on her fingers again. "You can leave right now. We never have to talk about it again."

She couldn't help her sardonic tone. "Because that worked so well the first time."

Lifting his chin, Jack leveled a ponderous gaze on her, appearing to turn something over in his head. Chafing in the prolonged quiet, Tura pulled her hands from his. "What? Do I have something in my teeth?"

"Sorry. I know it must've been going on for a while, but…" The ghost of a smile touched his face. "I can't figure out when I started falling in love with you."

A peculiar buoyancy went through her, as if someone turned off the gravity in her body for the briefest moment, and she experienced the strangest sense of vertigo. The phenomenon reversed itself when Jack stood up and closed the short distance between them. She started wafting downward like a piece of goose down floating in a warm pocket of air, the sudden change of elevation stopping just above the floor, leaving her at eye level with his thickly stubbled chin. The muscles in his throat flexed, his voice coming from somewhere above. "Did you hear me?"

Dragging her gaze upward to meet his, she felt her feet strike the ground, the ballast of his conviction bringing her to earth. She swayed, steadying herself with a hand on the solidness of his chest. "I'm sorry, I think I may be hallucinating."

Jack cocked his head, one corner of his mouth lifting in puzzlement. "Are there elephants? Are they pink?"

She laughed, overtaken by an unanticipated wave of giddiness, and stepped into the protective alcove under his chin, needing his arms around her. Pressing her face against the front of his shirt, she closed her eyes, wanting to remember everything about how this felt. The safety of being held by someone who truly knew her, all of her, even the tough parts. The smell of him, like warm cotton, soap, and something else, a rich, unnameable scent most concentrated at the center of his chest. She thought about how close she'd come to losing him only a day ago, and without warning, an unexpected bubble of conflicting emotion welled up, forcing a breathy sob from her throat.

"Hey." He leaned back, his brow furrowing. "What's this?"

"Don't mind me, I'm just coming *completely* unglued." She laughed at herself, dabbing her watery eyes with the sleeve of her sweater. "Geez. It's been a hell of a weekend, huh?"

"I know." Carding his fingers through her hair, he dusted his lips under her eye, kissing away the last trace of a tear. He stood over her for the longest time, lips parted, so achingly, exquisitely close without making contact. Exhaling a soft, shuddering breath, he shook his head, his voice dropping to a rough whisper. "Please, Tura. Just tell me what you want and I swear to God, I'll do it."

She started to tell him this was it, all she'd wanted for as long as she could remember, but somewhere between uttering that first syllable and his mouth coming down on hers, she forgot what she was going to say. She forgot *everything*, except the firmness of his lips, his breath on her cheek, and the taste of dry red wine lingering on his tongue when it pressed against hers.

A soft sound of astonishment rose from the back of her throat, and he pulled away, vivid blue eyes drifting open. He gave her a hooded smile, his focus snagged on her mouth. "Are we good?"

His thumb feathered along the bottom edge of her lip and she swallowed a moan, trying to think five moves ahead. Curiously enough, her rational mind appeared to have checked out for good. For the first time *ever*, her brain wasn't going at a thousand miles a minute, calculating for every variable.

"Are we good?" he asked again, his lips near enough to brush hers. She nodded, and he let out a gust of breath, bringing his mouth crashing down on hers, setting the last pretenses of their friendship alight.

fifty-seven
jack

JACK DIDN'T HAVE A LOT OF HAPPY MEMORIES FROM childhood, but there was one that did whisper through his thoughts from time to time. He was four or five, sitting on an elderly woman's lap in a bright sunporch, flipping through a worn cardboard picture book. He couldn't remember the identity of the person holding him, or the title of the book. They must've been a family member, though it hardly mattered now, since they had to be long dead. What he *did* recall with perfect, unshakeable clarity, was the feeling of wizened fingers touching the blond curls on his forehead, scraggy feminine laughter, a wilting trace of mothballs and cloying lily-based perfume in the air, and knowing he was unassailably safe. *Loved*.

Why would that memory flutter into his head at a moment like this, when he was kissing Tura, arguably the last person on the planet he *should* be attracted to? Maybe it was a response to that nagging voice in the back of his head, the one telling him this was wrong. It shouldn't feel good. The same voice that shrieked at him to stop eighteen years ago, only this time, he was able to dismiss it as easily as an annoyingly droning insect. *Thank you,* he thought, opening the screen door of his mind and letting the last of his doubts fly away. *I won't be needing you anymore.*

Snatching his glasses off, he tossed them onto the small table next to the bed. They skittered across the surface of the wood and clattered to the ground, but he didn't stop to look where they landed. Tumbling onto the bed, their mouths collided in a gasping, laughing, hair-pulling kiss that felt more like youthful indiscretion than the culmination of desperate adult passion. It was new, and awkward, and so right it made his heart swell with something frighteningly close to hope.

The headboard whacked against the wall with a hollow *thunk*, and Jack ripped his mouth free, whispering a muted curse as he reached up to stop it moving. Tura clapped her hand over her mouth, mirthful tears shining in the corners of her eyes. He held a finger to his lips and made a soft shushing noise, shoving her hand away from her face.

He smothered her giggles with a kiss. This was never part of the plan. He always imagined if he got this lucky, he'd take her someplace where he could make her scream without fear of getting caught. In his fantasies, Honey was out of state and he had all night to map this body and make it his, but here? Now? When a single squeaky bed spring would have the whole house pressing their ears to the door?

Slipping her arms around his neck, she nipped at his ear. "Grab the blankets. We can get on the floor."

They scrambled off the bed, giggling like mischievous children. He bundled the patchwork quilt into his arms, carrying it over to the fireplace. Spreading it on the braided rug with a game show host's flourish, he turned to see her already unbuttoning the front of her sweater and dropping it on the ground. Her thin thermal shirt and bra went next, and she hooked her thumbs under the top of her lounge pants, giving him a querying smile. "I'm sorry. Were you hoping to rip them off?"

Jack watched her skinning her pants down her legs and

started toeing off his boots, struggling out of his sweater and undershirt. "I'll live with the disappointment."

They came together in the middle of the quilt without preamble, mouths crashing, tongues tangling, toppling to the ground in a furious mass of limbs and breath. Closing a hand over the softness of a breast, he dipped his head to suck a nipple between his lips, plucking at it with his teeth until it stood firm against his tongue. She mewled softly, cradling his head against her chest with the flats of her forearms.

"Shh." He gave her a wolfish smile, bending to graze his teeth over her collarbone. "No screaming. No matter what."

Brushing his lips down her sternum, he chased that woodsy citrus scent into the valley between her breasts and over the concave of her belly, his eyes falling to the delicate monogram tattoo below her right hip. Studying the inter-twined letters without the aid of his glasses, the H overlaying the L in stylized victorian script, his mind churned with macabre curiosity. What did a man have to do to earn prime placement on this body? How much pleasure did he have to give her to earn that honor? A savage impulse sprung from some recently unbricked corner of his brain, releasing a fierce primal scream. He wanted to mark her, too.

"H.L.," she breathed, observing his rapt attention. "For Hattie Lamont's. We all have them."

The vines of avarice slackened, at least for the moment, and he traced his lips over the crease of her hip. Stretching out on his stomach, he arranged her knees over his shoulders, drag-ging his nose along the hollow of her thigh, peppering the silken flesh with kisses. He worked his way to the neatly groomed thatch of dark hair at her center and buried his face against it, sweeping his tongue over her slick flesh. She tasted amazing, aqueous and mildly tart, teasing at unripened fruit. Her hips jumped, and she let out a sharp squeak.

He chuckled, laying a soft kiss against her mound. "If you can't be quiet, I'll have to stop."

He had to hold on tight, locking his forearms around her thighs so she didn't jerk out of his embrace. Using his lips and tongue until he was drunk on the taste of her, the smell of her arousal, and sweet *fuck*, the way she moved. He was so hard it hurt, grinding into the quilt at the same cadence as her circling hips, but there was no way he was letting up until he tasted her climax. He wanted to see that loopy, pleasure-dazed look on her face and know he put it there. He drank in her every response, stroking with his tongue until she was slicked over his lips and chin and coming apart against him, flinging her crossed wrists over her face to stifle the moan erupting from her throat.

She was still pliant and humming as he crawled over her, feeling like a goddamn hero. Her lips parted when he kissed her, and she exhaled a faint moan against his mouth. He plunged his tongue inside and hers came to meet it in undulating swirls, making every synapse in his brain shoot off fireworks over his head. He laughed softly, brushing his fingers under her jaw. "Damn, you taste good."

Her breasts flattened against his chest as she looped her arms around his neck, pulling him in for another searing kiss. "*Now*, Jack. Please."

"What do you want to do about protection?" He lifted his head, *hating* that the first question to enter his mind was so damn responsible. For fuck's sake, this was *Tura*. He'd been waiting for this woman for almost twenty years, but as desperate as he was to be inside her, he needed her to feel safe with him. His mind went to the condoms in the care package. He could've deep tongue kissed every one of Tura's weird-ass friends, because he sure as hell hadn't thought to pack any himself. He sat up on his knees above her and cleared his throat, breathing hard. "I'm clean. I've been tested. But it's up to you."

"Just you," she sat up to face him, reaching for the front of his jeans.

His pulse spiked. "You sure?"

"I *trust* you, Jack. You're the only one I would *ever* trust." Her eyes burned into his, limitless and unflinching as she started popping the buttons on his fly. "I want to feel you."

Something changed as she dragged the waist of his jeans down, her gaze eclipsed ever so slightly when his naked cock sprung free between them. She looked down, a soft gasp slipping from her lips. He watched her tuck her hair behind her ear, wondering if she knew she had a tell. Probably not the best time to point it out, when she was staring at his cock like she'd come face-to-face with an unidentified life form.

He knew how she was feeling. He'd been very aware he was touching her in ways he was never meant to when he had his face buried between her thighs.

Mustering the last flinders of self-control, he dipped his head, capturing her gaze. "We don't have to do this tonight."

"No, I want to." Inching closer, she looked down again, sinking her teeth into her plush bottom lip. She reached for him and hesitated, lingering millimeters away for the merest instant, before skimming her fingertips over his shaft. First contact made, she opened her hand, weighing him in her palm. She smiled, adorably proud of herself. "Wow. Jack's dick."

He let out a strangled laugh, too lost in the sensation of her touching him to manifest anything even approaching umbrage. "Were you expecting me to be smooth below the waist, like an action figure?"

"I don't know. You think about something for a few decades, it sort of takes on a life of its own," she mused.

Emboldened, she closed her fingers around him, giving him an exploratory stroke. "This is a *very* nice dick, Jack."

"*Jesus.*" Jack's eyes rolled back in his head. Seeking to anchor himself, he tangled both hands in her hair, shaking with tightly reined restraint. "Well it's yours if you want it."

She nodded eagerly, mouth open, seeking his. "I want it."

She'd barely uttered the words before he lunged, slamming his mouth down on hers and falling on her like a starving animal. He pried her knees apart and crushed her body under his, ravaging her mouth with his tongue.

They aligned naturally, as if they'd been doing this for years. She jumped the first time he nudged against her center, exhaling the tiniest squeak against his mouth, then relaxed under him, allowing him to ease inside, moving in agonizingly slow motion. The breath rushed out of his lungs in a rasping, needful groan as the taut stretched perfection of her body molded around him like a second skin. She let out a soft whimper, her fingers gouging into his shoulders, the first tiny shift of her hips sending shivers darting over his spine, mingling with the desperate urge to thrust.

Burying his face in the dark refuge of her hair, he snuffed the thought that this was the first time he'd been with anyone in what felt like forever. He couldn't afford to anticipate the vital relief of a climax he didn't deliver himself. He wanted to be present, with Tura, because this was different. It *had* to be.

fifty-eight
tura

WAKING TO THE PASTORAL WOODNOTE OF WINTER birdsong, Tura pushed back the blankets and sat up slowly, careful not to disturb Jack where he slept. Stealing a throw off the back of one of the chairs, she crept over to sit on the cushioned bench under the window, watching the wind whip up ghostly moonlit funnel clouds of dry snow on the dark side of the hill. To the east, the first faint pastel-apricot filament of dawn engraved the blackened tree line against the sky.

A soft snort rose from the bed. Jack turned, one hand skating over the vacant side of the mattress. His posture changed, overtaken with sudden, wakeful tension, and he hoisted his face out of the pillow. He squinted around the room, a languid grin spreading over his face when he found her sitting in the window seat. "What are you doing all the way over there?"

"Watching the sky turn colors." She smiled, pulling the blanket closer around her shoulders. Jack left for college as she was becoming fully aware of her sexuality, sparing her the daily ordeal of bumping into him on the way to the bathroom, fresh from the shower with a towel wrapped around his lithe hips. The sight of him now, bleary eyed, pillow creases on one cheek, and a wicked case of bedhead, might've gone a long way to humanizing her young idol.

He rubbed his eyes, reaching for his phone. Blinking at the screen, he tossed it onto the side table again. "It's not even seven yet. Come back to bed."

He lifted the covers so she could crawl in, giving her an improbable view of his recumbent body. She felt the vestigial stain of sin slither through her, that spiteful little voice chiming in to tell her this wasn't for her to see. Dropkicking that thought out one ear, she burrowed against his side and threw a leg over his, passing the arch of her foot over the coarse hair on his calf. Jack heaved a contented sigh, his fingers closing over her shoulder. "I don't want to think about anything outside this room for at least another hour."

Tura hummed serenely, nuzzling into the sandy blond curls adorning the solid planes of his chest. "What happened? You never used to be this furry."

"A lot of shit can change in twenty years." A low chuckle rumbled through the silvery predawn shadows. "I used to have an eight pack and a soul patch."

"I'd successfully blocked out the soul patch." Tura cringed. "You really did tick every box for being a stereotypical nineties douche-canoe."

She felt him smile against the top of her head. "So you don't miss the eight pack? Because I sure as hell miss staying cut living on popcorn chicken and fried cheese."

"Not really." She skimmed her hand over the flat expanse of his stomach. It was true, he'd filled out since his teenaged years, packing at least forty pounds onto his previously rangy frame, but it was solid, muscular bulk. Maybe he didn't have individual abs, but he clearly took care of himself. "Unhealthy body standards aren't just for women. Every time I see a guy with visible abs, all I want to do is give him intravenous fluids and a cookie."

He laughed again, his fingers combing through her hair in lazy strokes. She lifted her head and propped her chin against his heart, admiring him at his most unguarded, eyes closed, a gentle smile playing at the corners of his lips. Morning Jack was a far cry from the untamed titan who'd pinned her to the floor last night, sliding into her as if he knew the way.

"Don't close your eyes," he ordered, breathless, but stern. He cast an entranced stare between their bodies. "Look. Look at us. You feel how good we fit together?"

She followed his gaze to the place where they joined and marveled at the unreality of the sight. This was happening. There would be no going back from here. His hand slid up her throat and nocked under her chin, the other sinking into her hair as he took his weight on one elbow and started to move, his first thrusts measured and slow.

Jack watched her with eyes tinted a warm caramel green in the firelight, allowing her to set the tempo, the hair on his chest and trailing down his abdomen gently abrading the length of her body. He picked up speed gradually, that studious gaze locked on hers until all that deliberate, practiced reserve finally fell away and he started fucking her like a man possessed; punctuating every punishing thrust with a feral snarl.

Don't scream. Digging her nails into his back, Tura buried her face against his muscular shoulder, a nest of searing sparks building at her center. *Don't scream. Don't scream. Don't—*

"Shh. Don't worry. I've got you." A firm hand clamped over her mouth, and he spoke in a gravelly husk against her ear. "Come on, baby. Show me what you can do."

It came out of nowhere, her orgasm making her entire body clutch under him with such violence it momentarily stole her breath, reducing her shriek to an ineffectual *eep* against his palm. Soul-rocking spasms oscillated through her body, frizzling through every nerve and wringing every last deep, crushing squeeze from her core. Her back bowed, and Jack stirred his hips, the pleasure amplified by the rich, masterful praise flowing from his lips. "That's right. Give it up to me. Fuck, that's good. That's so *fucking* good."

His teeth sank into her shoulder, one arm bound around the back of her neck like a boa constrictor as he spilled into her, hammering it home with a few final thrusts. He muffled a triumphant growl against the curve of her neck, his body seizing and shuddering for what felt like *minutes* before going boneless, pleasure sapping all the strength from his body.

Running her fingers over the tender, half-moon shaped bruises on her skin, Tura replayed the euphoric moment he laid his damp forehead against hers and closed his eyes, breathing her name like a prayer. "Oh Tura. Tura, Tura, Tura. I never knew."

At length, he'd rolled off and stretched out on his back next to her, beaming with joyful release. "Ten minutes, then we're going again."

Jack was a creative man, and once they were past the initial awkwardness, he seemed determined to take her in every configuration possible. She still had friction burns on her knees from the quaint braided rug in front of the fireplace, and they'd finished the marathon on the bench under the window, where she'd watched the sun come up a few short hours later. He pulled her into his lap and told her to ride him, all the while whispering the sweetest, nastiest encouragement she'd ever heard. Then, when they were both spent and sore, he rolled onto his front and slept, one arm thrown across her stomach, his breath a cool breeze on her sweaty skin, lulling her into the abyssal rest of the satiated.

Sensing her current abstraction, Jack spoke without opening his eyes. "Something on your mind?"

Tura worried at her lower lip. *Oh, the irony.* After a lifetime spent traveling to and from hostile places, this was the first time she felt as if she were lost in an unfamiliar country where she didn't speak the language. "The thing is, I'm between ninety-one and ninety-two percent sure I love you."

His eyes fluttered open, shining at her in the expanding dawn. "Not a hundred?"

"I like to allow for a margin of error."

He closed his eyes again, his voice filled with humor. "Oh, well. Keep me updated."

The doorknob rattled, and Jack pushed himself to his elbows. Honey's soft voice filtered into the room, and their eyes connected, sending a frisson of shared panic jagging between them. "Baba? Can I come in?"

"Fuck me!" Jack hissed. He was off the bed in an instant, diving for his discarded clothes. Hopping around whilst attempting to shove one leg into his jeans, he flung her cardigan backward, catching her in the face with it.

"Should I hide?" she asked, snatching her lounge pants off the rug and yanking them on. She still had time to crawl under the bed, or wedge herself into the armoire.

Honey knocked again, a childlike quaver in her voice. "Baba, are you awake?"

"Yeah, hold on, bug," Jack called back. He spun in a circle, located his shirt, and shrugged it over his head. Catching Tura's arm before she could climb under the bed, he pulled her to her feet, whispering sharply, "Don't be stupid. You're not hiding under the bed like a fucking criminal!"

"Well what do you want to do, because we can't exactly tell her we've been up here honking each other's horns all night!" Tura shot back, hastily buttoning the front of her sweater, only to realize the open V neck fell all the way to her belly button when she wasn't wearing anything underneath. "Have you seen my shirt?"

He tossed it to her and checked himself in the mirror above the bureau, raking both hands through his hair in an attempt to tame his cowlick. He fixed her with a gleaming smirk, pointing to the side of his head. "Why couldn't you tell me about this before? Shit, Kaplan. I thought we were friends!"

Tura finished dressing and threw up her hands, unrepentant. "Because I'm a vindictive monster, Jack. Hate me later."

Jack took a halting step toward the door, flicked the light switch, and unlocked the doorknob. Honey stood on the other side in her fleece pajama pants and tee shirt. Genie stood behind her with a bath towel thrown over one shoulder, having taken an apparent detour to investigate the unfolding melodrama. Honey's gaze slid between father and unexpected guest, her mouth flattening into a mystified frown. "Why are you here?"

"I agree." Genie beamed with pure, undiluted glee, taking on the affectation of a startled school marm. "My goodness, Tura! What in *heavens* are you doing in Jack's room?"

Jack sent Tura a look of confounded stupefaction. "We were just... Uh..."

Professional instincts taking over, Tura shifted to crisis management mode. Pasting on a lethal smile, she stared directly at Genie, infusing every syllable with the promise of swift, merciless retribution. "Wrapping Christmas presents. Yours is especially nice, Imogen. You'll *die* when you see it."

fifty-nine
tura

THE WIND TOOK ETHAN'S TIE AS HE CROSSED THE street, sending it flapping over one shoulder. He wore a look of grim determination, the expression overshadowing his kind features. He'd been gazing down the street when she opened the door, but he slowed his steps when he saw her, an incredulous laugh bursting from his mouth. "Tura?"

She clutched the front of her silk robe closed for what little protection it provided against the cold, mindful to not smear the paint covering her skin. "Ethan."

"What the fuck are you supposed to be?"

"We're holding a body painting exhibition. All proceeds go to the battered women's shelter." Unable to bite her lip or touch her hair, she was reduced to staring at him. "You said you had some things you wanted to return?"

"Right." He passed her a crumpled paper bag. "Just some stuff you left at my place."

"Thanks." She folded open the bag, unsurprised to discover all it contained was a toothbrush, a bra, and a travel-sized bottle of facial toner. She didn't know why it never registered in her mind that she'd taken such care to leave nothing behind.

"So this is it, huh? Figures I'm only finding out now." He surveyed the Federal brick façade of the boarding house, his features darkening. "I told myself you were a private person, and you'd open up when you were ready. But I'm not sure I could've handled seeing you all turnt out like—"

"Somebody else's fuck toy?" she finished for him, unable to banish the critical edge in her voice. "It's just window dressing, Ethan. I don't participate."

"Well that's a *relief*." Ethan scoffed. "It's great to know you chose watching other people fuck over spending time with me."

"They're not *all* sex parties." A piss-poor argument if ever she heard one. Ethan was right. Every event she'd attended during their time together meant a missed evening with him. She sighed. "I'm sorry. None of this is your fault. You were great."

"But I wasn't enough," he concluded, the wounded look in his eyes enough to make her stomach twist.

"That's not true." She wrung the paper bag closed again. "This is *my* problem. I had no business getting involved with anyone, especially not a man who could be the best thing that ever happened to someone else. I wasted your time, and that's on me."

"There's someone else, isn't there?" he demanded, his jaw flexing. "That Avi guy, right? I knew the second I saw you with him. I wanted to be wrong, but I knew."

"No, he's—" She broke off, slicing her gaze to the side. There was a humane answer to that, but Ethan was going to believe whatever helped him get from one moment to the next. Right now he *needed* to hate her, and she owed him a partial truth, at least. "We've known each other since we were kids."

"That's real fucking sweet." Ethan sneered, waving his

hand at the house, and her. "And does he know about all this?"

"He's inside."

"I guess he must have the edge, since he's known you for *so long*." A look of vehemence shaded his face. Pivoting on his heel, he started down the stairs, sending one last jab over his shoulder. "I feel sorry for you. You're going to have a lonely fucking life if you don't learn to let people in."

I'm trying. Tura watched him go, waiting to feel offended, or even remotely surprised by this side of his character, now that he was under no obligation to be nice to her anymore. All she found was a widening gulf of detachment.

Rikki caught up with her inside, halfway down the hallway to the ballroom. "Hey. You okay?"

"I'll get there." Tura slipped the robe off her shoulders, passing it to them for safekeeping.

"Whoa, there." Rikki shouldered around her, blocking her escape. Pursing their lips, they gave her a sad, coaxing smile. "I know you feel shitty, but you were due for a change. I never got the impression that boy was throwing god-tier dick."

She flinched. "Can we please leave Ethan out of this? I feel like I did him dirty enough."

"As you say." Rikki lifted their hands as if to lay them on her arms, then paused, unable to touch her without mussing her paint job. They settled for taking a step closer, their voice dropping to a low, clement timbre. "You did the right thing, cutting him loose."

Tura closed her eyes and drew a deep breath. It'd been five days since they'd arrived home from Maine. Five days since Jack walked her to the door of her building and pulled her into his arms, mindful of the little girl watching from the backseat of his car.

"I'm sorry. I'm trying to let you go," he'd murmured in her ear. "When can I see you again?"

The right thing would have been to go upstairs and take some time to recover, to get her head screwed on straight before she fell back into his arms and drowned in the warm, encompassing security of his love, but she heard herself promising to stay late after Honey's lesson on Tuesday night. He smuggled her in on Wednesday, and on Thursday, he arrived home without announcing himself, catching her stepping out of the downstairs shower after an especially strenuous afternoon of escape drills.

Tura was wrapping a towel around her chest when she heard a gentle tap on the door. She sighed, unlocking the knob. She didn't know if it was a kid thing in general, or just Honey, but she always seemed to time her toilet emergencies for when the bathroom was already occupied.

Tura was impressed by Jack's stealthiness as he ducked into the tiny room. She backed up against the wall, giggling at his brazen maneuver. "What are you *doing?*"

"I've been thinking about you all day." He pushed the door closed and locked it, rounding on her with a ravenous glint in his eyes. Ripping the towel away from her body, he spanned her waist with his hands and snatched her off her feet. She snuffed a yelp of laughter as he swung her onto the edge of the sink, stepping between her knees. "If I can't have you right now, I'm going to lose it."

She made a perfunctory attempt to remind him of the little girl doing her homework on the other side of the wall, but he only grinned, hitching one elbow under her knee and unzipping with his free hand. "Then we'll have to be quiet, won't we?"

She could still feel the abrupt, ruthless way he surged into her, tilting her backward until her shoulders met the cool surface of the mirror. See the way he loomed over her, one hand braced on the wall, the other pinioning her thigh against his shoulder as he pounded into her. Hear the muted echo of flesh slapping flesh in the tiled room.

That was the first time they finished together, Jack whispering he couldn't hold on much longer, Tura pleading for him to wait, craning her neck, angling her body so his every movement hit just right, creating the perfect amount of friction. He knew her body so well already, knew exactly when to clap his hand over her mouth as the first flutters bloomed into full-blown explosions, and he was right there with her, exhaling a hushed groan against her ear.

Later, after Honey was safely tucked away and they'd gone two more rounds upstairs, Tura was falling asleep above the covers, a sheen of hard-driven sweat drying on her skin. He was tracing delicate circles on her back with his fingertips, and it hit her: He'd ruined her for anyone else.

She gave Rikki a pained smile. "I think I'm in real trouble."

"As the person who's held your hand through every up and down for the last twenty years, I like to think I'm uniquely positioned to provide some perspective on this one," Rikki murmured, folding their arms. "But I don't think you're gonna like it one little bit."

She sighed. "All right. Out with it, whatever it is."

"It was always going to be Jack, dumpling." Rikki gave her a contrite smile. "There was never room for anybody else. We all saw it, even when you couldn't."

sixty
jack

THE MAN TO JACK'S LEFT DUG HIS ELBOW INTO HIS side as a statuesque woman painted to resemble a Xenomorph Queen slithered down the catwalk in an immense black head-piece and segmented tail. Pausing at the end of the stage, she arched her back, bending her arms at her sides like a T-Rex, and flashed a set of chrome grillz at the crowd. A wave of cheers went through the room, and she turned, flanks thunder-clapping in time with the driving electronic music. Jack took another sip of anemic draft beer as the lights faded, allowing the next exhibit to take their place at the far end of the catwalk.

Tonight was an impulse join. A new friend from school had invited Honey for a sleepover, so Jack accepted an invitation to a charity event at Tura's social club. He'd been looking forward to spending a proper night out with her and being able to touch her without worrying Honey might see. He knew he was bound to see some whacky shit, including a fair amount of spontaneous sexual activity. What he *hadn't* antici-pated was being crushed butt to nuts with three hundred screaming, sweating spectators, watching naked people strut around in head-to-toe body paint with no sign of Tura.

The house music faded out and the first gritty, warbling notes of a single electric guitar split the air. The lights came up, revealing a fantastical piece of living art perched atop a set of lemon yellow spike heels. She stood motionless, a long carnival colored whirly pop held over her head like a drum majorette's baton. Her face and body were a hotchpotch of magnified star mints, ribbon candy and pastel nonpareils, and her bright lilac hair was styled into Marilyn Monroe waves, topped with a crown of sugared gumdrops.

The ferocious grind of reverb and heavy base drums kicked in, and she broke into motion, prowling down the long tongue of the catwalk, the open cage bustle around her hips switching with each step. She leaned on the long stick of her oversized lollipop like a cane, taking her time, feeding off the undivided attention of the crowd. Raking an imperious gaze over the people seated below, she paused at the end of the stage and spun, crossing one ankle over the other, and bent deeply, displaying the candy heart airbrushed onto the two perfect globes of her ass, the words BITE ME printed in hot pink block letters.

The room erupted onto its feet, a cacophonous riot of cheers and wolf whistles drowning out the music as people leapt onto tables with their hands in the air. She spun again, peeling the clear cellophane wrapper off the candy walking stick. The ebony orbs of her eyes settled directly on his, and she gave the whirly pop a long, languorous lick. *Holy shit!* He choked, coughing against his forearm as she tossed the walking stick into the air and caught it, strutting away. She glanced once over her shoulder, shot a final wink at the crowd, and disappeared behind the curtains.

The show ended, and the models emerged from the back-stage area to give the audience a chance to take a closer look at the exhibits. A figure moved in his peripheral vision and the candy princess appeared at his shoulder, regarding him from under a fringe of purple foil false eyelashes. She leaned in, her expression tinged with devilry. "Enjoying the show?"

He grinned, giving her a slow once over. "It's been quite an experience."

"You want a tour?" She took his hand, leading him out the ornate rococo doors next to the stage. Crossing into the common areas of the boarding house, they passed the red damask wallpapered sitting room, where a full blown orgy was already beginning to foment, and turned up a set of old servant's stairs at the back of the house.

He traveled in her wake, keeping his eyes glued to the curves of her painted backside as they turned down a long hallway. "You should know I'm seeing someone."

"Oh?" She glanced at him over her shoulder, fixing him with a coy smile. Selecting a door, she drew him into an unused lounge area. The only light issued from a set of high arched windows at the front of the building, casting an eerie moonlight glow over the rows of theater seats and stage sets stacked to one side. Racks of old costumes hung in the dark, the sequins glittering like gemstones embedded in the walls of a cave. The distant noise of the party faded into the background as she flattened her palms to his chest, backing him up against the dusty velvet curtains on the wall. "Is it serious?"

"It is for me." He looked down at her wildly painted hands as she slipped his belt free of the buckle and lowered his zipper. "I think she's still deciding."

She slid her hand inside his pants to pull him free, a query lingering in those expressive midnight eyes. "You want me to stop?"

His laughter rumbled in the quiet. "*Hell* no."

She kissed him once, leaving the candy sprinkles from her lips dancing over his tongue as she sank to her knees in the dim light. Then, without taking her eyes off his, she extended her tongue and licked him like a candy cane.

"*Shit,* yeah. Like that." Jack sucked a sharp breath through his gritted teeth, his voice gravelly and hot in the quiet. He knew he was destroying hours of work when he snared his fingers in her hair, but the visual of her kneeling between his feet and taking him into his mouth was just too *good*.

Before long his hips were moving in shallow thrusts and he was panting like a rabid animal. He was almost too distracted to care by the time he heard voices traveling down the hallway, illicit laughter and running footsteps passing the door. Jack tensed as he heard them approach, the threat of being caught enough to make a fist of instantaneous release clench in his belly. He threw his head back against the scratchy velvet curtains, letting out a guttural roar of delirious, knee-buckling pleasure he was sure the whole house could hear. In the hallway, the giggles redoubled, and an amused masculine voice observed, "Someone's having a good night."

Tura grinned like an avant-garde succubus when he slid down the wall to face her, feeling like a reckless teenager caught skinny dipping in a stranger's pool; a little embarrassed, yes. But proud, too. His ragged laughter echoed in the empty lounge."Fucking hell, Tura. I love your mouth."

sixty-one
tura

Tura's painted skin buzzed with provocation as she led Jack into her apartment and caught the unmistakable sound of the shower running. Holding up a finger, she signaled for Jack to wait and paced to the bathroom door. She knocked, addressing the woodgrain composite. "Avi? Come on, man. You said I could have the apartment tonight."

A discombobulated moan echoed from the other side. *God damn it.* This time, she lifted her hand and banged on the door with a closed fist, waiting for an answer. Another lethargic moan met her ear, and Tura set her jaw, wrapping her fingers around the doorknob. "You better not have used up all the hot water, dickhead."

The door swung inward to a tableau of open mouths and water-lubed skin. Tura stumbled back, flinging her arm across her eyes. "Instant regret. Avi, you jackass! It's a shower, not a clown car!"

"What the fuck did you *expect*, Tura?" Avi's humor filled retort ricocheted from the tiled shower enclosure. "You knew someone was in here!"

"I thought you passed out!" she shouted back.

Avi was laughing in earnest now. "Close the fucking door!"

Tura groped for the door and slammed it closed. Drooping against the wall, she addressed Jack where he stood, observing her mortification. "Get a fork. I need you to blind me."

Jack chuckled. "How many people does he have in there?"

"You think I stopped to count?" Tura shuddered. So many fingers in *so many* places. Levering her shoulders against the wall, she pushed to a standing position again, shambling into the kitchen to wash the taste of abject horror from her mouth.

Avi emerged a few moments later, hiding what remained of his modesty behind his cupped hands. Stomping into the kitchen, he engaged her without stopping to comment on her painted over features, or the temporary purple dye coloring her hair. "You know, you're mighty judgey for someone who spends so much downtime at the horniest place on earth."

"It doesn't count as kink shaming when you walk in on a close relative having unsanctioned group sex in *your private home,* you narcissistic cockpoppet," Tura seethed, slamming her empty glass down onto the counter. "You are *getting* your own place."

"Actually, I am." Seeing the dubious expression on her face, he pointed with his chin in the direction of the bathroom. "What? I'm pretty sure one of them is a realtor."

A faint snort reached her ear, and she leaned around her brother to glare at Jack. "Don't you *dare* take his side!"

Jack held up his hands, giving her a blameless smile. "Hey, you know I'm on your side, but funny's funny."

"I changed my mind. I like him." Avi pivoted to address her companion. "I like you."

"No way. Uh-uh. The two of you need to stop bonding *immediately!*" Tura demanded.

"Excuse the shit out of *me*." Avi rolled his eyes, freeing one hand to pick up her glass and pour the last of her water down his gullet. "I thought a woman appreciated when her family got along with her boyfriend. Guess I was wrong."

Boyfriend... Tura scoffed, curbing her response at the sound of the bathroom door opening. A shapely redhead came scuttling down the hallway in a lacy green bralette and matching panties, carrying the damp bundle of her clothes against her chest. She blushed furiously, creeping out the door without an upward glance. A beat later, two others showed themselves, a fine-boned Asian man, and a stocky Slavic specimen with disjointed boxer's nose, the latter uttering a string of quiet apologies. Finally, a breathtaking woman with rich carbon umber skin appeared, slipping a figure hugging white bandage dress over her curves. She lifted her long silver balayage ponytail and turned, offering her unzipped back to Jack. "Would you mind?"

"Here. Let me." Avi was quick to step between them. Tura and Jack turned their eyes heavenward as Avi released his junk, freeing his hands to draw the woman's zipper upward. He bent to press his lips to the curve of her neck. "I'll call you later."

She bent to fit her shoes onto her feet, casting an adroit smile over her shoulder. "Yes. You will."

They watched in silence as the woman showed herself out. The door clicked shut, and Avi spun to face Tura again, concealing himself with one hand. His eyes flashed, his voice taking on a low, condemning edge. "*This* is why we can't have nice things."

sixty-two
jack

"I've been thinking," Jack mused from his seat at the kitchen table, watching Tura dig through her freezer. She was wearing his shirt, the tail riding up high enough to flash a sleek length of creamy thigh when she stood on tiptoe, sticking her whole head and shoulders into the freezer.

"About what? Ah-ha!" she crowed, coming up with a family-sized box of vegan black bean-sweet potato patties. Unfolding the top and reaching inside, she produced a pint of ice cream. "Suck it, Avi!"

He smiled, savoring the triumphant glee on her face. "I enjoy waking up next to you."

She opened a drawer and grabbed a pair of spoons, taking the chair next to his. "It *is* nice. As long as you don't breathe on me with that ungodly morning breath."

"I'd like to do it more often," he told her, pulling her chair closer so he could tease at the delicate hairs along her nape with his thumb. "I'd like to do it everyday."

"I woke up four out of the last seven mornings in your bed," she reminded him. Prying the top off the container, her smile dampened, and she turned it so he could see the message written in magic marker on the underside: *Marsh-*

mallows are bullshit. Get better ice cream. She rolled her eyes, tossing the cover onto the table and licking her fingers clean. "Curses, outflanked again." She passed him a spoon, offering him the first taste. "Wouldn't you rather enjoy sneaking around for a while? It makes everything so much hotter."

"The sneaking is hot," Jack admitted, speaking around a spoonful of chocolate s'mores ice cream. "But you know what'd also be cool? Spending all night with you in my bed and not having to smuggle you out before dawn."

"Which brings me to my next question." She dug a hunk of fudge out of the carton in his hand. "Has Honey ever walked in on you with an overnight guest? Because I love that kid, but she doesn't seem to appreciate the concept of a closed door. I keep picturing waking up nose to nose with a six year old, asking me why Baba's pants are hanging from the ceiling fan."

"I never had any overnight guests. My daughter lives there." Nuzzling into her hair, he dragged his nose along the curve of her jaw, placing a kiss behind her ear. "But I always lock the door when you're over."

"That's a relief," Tura said, darting an unexpectedly tender, playful smile in his direction. "I feel special, though. You done good."

Sensing his moment, Jack set the ice cream aside and stood up, lifting her out of her chair to the accompaniment of a surprised yelp. Carrying her over to the counter, he set her down and braced a hand on either side of her knees, staring into her eyes for a long, deliberative moment. "When the time comes, I think you should let Avi keep the apartment and move in with us."

She reared back to look him over, suddenly circumspect. "For real?"

Jack nodded, keeping his gaze leveled on hers. "When

we're done sneaking around, I want to wake up next to you every day for the rest of my life."

"And how would that look, Jack?" Angling her shoulders against the cabinet, she gave him a dry smirk. "You think I'll be taking day trips to Lisbon, or Dublin, or Johannesburg, handling my business, then coming home in time for dinner?"

"I don't care, as long as you're coming home to me."

"But I wouldn't be coming home to *just* you. Would I?" She draped her arms around his neck. "Remember Honey? She would *definitely* notice when all my stuff turned up at the house."

"I spend three hundred sixty-five days a year stepping on Legos and scraping stickers off my car windows. Is it so difficult to believe I want to spend my nights with you in my bed?" he asked, pushing the open collar of his shirt off her shoulders. He bent to bury his face against her neck, the scent of her cologne drawing a contented sigh from the depths of his chest. "Fuck me, I smell you in my *sleep*."

"Come on, Jack." The soft ripple of her laughter buzzed against his lips. "Being a part time good influence is one thing, but I can think of about a million ways I could fuck it up. Just look at *tonight!* And my friends. And oh, my god, Avi. What about Avi? We might as well beam the deviancy directly into her brain."

"Fuck's sake, Tura!" Jack laughed. "You think I don't lie awake at night, scared shitless that I'm fucking up my kid in some irrevocable way? She's already in therapy, I don't even want to *speculate* about the shit she's gonna be blaming me for in twenty years." He shrugged, channeling the sibylline wisdom of drunk Genie. "Look, we'll figure it out when the time comes. But if you really think you're any worse suited for the gig than I am, I've got news for you. My life was one nervous breakdown after another *before* you came along."

A myriad of thoughts whirled behind those intense black

eyes. He loved that look; the irresistible stage right before the cagey glint gave way to the lambent sincerity within. Seizing the opportunity, he ended the debate with a kiss, stroking his hands up her thighs and sliding them under her ass. The novel thrill it gave him blew his mind, being allowed to explore her with such casual freedom.

"Tell you what," she purred against his lips. "I'll consider it, if you'll do the thing."

He shook his head, chuckling. He'd created a monster. Now even when they were all alone and free to fuck the bed off its moorings, she begged for his hand on her mouth.

"Anything you want. You know that," he murmured, plaiting his fingertips together at the nape of her neck, his palms framed at the pulse points beneath her jaw. Pulling her forehead to his, he released a deep, prayerful sigh, letting his eyes fall shut. "Tell me you love me. I need to hear you say it, just once."

She responded by winding herself around him, legs around his hips, arms draped around his shoulders, and gave him a soft, eloquent kiss. This time when she spoke, he heard the temperate smile in her voice. "I've *always* loved you, Jack."

sixty-three
tura

Tura met Honey at the bottom of the bus steps and slipped the inhumanely heavy backpack off the girl's shoulders, carrying it for her as they trudged back to the house. Honey was showing her the giraffe painting she made in art class and detailing the minutiae of her day when Tura felt it again; that tingling alertness at the base of her skull. A burgundy sedan came crawling around the bend in the driveway, and Honey stopped, a hint of anticipatory concern scrunching across her brow.

"You know who this is?" Tura asked, eyeing the woman behind the wheel. Late sixties, big hair, designer sunglasses, and deeply weathered skin, most likely from cigarettes and too many years spent sun worshipping, dyed an unnatural shade of tangerine. Nothing remarkable or dangerous that Tura could see, and yet, something prodded at her, warning her to stay on guard.

Honey nodded, swallowing heavily. "Nana Kathy."

"Oh, *this* is Nana Kathy!" Tura said with false cheer, bending to address the woman as she pulled alongside them. The woman rolled down her passenger side window, releasing a gust of stale cigarette and sweet brown liquor-scented air, the stench threatening to unpin Tura's rigidly fastened grin. "Hi, can I help you?"

"Hello there." The woman met her with an equally precarious smile. "I'm Honey's Grandma Kathleen." Sliding her sunglasses down her nose, she flapped her fingers at the little girl. "How are you, sweetheart? Have you been missing your nana?"

Shifting from one foot to another, Honey gripped her painting in front of her, crumpling the edge of the paper. She nodded at the ground, the slightest trace of a wobble in her chin. "Uh-huh."

"Ahh, don't be that way," the woman cooed, giving Honey a wide, cajoling smile. "Hey, you remember that place we used to go for cupcakes in Warwick? I was thinking maybe we could go get some. We haven't done that in a while." She patted the empty passenger seat. "Come on, hop in!"

Honey's eyes slid to Tura's, concern melting to unbound terror. She wasn't afraid Tura would actually let her *go*, was she? Taking Honey's hand in hers, Tura gave the woman her most apologetic smile. "You know, that's so thoughtful, but Honey has about fifteen pounds of homework today." She lifted the backpack for emphasis. "Maybe if you call her dad, you two can set up something for this weekend."

Kathleen's smile slipped by a fraction, something bright and deranged flashing in her eyes, but she recovered quickly. "Oh, come on. I'll have her back in an hour. Jack doesn't even have to know."

And you just said the magic words. Tura flattened her hand between Honey's shoulder blades, urging her toward the house. "Hey young lady, my phone's on the counter inside. Why don't you run ahead and call your daddy? Maybe we can all go."

Honey hesitated for a beat, conflicted about leaving Tura alone with her grandmother. Taking the painting from the girl's hands, Tura gave her a light push. "Are you listening to me, *young lady*? I said go inside and find my *phone.*"

Kathleen made a loud squawking noise when Honey took off at a sprint, running the final fifty feet to the deck and up the stairs. The emergency brake cranked sharply as the woman ratcheted it upwards and climbed out of the car, marching around the front bumper to confront Tura. "I don't know who you think you are, but you have no right to come between me and my granddaughter."

Tura lifted her hands in apology, turning to walk back to the house. "I promise you ma'am, I have no interest in coming between you and anyone else. I'm simply making sure Honey takes care of her schoolwork first."

"Don't you 'ma'am' me! How dare you?!" Kathleen charged after her, arms pumping like a speed-walker. "Hey! Get your bony ass back here. We're not done!"

"Respectfully, I don't see what else there is to talk about." Tura almost made it all the way to the stairs before Kathleen latched onto her arm. Catching a strong whiff of alcohol on the woman's breath, it took all her self control not to belt her in the face with Honey's backpack.

"You're the new one, right?" Kathleen raked her with a sneer. "Let me tell you something. He's going to ruin your life, just like he ruined my daughter's."

"You're probably right." Pulling her arm free, Tura started up the stairs.

"Don't you walk away from me!" Kathleen stomped after her again. "You ungrateful little bitch, I'm trying to *help* you!"

"Yeah well, you can't tell me nothin' because I'm from Missouri. It's the Show Me State, don'cha know," Tura finished on a caricatural Midwestern accent, reaching for the door. She could see Honey inside, eyes large as saucers, holding the phone clutched against her ear. Pressing down on the latch, Tura pushed the door open at the same moment Kathleen grabbed a fistful of her hair and yanked her backward, slamming her other palm into the side of Tura's face.

"Are you fucking kidding me?" Tura scoffed, dropping Honey's bag to take hold of the woman's wrist. All she'd have to do was twist; she could force her to her knees and hold her there until help arrived. She'd performed the maneuver a thousand times, but before she could execute it, Honey rocketed through the door, pelting the older woman's back and kidneys with purposeful fists.

It happened so quickly. The three flailed in a graceless dance, Honey advancing and Kathleen ducking away, body-checking Tura backward. For one brief moment, the thought that this would be funny if the stakes weren't so high flittered through Tura's brain, and she let out a bark of capricious laughter.

With a childlike war cry, Honey aimed a powerful side kick at Kathleen's kneecap, sending her pitching sideways. Kathleen took Tura with her, releasing her grip on her hair an instant before plunging both hands through the tempered glass top of the patio table and somersaulting over it, pulling the frame onto its side. Tura came down on top of the over-turned table with her full body weight. There was an odd popping sensation, a fulmination of white hot pain knocking the air from her body.

Honey screamed. Kathleen kicked at Tura's shoulder, trying to dislodge her dead weight from where she'd toppled against the other woman's badly injured knee. Gulping for air that wouldn't come, Tura laid immobilized by excruciating, nauseating pain like she'd never felt before. It radiated through her midsection, somehow magnetizing the warped frame of the table to her side. Her ear scraped against craggy pebbles of glass as she angled her head to look down, vision pixelating. A prong of aluminum plunged through the fabric of her coat, a thin ribbon of blood pouring down the groove in the metal.

sixty-four
jack

A SEA OF FIRST RESPONDER VEHICLES LIT THE YARD, the flashing blue and red lights filtering through the trees in the gloaming light of afternoon. A passel of uniformed police officers stepped out of the way as he careered up the drive and skidded to a stop, spotting his daughter sitting on the tailgate of an ambulance between a paramedic and a somber-faced detective in a gray blazer. He was out of the car in an instant, dashing across the grass without bothering to close the door.

"*Baba!*" Honey screeched, dissolving into tears the moment he lifted her in his arms.

Jack dropped to his knees, setting her on the ground and checking her over. "Are you okay? What happened?"

"According to your daughter, her grandmother tried to abduct her." The bullish, square jawed detective loomed above them. "The sitter tried to stop her, and they both fell through the table on the deck."

"Where'd they take her?" Jack was on his feet again, casting a frenzied glance around. "Is she okay? Did they say—"

"They're both en route to the hospital, but I can't speak to the condition of either." The officer gave him an ineffectual shake of his head, withdrawing a black notebook from his breast pocket. He clicked his pen. "Can you tell me if—"

"No, someone has to know!" Jack shouted. He pressed his hand against his clavicle, feeling suffocated. He staggered to the stairs, pulling a weeping Honey along with him, and sat down, clinging to the handrail overhead. His eye went to the place where the table used to stand, shattered tempered glass scattered in safe little cubes, and the ominous pool of blood — *Fuck, too much blood* — dribbling through the decking. "Why the fuck was Kathleen even here?"

Breathe, Jack. Think of Honey. Nessa's benevolent tone echoed in his head, the aptness of her timing temporarily overriding his distress. Now? She chose *now* to come back?

The sound of his ringtone made his heart stutter in his chest, and for an instant he fumbled around, feeling his pockets. Realizing he'd left it in the front seat, he dropped Honey's hand and bolted for the car, diving across the driver's seat. "Hi? Hello?"

"Hello sir," an assiduous feminine intonation fed down the line. "I'm calling from Providence Rishona Hospital. Is there a Jack Aldridge at this number?"

"Yes, this is Jack." He gasped.

"We have a Tura Kaplan here. You're on her list of emergency contacts."

"Providence Rishona?" Jack repeated, crawling backward out of the car to rest a shaking hand on Honey's shoulder. "Do you know—"

"I'm sorry sir, we're unable to give any information over the phone."

"Right, I'm coming." Hanging up without saying goodbye, Jack swung Honey into his arms. The detective was behind him as he flung open the rear door and deposited his daughter into her booster seat, reaching across to buckle her in.

"Sir, there are a number of questions we have to ask..."

"God damn it, I don't have *time* for this!" He reached into his back pocket, intending to give the detective a card, only to realize he'd rushed out of the office so fast he'd forgotten his wallet and briefcase. If he hadn't been grasping his phone against the side of his face hard enough to make his ear ache, he doubtlessly would have left that, too. Slamming the door, he rounded the car and paused, resting his hand on the roof. "You can follow me to the hospital and I'll answer your questions there, but I have to say, if this is about Kathleen, I don't care if you burn the bitch at the stake."

He slid behind the wheel, catching eyes with Honey in the rearview mirror. Gobsmacked, she let out a single hiccup in the oppressive quiet of the car. Jack ground his teeth and turned, reaching between the seats to rest his hand on her knee. "I'm sorry, baby girl. I shouldn't have said that."

Starting the engine, Jack executed a breakneck three-point turn, the wheels kicking up a cloud of clay dust, grass and rocks as they sped away. They drove in silence for a few minutes, until Honey spoke in a shaky voice from the backseat. "Baba? It's my fault."

"No it's not, Honey. God damn it, *move* you son of a—" Jack slapped the steering wheel, pulling around a powder blue land yacht crawling down the highway at forty-five miles an hour. He clenched his jaw, drawing a shuddering breath. "None of this is your fault, okay? Your Nana knew she was supposed to stay away."

"No." She sniffled. "Tura said if she ever called me 'young lady' I was supposed to run away as fast as I could and call 911. And she said it *twice*, but I was too scared."

"Tura told you that?" Jack asked, watching her hang her head in the rearview.

She nodded limply. "Nana Kathy hit her, and then I hit Nana Kathy, and they fell, and Tura—"

Damn it, she was crying again. The big, honking baby sobs that just *flayed* him alive. Jack steered the car onto the shoulder. Climbing into the backseat with her, he lifted his little girl into his lap, enfolding her in his arms. He laid his chin on top of her head, eyes burning as he petted her soft bronze curls and rocked her from side to side, the way he used to when she was tiny enough to fit in his two hands. Eventually, the sobs slowed to gentle gasps, and he leaned back to look down at her.

"Listen to me, bug." He pushed her hair out of her face, his chin trembling with the effort of holding back the flood of his own heartbreak. What had he done, bringing Tura into their lives? He should have *known,* he chastised himself, they wouldn't be allowed to keep her. He sucked a sharp breath through his nose, unable to fully banish the quaver in his voice. "Sometimes, terrible things happen and there's nothing we can do to stop them. But Tura wouldn't blame you for any of this. Do you hear me? Not *ever.*"

Honey let out another shallow gasp and nodded up at him, her lashes matted with tears. Jack pulled her close again, holding onto her like a life preserver, the only thing keeping his head above water.

sixty-five
jack

"SHE'S GOING TO FUCKING HATE THIS," AVI GROUSED at the ceiling, drooped so low in his chair he was practically sliding off onto the floor. It was dark and visitor's hours were well over, but Rikki had reached into a bottomless bag of favors owed by powerful people. When they wheeled Tura out of surgery, unconscious and blanched to a sickly green, they brought her here, to a private room where they could sit bedside without being shooed out.

"That is not helpful," Rikki replied with torpid humor, the very model of genteel southern dignity. Leaning against the wall, they ignored the late night cable infomercials playing on the television and kept their attention directed out the window, twirling the drawstring end of their loose-fitting hoodie.

"Seriously, I've never seen her take a fucking aspirin!" Avi shot to his feet, pointing with a flat, emphatic hand at the motionless form in the bed. "You know how she'll react when they try to give her *morphine?* She's gonna go apeshit!"

"This. Is not. The *time,*" Jack bit out, keeping his eyes on the floor. He didn't begrudge Avi his anger, in fact they'd all three shared some very colorful opinions on how best to deal with Kathleen when the police came to ask if Jack wanted to press charges. It was a damn good thing Genie had already come to collect Honey, because she'd never feel safe again if she heard them shouting all at once, competing to outdo the Spanish Inquisition for torture methods. Now they sat in the same room like a trio of caged tigers, with nothing to distract them but the beeping of the heart monitor and the bombastic idiot flogging high-tech food dehydrators on channel seven.

Rikki heaved a despondent sigh. "I could use some air. Anyone want anything from the coffee place?"

Neither man spoke for a long time after Rikki departed. Avi sat across from him, resting his elbows on his knees, twisting the chunky silver ring around his right middle finger, staring into nothingness. Jack leaned back against the wall, watching the way the light slanted through the window and formed a mottled splotch across the scratchy blanket over Tura's legs. Praying. For a twitch. Or a moan. The flutter of an eyelid. Anything to indicate she was okay in there. That she was coming back.

"You know about our mother?" Avi broke the silence without looking at him. "What she did to us?"

"Not much." Jack shook his head. "I know she tried to sell you."

"Yeah. I'd give my left *nut* to find whatever fuckwit family court judge thought it'd be a good idea to give a junkie her kids back after that." Avi's head sagged low between his shoulders, his dark hair falling over his face. "She tell you how we were born?"

"Seven minutes apart."

"That, and..." Avi laughed morbidly. Sitting back, he crossed his ankle over the opposite knee, still twisting that ring. "You see before you two genuine crack babies."

"Shit," Jack breathed, absorbing this newest revelation. "Does anyone else know?"

"Pretty sure Rikki does. But I doubt she told the rest of 'em, given the way they party at the house. Sometimes I'd swear she hooked up with those freaks just to prove she could stay sober." Avi folded forward again, lacing his fingers together and resting his chin against his thumbs, like a man at church. After a few seconds, he scrubbed both hands over his face, releasing a rough, wounded sigh. "They might as well take the needle out before she tries to do it herself. No alcohol. No nicotine. No pot. Fuck, she won't even drink *caffeine,* because she got it into her head we're predisposed to substance abuse, and nothing scares her more than that. It doesn't matter what the doctors say. She's gonna try to gut it out, because she's Tura, and she's the smartest person in every goddamn room."

Jack's mind went to Honey, and all the irrational fears that'd been eating him alive for the past six years. All the times he'd grilled her pediatrician, and even Portia, about Honey's risk factors. The heart-stopping knowledge that having a family history of alcoholism meant he might've damned his daughter with his own genetics. It didn't matter he was doing exactly what he should to keep her safe, he knew that fear better than anyone. Conversely, there was a part of him that was hurt, even angry, to know Tura didn't feel she could share that part of her history with him.

A nurse shuffled in to check Tura's vitals and hang a fresh IV bag. Avi announced he had to take a piss and exited the room, leaving Jack alone with the strange woman in pink nurse's clogs.

"You should try talking to her," she suggested, making a note on Tura's chart. "It might help."

Jack tamped down the urge to inform the woman how

little faith he had in the power of his voice to bring someone back from across the *street*, let alone whatever lightless abyss Tura was killing time in, but he felt so useless sitting there doing nothing that when she left, he picked up his chair and moved it closer. Lifting Tura's limp, cold hand and sandwiching it between his, he swallowed the rough feeling at the back of his throat. "Tura. Baby. I need you to wake up, okay? Please. I don't know what we'll do without you." He pressed his lips to each of her fingertips, exhaling a wretched sigh. "I'm sorry. I'm so sorry, baby. Just please."

He could feel his heart pulling him in separate directions, trying to cleave itself in two. One part held fast to the woman in front of him, this superhumanly brave woman who would go to war for his daughter. The woman with whom he could see his life unfurling into the future, growing and changing and becoming someone new and better everyday, just for knowing her. The other part couldn't forget how he'd whispered this plea a thousand times before. That part of his heart still mourned, would *always* mourn, for Nessa. He'd fought with everything he had, but he lost her long before she'd left this world, and he was tired, so fucking *tired*, of carrying that hurt. "Fuck, I can't do this anymore, Ness. I can't lose her, too."

I know. A strange sensation floated over him, and for the briefest instant, he almost imagined he could feel the tethers on his heart snap.

A shadow moved in the doorway, and Jack lifted his head, half expecting to see his wife standing in a halo of light. It took a few seconds for his grief-drenched brain to identify the tall, nattily dressed silhouette in the doorway, but by then Noel was already setting his attaché case on the bench against the wall and draping his long camel coat over the top of it. Picking up Avi's vacant chair and moving it closer to the bed, he looked Tura over in the shadowy room. "How is she? Do they know anything yet?"

Jack straightened, struggling to comprehend Noel's sudden presence in the midst of all this awfulness. "What are you doing here, man?"

"The hospital called." Noel ran his hand over his fastidiously styled hair, breathing out a long, tight sigh. "I was in Chicago for business. Caught the first flight I could out of O'Hare."

"Oh," Jack said, any further conversation felicitously halted by the entrance of Avi and Rikki, the latter arriving with a bag of assorted pastries and a travel carrier of coffee. Rikki passed Jack a paper cup and a scone, extending a compensatory apology to Noel for not having enough to go around.

"Forget about it." The legs of Noel's chair scraped the floor as he stood up, appraising the newcomers. "Noel. Another one of Tura's foster brothers. You're friends?"

"Nope." Avi stepped to the side, removing himself from Noel's direct line of sight. Lifting his coffee to his lips, he flicked a furtive look in Jack's direction, the expression so familiar, so much like Tura, that it made Jack's heart throb with longing.

"This is Avi. He's Tura's biological brother, in case his atrocious manners weren't a decent enough hint," Rikki supplied the introduction, their voice taking on a pointedly reproachful note. "And I'm Tura's friend Rikki. We've met."

"Tura's brother," Noel repeated, sizing Avi up for a second time. "Sorry, man. I didn't realize you were in the picture."

"It's cool." Avi reclaimed his chair, propping one foot up on the bottom railing of the bed. Evidently rattled by the chilly reception, Noel stepped to the side, hands on hips.

"What'd the doctor say?" Noel addressed his question to Rikki.

"She fell through a table," Rikki synopsized, casting a doleful look at Tura. "Broke a few ribs and punctured a lung. She lost a lot of blood at the scene, but she's scrappy. She made it through surgery all right, and she's breathing on her own. All we can do now is wait."

"Was she drunk?"

"She doesn't drink," Jack and Avi spoke in unison.

Noel went quiet for a beat, finally picking up on the strange vibe in the room. He started unbuttoning his suit jacket, sweeping an impatient gaze around at the others. "All right. What am I not being told? Come on, I wouldn't have flown all the way here if I didn't *care*."

"My mother-in-law pushed her," Jack said, the truth bitter on his tongue. "Tura was watching Honey, and Kathleen came to the house while I wasn't there."

"Your house..." Noel's voice trailed off. His gaze tumbled to the place where Jack clasped Tura's hand in his. "I didn't know you were speaking."

"We reconnected after Nessa's overdose." He gave Noel a pained look, willing him to understand. "She's been there for us a lot, the last few months."

Noel's upper lip bulged as he ran his tongue over the front of his teeth, staring into the middle distance for a protracted instant. He dropped his chin against his chest, his pronounced brow puckered with comprehension, and made a soft, disapproving *chuff* under his breath. "That's our *sister,* man."

Seeing things going down exactly as he'd predicted eighteen years earlier, Jack exhaled a defeated sigh. He'd wasted a lifetime flagellating himself for this same point. Having finally made peace with his feelings, it all felt so pointless. Weren't they all here for love of the same person in one way or another? "Did you think I forgot?"

Avi precluded any retort from Noel by taking his foot off the side of the bed, bringing it to the ground with a categorical *bang*. Leaning back to stare at Noel, he curled his hands loosely over the knees of his black jeans, his casual posture belying the menacing tenor of his words. "She's not *your* sister. She's *mine*. And I don't feel the need to police her pussy, so why should you?"

sixty-six
jack

DAYS PASSED. THE OTHERS COVERED THE EVENINGS and overnights when Jack went home to take Honey off the bus and feed her dinner. Once she was down for the night, he'd shower and climb into bed, sleep for a few dreamless hours, then wake up to feed his daughter breakfast and send her off again. He ran on autopilot, performing all actions in precise order, hating himself a little bit more every time she looked at him for reassurance and he had none to give. No, he didn't know when Tura would be better. No, he didn't know what was going to happen to Nana Kathy (though if he had any say about it, she'd never see daylight again).

Noel had taken the early morning watch. He was there when Jack arrived, clacking away on his laptop at the table in the corner. They sat in thorny silence for almost an hour, Noel shuffling paperwork and entering figures onto one spreadsheet or another, Jack sitting in disconsolate misery next to the bed, nursing a cup of scorched hospital coffee. When Noel finally spoke to him, he did so in an absentminded monotone, as if he were giving a stranger the time in an elevator. "How long we gonna do this?"

Glancing over at Noel, one corner of Jack's mouth

quirked up. "You want to fight about Tura and me? That why you're here?"

"Fuck off, dude." Noel hunched forward, resting his elbows on the tabletop. He pressed his upturned thumbs to the bridge of his nose, chuckling at some private amusement. "We both know if I took a swing at you, she'd sit straight up in that bed and start harping on me about 'diminishing her agency,' or whatever."

"Shit, if you think that'll work." Jack laughed to chase away the raw, acrid feeling in his gut. "I'm game."

They sat grinning to themselves, lost in the memory of a thousand companionable moments before they remembered where they were, their smiles falling away. Noel tapped on the table with his index and middle finger, ruminating. "Is it fucked-up to say I'm not even that surprised?"

"Then you're the only one." Jack gazed at the bed, his heart wilting. "I didn't go looking for this. She was there, and I hadn't felt any kind of way about anyone in such a long time. We sort of just—"

"Yeah I don't need details." Noel waved his hand, as if trying to bat away the thought of his foster siblings tripping and falling into bed together. "Just tell me you're not using her."

"I love her." Jack trained his eyes on Tura, praying she could hear him, wherever she was. "And Honey does too, which only makes it easier."

"And that's my limit." Noel pushed back his chair, gathering his papers together and stuffing them into his attaché case. He straightened, giving Jack a laborious smile. "You know I love you like a brother, and I'm gonna try to be cool about it, but right now..."

"Yeah." Jack sighed, a reluctant sense of understanding tugging at his heartstrings. It was an all-around fucked situation. This was probably as good as it was going to get for a long time.

Noel paused as he walked past, his hand coming down on Jack's shoulder. "You know she's gonna come through this and be an even bigger pain in the ass than before."

Jack reached up to pat his hand. "Thanks, man."

Portia arrived a few hours later, bringing a single-serve container of warm chicken enchilada casserole and a paperback romance novel. She put a fork in his hand and sat down against the wall to read, informing him she intended to wait until every bite was consumed. He picked at it for a few minutes and set it on the bedside table, earning a captious glare from the woman on the bench behind him. "How long has it been since you ate a full meal?"

"I ate with Honey last night."

"Bull. You think she doesn't talk to us?" Portia challenged him, retrieving the container and handing it to him again. "You aren't eating. You look like you haven't slept in days. You haven't been to work all week."

"I also took the lord's name in vain seventy-two times," Jack muttered, poking at the mass of congealed chicken and cheese without feeling a single stirring of appetite. "For real, I don't think I can eat right now. I'll only make myself sick."

"Humor me, Aldridge."

"Don't you have your own family to harass?"

Slapping her book shut, Portia scowled at him above the rims of her glasses. "I would, but they're busy keeping *your daughter* distracted while you're here."

"And I'm grateful." Jack forked a hunk of chicken, shoveling it into his mouth. "She knows I need to be here right now."

"Honey needs you too, Jack," Portia said quietly. "We get that you're going through it. We all know Honey's grandmother is a deeply unstable person, but she also played a major role in your daughter's upbringing. Honey hit someone she cared about. Not only did she contribute to the violence that almost killed Tura, now it appears it's killing her daddy, too. She's *scared*."

Jack stared at Tura's unconscious form. Tura was staying. He'd made his mind up sometime last night, when he was lying awake, waiting for sleep to take him. She was staying if he had to trek his ass to hell, play chess with death, flip the board and punch the fucker in the nuts. "Neither of us is dying."

"Tell *her* that, Jack."

"Tell her what?" a slurred voice rose from the bed. Stunned to open-mouthed silence, they sat forward to watch Tura fighting to hoist her ossified eyelids open, her head tossing from side to side on the flat hospital pillow. "Oww. *Hurts.*"

The container slipped from Jack's hands, not that he gave a flying fuck about the soupy chicken casserole spattered across the toes of his shoes as he leaned over the bed. Combing her hair back with his fingers, he searched her face. "Tura? Can you open your eyes for me? Open your eyes."

He was vaguely aware of Portia moving around behind him, jamming her thumb on the emergency call button. A pair of nurses in easter egg blue scrubs bustled around the other side of the bed, checking her pulse and taking readouts from the machines. The doctor, a youthful South Asian woman with a shag faux hawk and neck tattoos, shouldered past him and plucked a pen light from her pocket, shining it into Tura's eyes.

She spoke in a smooth, unflappable mezzo-soprano, explaining to the patient she'd been seriously injured and unconscious for eighty-seven hours post-surgery. Asking if she remembered any part of the accident. Jack held his breath, his eyes trained on the bridge of Tura's nose, scrunched with drowsy annoyance.

"Drunk lady," Tura croaked. She swallowed roughly, squinting at the light. "Pulled my hair."

"That's a good start." The doctor put away the pen light and smiled, slipping her slender hands into the pockets of her white coat. "Anything else?"

"Honey was—" Tura's eyes flew open, inundated with panic. "Where's Honey?"

"She's safe," Jack said, leaning over the doctor's shoulder. "She's home."

"Good." She closed her eyes, letting her head fall back against the papery pillowcase. "*Thirsty*."

sixty-seven
tura

Nothing like waking from a coma to help a person appreciate their porous relationship with time. The present slid into focus gradually, arriving in flashes and flickers, like viewing reality through the aperture of a stop-motion camera. Every smell, sound, image felt brand new, the tiny pinpoint of her consciousness widening to absorb each added stimuli. The pain came first, assaulting her senses like hurricane-stirred waves pummeling a beach. The pocked expanse of the drop ceiling above the bed. Jack's fingers interwoven between hers. A kind-eyed doctor asking her questions. The squeaky wheel on the nurse's cart, and Jack's breath tickling her forehead when he kissed her face. And pain, and pain, and *pain*. Put it in a box. Seal it up tight.

No, not on the mouth. She whined, face twisting as Jack pressed his lips to hers. Her mouth tasted like the floor of a public restroom. Definitely not sexy.

He kissed her anyway, pressing his lips to hers hard enough to make her flinch, until she jerked her face away and begged for water. She licked her lips. Parched, like salt flats. Her eyelids felt like they were weighted with manhole covers, but she opened them anyway. His eyes were wet. "My breath that bad?"

Someone laughed, and she swiveled her attention to the face hovering above his shoulder, recognizing her weepy visage before the name alighted on the tip of her tongue. "Heyyyy... Portia's here. Now it's a party."

More people came, what felt like an unbroken stream of faces and voices spooling past the foot of her bed. *Noel* was there, which was weird. He came bearing a stuffed raccoon, the critter sticking it's pointy snout from under the lid of a plush silver lamé garbage can. Only after Rikki gave her the full story was she glad she hadn't made a joke about the message inferred from a toy trash panda. She thought she'd imagined the trepidation on his face, but there was no missing the way he kept his body angled toward the door, or the stiffness in his posture when he bent to kiss her cheek.

Rikki made it sound *rough*, like Jack had to walk the poor horse right up to the water and hold his head under before Noel caught on. To his credit though, he'd stuck around, even after Avi had, by all accounts, snapped it off in his ass. Perhaps she would have to revisit her feelings toward her hard-assed foster brother. Sure, he could be a dick, but he showed up, even when it was awkward. No small thing, that.

On the much less pleasant end of the spectrum, there were the daily battles over morphine. She liked Dr. Kumarage. She was appreciative of the unorthodox young doctor's tactful nature and cockeyed smiles, but she didn't want the drugs, and Dr. Kumarage couldn't *make* her consent to the morphine drip.

A few times a shift, the doctor would stroll through the door with her trademark casual flair, holding her stethoscope looped around the back of her neck like a gym towel. She'd enquire about Tura's pain levels and offer her something stronger than the horse-tranquilizer sized Ibuprofen tablets she was choking down every six hours. Tura would lie, dividing her summative pain by at least half, and Dr. Kumarage would promise to monitor Tura's dosages with the scrutiny of a mafia bookkeeper. It would end, as always, with Tura assuring the doctor such efforts were not necessary while simultaneously squelching the urge to blot the sweat along her hairline.

So it went for almost a week, until the morning the doctor tired of the daily square dance and discharged Tura with strict orders to avoid falling through any furniture for at least six months.

"Promise me the thing at the hospital was it." Tura took Rikki's arm, pulling herself out of the side of their car with a lock-jaw grunt and standing, waiting for her vision to stop swimming.

She'd left the hospital that morning to the accompaniment of a dozen tunelessly trumpeting noisemakers. Honey jumped up and down, waving a hand drawn WELCOME HOME TURA sign high over her head as Tura's friends pelted her with fistfuls of confetti. All she could think about was how the orderly seemed to be aiming directly for every crack and dip in the sidewalk.

Rikki snorted quietly, slowly guiding her up the stairs on Jack's deck. "Lemme tell ya buttercup, I was ready to hire a kick line of rollerskating drag queens, but your boy was all, 'No, she's *hurt*. She just wants to *rest*.' That man could suck the fun out of brunch at a gay rodeo."

"He has his uses." Tura's smile was shaky. Clinging to Rikki's arm, she shoved the searing pain in her side to the back of her mind and concentrated on putting one foot in front of the other.

"Girl, you better watch yourself." Rikki side-eyed her something fierce. "They get you with the good dick, then one day you'll wake up and your life is all carpools and school plays. You'll start to wonder if maybe you mighta caught a touch of the brain damage, all those nights he rabbited you into the headboard."

"My god." Tura snickered at the notion of anyone trusting her to drive a carpool. "You're such a *troll* when you don't get to rent a glitter cannon."

"You could still come home with us, if you want."

"We talked about this," she replied through gritted teeth. This was one of the conditions of her release. She couldn't stay alone. It was tough enough working up the will to limp to the bathroom. She couldn't be dragging herself back and forth to the kitchen, risking re-puncturing her repaired lung. Staying in her tiny apartment and relying on Avi would only result in bloodshed, and as much as she knew she'd be showered with love and attention at the boarding house, she didn't have the bandwidth for that level of pandemonium. That made Jack's place the most logical solution.

The door swung open to reveal a room blessedly free of crowds and paper streamers, distant strains of a mid-nineties rap anthem drifting from somewhere at the back of the house. Depositing Tura's overnight bag inside the door, Rikki looked around, letting out a low, appreciative whistle. "Your boy did this? Okay, I guess I can see it."

"Glad you approve." Jack sauntered around the corner, carrying a full laundry basket on one hip.

"Speak of them and they appear." Rikki shot Jack a surprisingly altruistic smile. "Got it from here, doll body?"

"Sure thing, tiger." Jack answered, cool-headed as always.

"Not that I'm not overjoyed to see everyone has been getting along during my unscheduled sojourn from cognizance, but my ribs hurt like a motherfucker. Could we please move this the *fuck* along?" Tura bit out, shaking with the effort of holding her body upright while standing in one place.

"And you dare criticize my love of glitter cannons," Rikki taunted, angling their head to drop a quick peck on her cheek. "I'll pop by tomorrow, after you've gotten settled in. Call if you start feeling the overwhelming urge to join the PTA."

"Hey, don't joke about the PTA." Jack set down the laundry basket, dusting off his hands. "Those folks'll fuck up your whole world."

The haughty noise Rikki summoned from the back of their throat spoke volumes. Jack watched them leave and grinned, oceanic blue eyes sparkling with amusement. "I don't think they actually know anyone's name."

Tura started limping toward the stairs. "The day Rikki stops making up cute nicknames. That is the day they decide you're trash."

"Hey, slow down." Jack was at her elbow, laying one hand flat against the small of her back.

"Jesus fucking Christ, I'm already moving at a snail's pace. What do you *want* from me?" Tura sniped, her patience already beginning to fray. This was a terrible idea.

sixty-eight
tura

She instinctively gave Jack the straight arm when he moved to pick her up; flashing her teeth like a coyote with its paw caught in a trap. The sudden movement sent an acute pang stabbing through her midsection. Clutching her side, she pressed the back of her hand against her mouth, fighting the impetus to retch. Jack stepped back, the harshness of his tone betraying a combination of stymied protectiveness and pure irascibility. "Look, this is going to take a hell of a lot longer and hurt a hell of a lot more if you try to climb the stairs on your own, so stop being a stubborn little brat and let me *help* you."

They stared each other down for a beat, then Jack heaved a tormented sigh.

"Please, Tura," he implored her. "I'm not going to ask you to take anything for the pain, but don't make me watch you suffer just to prove a point."

Accepting the impracticality of rabid self-reliance in these circumstances, she relented, dropping her hand. Jack moved closer, presumably formulating a plan for how best to pick her up without causing more damage. Wrapping one arm around her back as gingerly as he could, he slipped the other under her knees and lifted her as if he was trying to cup his hands around a bubble, hefting the uninjured side of her ribs against his chest. She smothered a yelp, the sound reduced to a whimper at the back of her throat.

"I know, baby. I'm sorry," Jack soothed, brushing his lips over her temple. Adjusting his hold to carry her slightly away from his body, he flexed his jaw, directing a stoney glare at the top of the stairs. "Don't worry. You can go right to bed and stay there. You won't have to move again unless you want to."

"At least until I have to pee again." Tura allowed herself the tiniest laugh, inviting another cruel twinge to crush the breath from her lungs. She winced, replacing the lost oxygen with a torturously inadequate inhale. "I miss air."

"Almost there," he said, doing an admirable job of masking how much he abhorred causing her discomfort. "There are clean sheets on the bed, and Honey and I had a talk about giving you lots of space, so all you have to do is relax and get better."

Tura wanted to weep with gratitude when he finally set her down. She sunk into the pillows, allowing him to unlace her shoe without complaint. Putting them on at the hospital had been such a trial, one of the nurses had to finish the job for her, cheerfully reciting the old nursery rhyme about rabbit's ears and trees as she tied the knots. "I can already tell this whole invalid thing is going to be *great* for my self esteem."

"Just stop." Jack slid the shoe off and set it on the floor, then started on the other. "I know what a broken rib feels like."

Tura bit her lip, studying the taut crimps of concentration between his eyes. She wondered who taught him to tie his shoes, or do the laundry. Whether he was born with empathy running in his veins, or, like all his other best qualities, he credited it to someone else.

"When will Honey get home?" Tura asked, redirecting her thoughts to less arduous topics.

"Portia said she'd drop her off in a few hours." Unfolding the blanket from the foot of the bed, he stood up and draped it over her legs. "I was thinking we could order out for dinner, but I can make you something if you're hungry now."

"I can wait."

"In that case." He pointed, itemizing the supplies on the side table for her benefit. "You've got Ibuprofen, water, books, there's your laptop if you want to watch a movie, and if you need anything else, I'm right downstairs. I'll come up and check on you when it's time for dinner."

She took hold of his wrist. "Stay for a minute?"

Jack gave her a faint smirk, settling onto the edge of the bed again. "What happened to, 'I've been stuck in the hospital for a *week*, Jack. If I don't get some privacy, I'm going to lose my shit?'"

"I know what I said." She twined her fingers with his. "But Honey will be home soon, and you'll be sleeping on the couch."

Jack slid back on the bed, laying his arm across the stack of pillows behind her. "If you want me to sleep up here, I'll sleep up here."

"We agreed that was a bad idea," she reminded him. Sure, Honey would turn handsprings to have them together, but there was still the matter of Jack's sleep cuddling to contend with. In the state she was in, all he'd have to do was roll over and throw his arm across her torso and she'd wake everyone in a five mile radius with her screams. "And it's not like I'm up to fooling around anyway."

"Because that's the *only* reason I like having you around," he replied, sounding unexpectedly combative.

"Do you want to fight?" She let her head fall back against his arm, smiling inquisitively. "It feels like you want to fight."

"No. I just..." He stared down at his lap for a beat, the muscle at the corner of his jaw flexing. "I hate this. I hate watching you suffer. I hate that I can't even touch you without making it worse. I *hate* that after everything drugs have cost us, I'd still crawl over broken glass to get you Oxy if you would only take it." He dragged in a harsh breath, gazing down at her. Lifting one hand, he grazed his knuckles over the curve of her cheek. "And I really fucking hate that you didn't trust me enough to tell me why you wouldn't."

Her eyelids fluttered, the cogs in her brain grinding listlessly for a few seconds before a fully formed thought spun free. "I'm going to kill Avi."

"No you're not."

"Yes I am," she insisted. "This time I mean it. That was not his information to share."

"No. You're not." Jack kissed the top of her head, his breathy chuckle stirring in her hair. "He's an asshole, and your shared love language is...well, it's totally fucked. But he'd be the first one to volunteer to take the pain for you if he could. Shove me right out of the way and put his hand up."

She gave him a grudging smirk. "I thought I warned you. Nothing good can come from bonding with my brother."

"Hey, I tried to fight it, but you really put us through hell." He laughed, the hand draped behind her stroking gentle circles on her shoulder. "Just be glad you came out of it before we got drunk and woke up in Vegas with matching tattoos."

"That's it." Tura pointed to the bathroom door. "Go wash your mouth out with soap."

sixty-nine
jack

Eleven Months Later - 1:23 a.m.

JACK STIRRED AWAKE AS SOMEONE PEELED BACK THE covers, the draft of cold air sluicing down his spine carrying a siren's song of citrus zest, rosemary and cedar. Warm hands slid over his shoulders, accompanied by the press of lips on the back of his neck, rousing his sleep-dampened senses. Arms slithered around his waist in the murky darkness, molding satin curves against the length of his back. She wasn't supposed to be home for three days, yet here she was, rolling him onto his back and climbing astride, her weight settling on either side of his hips. He smiled dreamily, bringing his hands to rest on her thighs. "Are you home?"

"Finished ahead of schedule." She stroked him to fullness, bending to nibble at his lip as she did. This was the best part of her leaving; coming back together after the deprivation of her absence. Feeling everything else fall away as they made each other whole again. A blissful purr wound from her lips as she sunk down on him, one hand flattened over his heart. Jack hissed at the unheralded rush of heat, arching his neck. Wanting to go deeper.

"Fuck, I missed you," he groaned, taking hold of her hips, urging her to a canter above him.

"Say it," she said, her voice hitching.

Jack forced his eyes open, watching the way the moonlight illuminated her skin, making her glow like an angel. She was touching herself. *Christ,* that was hot, watching her getting herself off while she rode him like a fucking Valkyrie. "I love you."

"Again!" she demanded, scoring his chest with her nails.

"I *love* you!" He growled through gritted teeth, his shoulders lifting off the bed as he reached up to gather a fistful of her hair and yank her head back, clapping one hand over her mouth. She yielded, sinking her teeth into the meat of his palm and shrieking like a falcon, shattering around him. Her hands fisted in his chest hair, the bite of pain enough to put him over the edge and blur his vision.

They lay in a sweaty, limbless heap for a few minutes, Tura gasping against his chest as he waited for the tremors in his legs to stop. He let out a hoarse bark of laughter. Even if he wanted to move her, he wouldn't have the strength. "So, how was Prague?"

"Some jackass let his shady uncle provide seed money for his investment firm, then acted surprised when they started laundering money through the side door. It turned into a whole thing," she answered with her typical lassitude where work was concerned, slithering off him and curling against his side. "How'd the meeting with the school go?"

Jack exhaled a gruff chuckle, letting her hair slip through his fingers like silk. His daughter, his sweet little girl, had engaged her second grade teacher in a debate regarding the volume of anachronistic lies in their history textbook before being summarily ordered to the principal's office. "She's going to have a note for insubordination on her permanent record."

"That's my little revolutionary," Tura murmured with

approbation, and goddamn if it didn't make him the happiest man in the world to hear the pride in her voice. "I think I'll take her go karting this weekend."

"Actually, I thought we could take a trip over Christmas break. Maybe Morocco?" He turned on his side to face her, pulling her to him, pelvis to pelvis. "We should go. You, me and Honey."

"Really?" Tura sat up on her elbow, worrying at her lip for a moment. "A friend of mine owns a hotel in Marrakesh. A nice boutique place right in the Medina. I think his chef just picked up a second star."

Jack mulled this over. His vision of the trip had been more budget friendly, leaving enough money left over to plan a midsummer visit to the little village in Sicily where Birdie's parents were from. What she was describing sounded like he should be deciding which kidney to sell. "How much would something like that cost?"

"Nothing, for a pretty little piece like you boo-boo." Tura gave his ass a playful slap. "Trust me. My travel rewards balance would make Marco Polo cream his pants."

Jack laughed, utterly astonished. He knew better than to wait for Nessa to chime in with an opinion. She'd stayed gone since that night in the hospital. Still, he liked to think she was out there somewhere, happily watching these moments unfold, when he took stock of his life and felt like the luckiest man in the world. "You're serious."

"Just think of me as your sugar mama." She slid closer, nipping at that spot under his jaw that sent shivers up his spine. "What do you think? Swimming in the private riad. Fresh fruit every morning. The smell of spices in the air. I bet we could even get Marzouk's mom to babysit for Honey one night and I can take you to this little restaurant I know, they make an eggplant tagine that'll make you weep salty tears of gratitude."

"Mmm. My favorite kind of tears to weep." Jack hummed, growing hard for her again. Without being asked, this beautiful, brilliant woman had reached into the fire and saved his daughter, his heart, and his faith in humanity with her bare hands, all without asking for any kind of compensation. Still, he intended to keep fucking her until he'd paid her back, which by his calculations would probably take several lifetimes. Rolling her under him, he buried his face against her neck, taking her deep into his lungs. "I wasted so much of my life without you."

"There are no straight lines, Jack," she reminded him, sliding her hands down his back in that slow, meditative way she did when she was trying to map every touch, committing it to memory for those nights they were apart.

He chuckled against her shoulder, relishing the feeling of having her there with him, exactly where she belonged. Right, as always. They'd found each other, and the distance traveled didn't matter. They were bound together by stronger stuff than space or time. Love, grief, or gravity, nothing in the universe traveled in a straight line.

epilogue

Honey

Rubbing the grains of sleep from her eyes, Honey sat up to greet the sassafras tree outside her bedroom window. It seemed the leaves turned red overnight. It would be her birthday soon, and the speckled yellow birds nesting in the tree's branches would fly away for winter. Baba would knock down the old nest with a stick, so the birds wouldn't catch feather mites when they flew home in the spring.

Kicking the covers back, she crawled down the ladder from her bed, the distance to the ground feeling so much shorter than it used to. Her favorite blue sweatshirt, the one with the cartoon stegosaurus on the front, was feeling a little tight around the collar, the cuffs stopping just above her wrists. She took it off and stuffed it into the donation box in the back of her closet, along with a handful of toys she'd lost interest in and a stack of picture books she'd begun to regard as "too babyish" since starting second grade. When it was full, she and Baba would take it to the Women and Children's Center downtown and get ice cream sandwiches on the way home, as a reward for doing a good thing.

She scented the air as she shoved her feet into her slippers and scuffed into the hallway. Someone was awake in the kitchen. She could hear the popping of freshly lit firewood and the *tap-tap-tap-kssh* of eggs breaking into a frying pan. She smelled sizzling garlic, and the piquant Aleppo pepper flakes Tura kept in the cabinet. She was there, buttoned into one of Baba's big flannel shirts and standing over the stove, scrambling eggs with spinach and feta and slathering slices of pumpernickel toast with butter.

Honey knew before Baba told her, of course. She was a kid, but she wasn't *stupid*. She could see the way they put their heads together when they talked, and the devious little smiles they tried to hide. She worked hard to appear oblivious when her father's hand brushed Tura's hip in passing, or a goodbye hug went on for a little too long. That one time she turned a corner and they'd sprung apart like two magnets aligned on like poles, radiating panting, round eyed guilt? Yeah. They *for sure* weren't kissing.

Months elapsed, but she played along. Then one day, Baba told her. They were driving home after school and she was wired, swinging her feet in high, bouncy arcs. Baba cleared his throat from the front seat. "Listen, baby girl. You know how much I love you, and how much Tura does, too."

"Yup." She'd nodded, meeting his eyes when they darted to hers in the rearview mirror.

"How would you feel if Tura and I were more than friends?"

"Like...boyfriend-girlfriend?" she returned, giving him that well practiced know-nothing look. Just a kid. Nothing to see here.

"Yeah. Exactly like that." Her father's hands slid to the top of the steering wheel, tightening their grip.

"Can she still keep teaching me fighting?" she asked, finally able to pose all the questions she'd been avoiding bringing up.

Baba grinned at her. "Absolutely. Just because she's my girlfriend doesn't mean she can't be your friend, too."

Honey mulled this over, because from her limited understanding of adult relationships, this was an outright lie. Every time Cecily Miller's mom got a new boyfriend, Cecily was suddenly saddled with a new set of rules; the incoming partner's expectations for how a child should act seamlessly overwriting her mother's own lackadaisical parenting model. Cecily learned to wait it out. The new guy would be gone eventually, and things would go back to normal.

Honey lifted her gaze to meet her father's again. "Is she gonna move in with us?"

Baba shook his head. "Not yet. But I hope so."

Honey gnawed a lip. Aurore Xiu had to share her bedroom with an older stepsister who liked to sniff markers and kept a jar of fingernail clippings under the bed, and when Harlan Alvez's dad got married again, his new stepmom moved her work desk into his room. Now when he visited on weekends, Harlan was sleeping in Missy's office. Fixing her eyes on the back of her father's head, she balled her hands up in the hem of her pleated skirt, her voice hard with determination. "I don't want to share my room."

Baba half-turned in his seat, shooting her a slightly baffled frown over one shoulder. "No one said you had to, bug."

"Then I guess it's okay." Honey shrugged, turning her head to look out the window.

It was an adjustment, learning to share Baba when it had always been just the two of them, and it was still weird to see them kiss. There were fights, and awkward moments, and Tura still went away, sometimes for days. The air around Baba would feel heavy at first, then the phone would ring at exactly seven-thirty, no matter where Tura was and what she was doing, and he would smile when he heard her voice, the world tilting back to its proper axis. They hung a map on Honey's bedroom wall, marking each destination with a thumbtack and counting down the days until she would appear again, folded seamlessly into their lives as if she never left.

Honey wound her arms around Tura's waist, nestling one ear against her ribs. Lifting one arm, Tura drew her into the cherished curvature of her hip and laid a kiss on the top of her head, her voice tranquil and tarnished with sleep. "Morning, little gem."

Pressing her face against Tura's side, Honey tightened her hold, inhaling the safe, familiar scent of laundry detergent and cotton and the clean, zesty warmth of Tura. She belonged to them, now. She was home.

about the author

Right now, Janet Poisonner is probably dancing around her apartment in bare feet and nerdy glasses.